ENTICED
BY YOU

Also by Elle Wright

The Wellspring Series

Touched by You

Published by Kensington Publishing Corp.

ENTICED BY YOU

Elle Wright

Kensington Publishing Corp.

www.kensingtonbooks.com

DAFINA BOOKS are published by

Kensington Publishing Corp.
119 West 40th Street
New York, NY 10018

All Kensington Titles, Imprints, and Distributed Lines are available at special quantity discounts for bulk purchases for sales promotions, premiums, fund-raising, and educational or institutional use. Special book excerpts or customized printings can also be created to fit specific needs. For details, write or phone the office of the Kensington special sales manager: Kensington Publishing Corp., 119 West 40th Street, New York, NY 10018, attn: Special Sales Department, Phone: 1-800-221-2647.

Dafina and the Dafina logo Reg. U.S. Pat. & TM Off.

ISBN-13: 978-1-4967-1602-6
ISBN-10: 1-4967-1602-7
First Kensington Mass Market Edition: September 2018

eISBN-13: 978-1-4967-1603-3
eISBN-10: 1-4967-1603-5
First Kensington Electronic Edition: September 2018

10 9 8 7 6 5 4 3 2 1

Printed in the United States of America

For Tanishia Pearson-Jones, my friend, the one who always encouraged me to keep going, to keep pushing. Hard to believe you're not here, but I know you're cheering me on in Heaven. Miss you, friend.

To Mom, I hope you're proud of me. I promise I don't cuss like this in real life. I love you and miss you.

Acknowledgments

Enticed by You was the book that stole Thanksgiving. Literally. As I grow as a writer, each book becomes its own rollercoaster, taking me up hills slowly and then dropping me down fast and flipping me over. I almost lost my shoes with this one, but I don't regret the journey. I pray you enjoy the ride that is Parker and Kennedi. I appreciate all of your love and support.

Giving honor to God, who is everything I need. Even when my world seems bleak, I can call on Him and feel His peace.

To my husband, Jason, I love you. After nineteen years of marriage, I am still enticed by you.

To my children, Asante, Kaia, and Masai, keep rising, keep striving to be more, to be better. I love you all so much. I am so proud of you.

To my Aunt Angelia, you once told me to write you in a book. So, I created Angelia Hunt with you in mind. I love you, my Anny. And I thank you for stepping in when Mom died and being who you are.

To my family and friends, thank you for your unwavering support. My life is brighter because of you. Thanks for being #TeamElle!

To my Seester sister, LaDonna, you roll with me without question. I am not sure how this would work without you. Thanks for traveling with me, listening to me, and loving me unconditionally. Love you!

To my lit sisters, and Once upon a Series crew, Sheryl Lister, Sherelle Green, and Angela Seals, let's get it. I can't wait to do more. Love y'all!

To my Book Euphoria ladies, you are #SoDope.

To my agent, Sara Camilli, thank you for being in my corner always! Appreciate you.

To my editor, Selena James, it was a happy day when you called and told me you enjoyed Enticed by You. Thank you for believing in me.

I also want to thank Priscilla C. Johnson and Cilla's Maniacs, A.C. Arthur, Brenda Kidd-Woodbury (BJBC), MidnightAce Scotty, King Brooks (Black Page Turners), Sharon Blount and BRAB (Building Relationships around Books), LaShaunda Hoffman (SORMAG), Orsayor Simmons (Book Referees), Tiffany Tyler (Reading in Black and White), Naleighna Kai (Naleighna Kai's Literary Café and Cavalcade of Authors), Delaney Diamond (RNIC), Wayne Jordan (RIC), Radiah Hubert (Urban Book Reviews), and the EyeCU Reading and Social Network for supporting me. I truly appreciate you all.

Thank you to my readers! You're pretty awesome! Nothing would be possible without you.

Thank you!

Love,
Elle

Chapter 1

For the last several hours, Parker Wells Jr. had been asking himself the same question over and over again. *What the hell was my father smoking when he married Patricia Lewis?*

Sighing heavily, he watched the movers cart box after box from his father's mansion. It seemed Patricia had made out quite well for herself considering she'd been a "reformed" stripper when she became wife number five to Parker Wells Sr. With her bright blond weave, long fake nails and lashes, and her enhanced face and breasts, he often wondered how she really looked under all of that . . . fakeness.

Gesturing to one of the movers, he grabbed the huge painting his father had commissioned of his latest wife. At least she got to keep it. The other four wives, including his own mother, hadn't fared so well. The paintings ended up in the incinerator the moment the divorce was final. Or, in his mother's case, the death certificate was signed.

Parker wondered if that was the moment he realized he didn't care for his father. Hell, he borderline hated him for most of his thirty-one years on this earth. For the life of him, he couldn't think of any redeeming qualities.

Senior, as they were instructed to call their father, had made it a point to not engage with his sons. His younger sister, Brooklyn, had a different experience as a little girl, when their mother was alive. She remembered their dad as kind and protective back then. Things didn't change for Brooklyn and Senior until Mama died.

On the other hand, Parker had never remembered feeling secure in his home, or even in his own skin. Everything about him had been picked apart since he could form a coherent sentence. His first memories of his father were painful ones, discipline for even the smallest infraction. His pants weren't ironed right, his hair was too long, he didn't enunciate his words properly, he wasn't smart enough, he wasn't fast enough on the football field. Never mind he had never received less than an A on anything, had made the All-State team and won MVP for every year he played football. After a while, he'd stopped even bringing home trophies or awards because they just didn't matter. And things had steadily gotten worse as he grew into adulthood.

After his mother died, he'd become a shield for his younger siblings, taking their punishments so they wouldn't have to be subjected to their father's wrath. Although, neither one of them had escaped unscathed. Most recently, his father had waged a war against Brooklyn for daring to say no to the arranged marriage Senior had set up. In 2018. *Who promises their daughter's hand in marriage for a buck?*

The last time his father had hit him was the one time Parker had ended up in jail. Parker could still remember the fury that had tightened his bones, turned his blood hot, yet cold, at the same time. He'd defended himself that day, and his father had never stepped to him again.

Of course, the punishment for that transgression had been banishment from the house and the family company, Wellspring Water Corporation. At the time, Parker didn't care. He'd considered it a blessing that he wouldn't have to be around Senior and his cronies.

Everything changed once he'd graduated from law school. He'd made it his mission to work his way back into his father's good graces, kissing up, going against his heart. It had chipped away at his soul.

But Parker had a plan. Inevitably, his father wouldn't be around much longer. And he would be able to run the company the way *he* saw fit. He would be able to do right by his grandfather's vision for Wellspring Water Corp. So, he'd bided his time, played the game. Now, it was his turn.

Parker Wells Sr. had suffered a massive heart attack several months earlier and was now comatose. The doctors weren't hopeful, but Senior was holding on for some reason. Maybe it was the old man's way of saying "fuck you" to all of them. As long as he was alive, the company would be his, the legacy would be one of darkness and corruption, not light and responsibility like Parker envisioned.

As the heir to the family company, Parker was next in line to take over as chief executive officer when Senior finally passed away. Recently, the board had voted him in as the interim CEO while his father was incapacitated. But there was more, so much more to the story.

Apparently, his father hadn't been content to cheat unsuspecting workers, steal land, and marry strippers. He'd actually committed a serious crime, forging their mother's will. Doing so allowed him to maintain control of a company that technically belonged to Parker and Brooklyn.

The scandal had rocked their small town of Wellspring, and he and his sister were currently working with a team of attorneys to fix the mess Senior had made of all of their lives.

A loud thump sounded from the sitting room in the front of the house. Next, he heard the crash of glass against the wall. Sighing, he rushed over to the room, where his sister had been arguing with Patricia for the last half hour—about anything and everything, from the priceless vase Patricia felt was owed to her to the Honey Nut Cheerios she wanted to take from the kitchen.

Brooklyn. Parker sighed when he thought of his little sis. She was petite, but she packed a punch. And she wasn't letting Patricia leave the house with anything that wasn't specified in the agreement they'd signed last week, no matter how petty and how miniscule the item was.

Pushing the door open, he scanned the room. Patricia was standing there, wig crooked and chest heaving. Brooklyn, on the other hand, was calm. There wasn't a hair out of place on his sister's head. Her clothes were pristine, like she'd just put them on. There was glass around Brooklyn's high-heeled pumps.

"What the hell is going on in here?" he asked his sister.

Brooklyn stared at him, amusement crackling in her brown eyes. "Patricia won't go quietly into the night like she agreed. She insists on breaking up all of Senior's shit. And what she fails to realize is I don't give a damn what she breaks. There is no way in hell she's going to walk out of here with anything not outlined in this agreement." His sister held up the divorce decree.

It had been their attorney's idea to offer a settlement to Patricia to divorce their father. Patricia had been happy to accept the offer, because they'd offered her a sum over and above what had been agreed upon in the prenuptial agreement and what would be bequeathed to her in the event of Senior's death. In fact, Patricia had been so eager to accept the terms of the agreement, Parker wondered if she had a boyfriend on the side somewhere.

The proceedings had gone well. There wasn't a lot of arguing, no real disputes over the terms. Ultimately, they'd come to an agreement. Which is why he was perplexed she was having so much trouble now that it was time to move out of Senior's house.

"Patricia, what is the problem?" he asked, arms out at his sides. "You knew this day was coming. You agreed to the terms."

Patricia glared at Brooklyn. "I can't stand that little bitch. I never could."

Brooklyn barked out a laugh. "Ask me if I care."

Parker cut Brooklyn a look that he hoped told her to shut the hell up so they could get the woman out of the house. Brooklyn got the message because she gingerly stepped away, avoiding the glass, and took a seat on one of the chairs.

Approaching Patricia, Parker said, "Is there anything I can do to make this transition better for you?" Parker ignored the muttered curse from his sister from her side of the room. "What's going on with you?"

A still seething Patricia wouldn't look at Parker. She was still throwing Brooklyn death glares. "I won't talk as long as she's in the room."

Sighing, Parker turned to Brooklyn. "Can you give us a minute?"

His sister's mouth fell open. "Parker . . . why?"

"Because I asked you to, Brooklyn. Go have Arlene make you some lunch or something. Call Carter, I don't know. Just leave us alone for a minute."

Shaking her head, Brooklyn did as he requested and left him alone with the latest Ex-Mrs. Parker Wells Sr. When the door was closed, and they were alone, Parker motioned for Patricia to take a seat.

"What can I do for you?" he asked.

"Parker, don't play me," Patricia said with a scowl. "You're not that nice."

He blinked. Nice? He'd never pretended to like Patricia, but he was respectful of her title. Despite how she'd treated him and his sister, he'd made sure he was cordial at all times. That was something he'd learned from his mother, Marie. His mother had been kind, giving. She had been all the things that no wife of Senior had been since.

"What is it, Patricia?" Parker asked, his patience dangling on a very thin thread. He didn't have time for this. He had to get to work and put out the seemingly endless fires his father had set in motion. "What do you need to say?"

"I expect to get what's owed to me."

"You'll get exactly what we agreed upon. Anything else?"

Patricia's mouth pulled in a tight line. "Yes, actually there is. I have information that's very valuable to you and that little ingrate you call a sister. Even your brother, Bryson."

Parker was admittedly curious. It was no secret that his father was into all kinds of shady business. He wondered what Patricia had in her back pocket that would be worth something to him. Would this information affect him and his siblings? Wellspring Water?

Unwilling to show his hand yet, he sat on the chair his sister had vacated a few minutes earlier, crossing his left leg over his right. "I'm listening."

Patricia let out a humorless chuckle. "Really?

Do you think I'm going to play my hand that fast and easy?"

"That would depend on a few things. One being if it has anything to do with my family. The other being if it has anything to do with my company."

"Your company? Senior isn't dead, Parker."

"Whatever he is, it's no concern of yours anymore." Parker took a deep breath. His mask was slipping, and he couldn't afford it at that moment. He'd prided himself on his ability to get the job done, and that meant being able to get to the thick of things without losing his temper.

"Oh, okay. It's like that?"

With raised eyebrows, he asked. "How should it be? You're not his wife anymore. You're free to leave with the money we gave you, money you wouldn't have seen if it had not been for me and Brooklyn. I'm not sure why you insist on dragging this out longer than it has to be. If you know something that would be of use to me and my family, why not just say it? If I feel that it's worth something, I'll act accordingly. Because I'm sure that's what this is about. Isn't it? Your bottom line? Cash."

Patricia was always after her next dollar. He knew the type, had even been fooled by a few women in the past. But he'd learned the hard way to never let his guard down, and never drop his card before his turn.

Leaning against the table, Patricia crossed her feet at her ankles and straightened her wig. "What is another sibling worth to you, Parker?"

The sneer in her tone when she said his name

wasn't lost on him. "If that sibling is from you, I cry bullshit."

Patricia was younger than Senior, yes. But she wasn't young enough to be pregnant with Senior's baby.

His ex-stepmother glared at him. "Not my child."

"Whose child?"

"Senior had another child. A daughter. I only know because he slipped up one morning at breakfast."

"Why should I believe you?"

The thought of there being another Wells sibling turned his stomach. Not that he didn't love his brother and sister. On the contrary, he loved them more than anything, anyone. He'd do anything for them, and had.

He assessed Patricia, who was watching him intently, a smirk on her augmented lips. *Fake.* She could be lying. He wouldn't put it past her to try to extort more cash from him with this long-lost sister crap. But something told him she wasn't lying this time.

Senior had made no secret of his penchant for mistresses. Bryson's mother had been a long-term mistress, and most of the wives he'd brought home were former side chicks. There could very well be another sibling out there somewhere. And if there was, he needed to find out.

"Name your price," he said coolly.

A smug Patricia threw out some astronomical number that made Parker's blood boil.

"Nice try, but hell no."

Her mouth fell open. "But this information is priceless."

"If there is another sibling, I will find her with or without you." He stood up and walked to the door, swung it open, nearly pulling Brooklyn into the room too. His sister braced herself on the door. Shaking his head, he asked, "Really?"

Brooklyn shrugged. "Sorry."

Parker turned toward Patricia. "Your belongings are outside in the moving truck. I suggest you follow it."

Kissing his sister on her forehead, he murmured, "I'll call you later. I have something to take care of." Then, he left.

Chapter 2

I can't believe I wasted all my pretty years on this idiot.
Kennedi Robinson shook her head as she glanced at the dollar amount on the last spousal support check she would ever write. It had been a long year, full of legal briefs, subpoenas, and surprise court dates, all designed by her shitty ex-husband to extort as much money as he could from her.

Luckily for her, the judge had dismissed her ex's last attempt to extend spousal support beyond the one-year time frame originally ordered. Now, that year was up.

After signing the check, she stuffed it in the envelope addressed to her attorney, her colleague and friend, Paula. "Here you go," Kennedi said, handing the envelope to Paula, who was seated across from her desk, engrossed in a file.

"You sure you don't want to deliver this yourself?" Paula asked. "Along with a 'fuck you' for good measure?"

Kennedi giggled. She knew Paula wasn't serious. The two were consummate professionals at work, and profanity while in the process of business was a no-no. "I don't want to give him any more of my energy. He already took my money; he won't take my dignity."

Paula eyed her. "Are you sure you're okay?"

"I'm fine. You know it would have never worked, anyway. He blames me for everything wrong with him." Kennedi stood and made her way over to her office window. It was a beautiful late summer day in Ann Arbor, Michigan. She'd had a chance to enjoy the weather that morning on her daily run, which she rarely missed. There was nothing better than the wind in her face, the burn in her legs, as she ran her route through Gallup Park.

The park was Ann Arbor's most popular recreation area, located along the Huron River and Geddes Pond. It was a runner's dream, and Kennedi took advantage of the asphalt trails every single morning.

She heard Paula approach her from behind. Soon, her best friend was standing next to her, offering her silent strength. The two had been friends since they'd enrolled at Michigan Law seven years ago. Since their first day of classes, they'd supported one another through everything, through the death of Kennedi's parents, through Paula's pregnancy, and now through Kennedi's failed marriage.

Sighing, Kennedi said, "I need to make a change, friend."

Paula turned to her, but Kennedi refused to meet her gaze. "What change do you need to make, Kenni Cakes?"

Kennedi smiled at the nickname Paula had given her during their first year of law school. "Change of scenery, Paula. I need a vacation."

Years had passed since she'd entered the workforce, with no spas, no resorts, no time off in her plans. Kennedi worked hard in her job as a corporate attorney, putting in long hours for her clients.

"Then, take a vacation, hun."

Kennedi folded her arms across her chest. It was almost laughable how easy Paula had made time off sound. In her mind, it wasn't so simple. She had commitments—to her clients, her firm, and her friends. "How am I supposed to do that when I'm pushing you down the aisle in one month?"

Paula smiled, a wistful look in her eyes. "I know. I can't believe I'm getting married."

Her best friend was engaged to Mark Hoover. The two had met during a golf outing last year, and the romance had blossomed into unconditional love and acceptance. Mark was the type of man every woman dreamed about—intelligent, polished, handsome, and a provider. Kennedi knew he was a keeper when he'd shown Paula's daughter nothing but respect and love from the very beginning. Kennedi's goddaughter, Lauren, was smitten with her future stepfather and that was a testament to Mark's willingness to love the three-year-old as if she were his biological daughter.

Kennedi squeezed Paula's hand. It had been years since she'd seen her friend so happy; years of tears, struggling to make ends meet, and raising her daughter alone. "You deserve to be happy, Paula. I'm so proud that I'm going to be standing up for you when you marry the love of your life. Mark is a good man. He'll be a good hubby to you and an amazing father to my Lauren."

"Kennedi?"

Oh Lord. She loved her best friend with everything in her, but she couldn't bear another "you'll find love again" conversation. Yes, Kennedi had been dragged through the longest nightmare divorce from hell. No, Kennedi wasn't sour on love. She just wasn't looking for it at this point in her life.

She'd spent a full four years dealing with her ex's antics, longer than the marriage lasted. What she wanted was a little peace and quiet, away from home, away from the demands of her job.

"Paula, I know what you're going to say, but it isn't necessary. Really."

Kennedi smiled at the worried expression on Paula's face. Her friend was gorgeous every day, but she was radiant with the glow of her impending nuptials. Paula's brown skin was sun kissed and smooth. She was a natural beauty, and Mark was the lucky man who'd better not ever forget that he was marrying a gem.

"I'm not sad," Kennedi added, hoping to alleviate her friend's concern.

Paula peered at her friend with suspicious eyes. "If you were, I wouldn't blame you. We all thought Quincy was the one for you."

"Well, turns out he wasn't. And I've made my peace with that. I truly appreciate your support. You were excellent in that courtroom." Instead of corporate law, Paula had chosen family law as her field of choice. Her friend's long-term goal was to become one of the top divorce attorneys in the state, and she was well on her way.

"Can I just tell you that you are my shero?"

Surprised, Kennedi took a step back. "Me? Why?"

"You could have let this man break you. He put you through the ringer, with one motion after another, false accusations, going after your family business. But I watched you walk in that courtroom every day with your head held high, your shoe game fierce, and that uncanny ability you have to turn off your emotions. He tried everything he could, threw anything and everything at you. But you never let him see you sweat. That's why you're my shero. I don't think I could have done it."

It wasn't an uncanny ability, Kennedi thought. It was a learned behavior she'd been able to perfect as the result of losing both of her parents at the same time to a horrible crime. Kenneth and Yolanda Robinson had been the unfortunate victims of a home invasion. The culprit was an older man, high on drugs. The man had broken into her parents' home, in their middle-class neighborhood, and killed them for daring to be home while he stole everything they'd worked hard for.

"Kennedi, you're the strongest person I know. But even the strongest person needs time to regroup, to relax, to release. So, if you need a break, please take one."

Her bestie had given her a lot to think about. She'd spent years being strong for everyone else around her, for her sister, for her friend, for her aunt. For the past few months, she'd felt bogged down. Her aunt would say she was *kicking but not high and flopping but can't fly*.

"I think I'm going to head to Wellspring," Kennedi announced.

Paula grinned then. "Good. You need to visit."

Wellspring, Michigan, nestled between Kalamazoo and Grand Rapids, was Kennedi's hometown. She'd been born in the small, mostly African American town. Although her parents had moved away before she hit high school, she'd visited many times over the years, spent summers there with her Aunt Angelia.

It was just what she needed, time away to renew, to relax, and begin the process of rebuilding her life. "I'll talk to my boss this morning."

"Maybe Jared will take some of your workload from you."

Jared Smith was a junior partner at the firm, and her senior. He was the first African American partner, junior or otherwise, at their firm. They'd met during law school, when he'd mentored her through her first year. After a disastrous start at another firm, he'd brought her in and helped her find her footing there.

"I don't know. He's busy at home, with his family." Jared was proof positive that attorneys could lead fulfilling lives outside of the office. He was happily married with two lovely children, and part owner of one of her favorite after-work destinations in Ypsilanti Township, Michigan—the Ice Box.

Ypsilanti was located six miles east of Ann Arbor, and approximately forty miles west of Detroit. It was home to Eastern Michigan University, and where Kennedi currently resided. Her mom and dad had moved to the area when he'd taken a job as an attorney for an automobile manufacturer in Detroit. She'd followed in his footsteps when she'd decided to go into corporate law. Kennedi couldn't say that she'd done it because she loved the work, though. Mostly, she'd done it because that's what he'd wanted for her, what he'd groomed her for.

"It doesn't hurt to ask, Kennedi," Paula added.

Paula was right. She'd ask, and hope for the best.

Later that evening, Kennedi turned down Main Street in the downtown Wellspring area. After she'd talked to Jared, he'd worked everything out with her, agreeing with Paula that a vacation was long overdue. He'd worked so efficiently that she was able to leave the office by noon. Kennedi decided it was better to get on the road right away, or she'd definitely change her mind. So, she'd sped home, tossed several things into her suitcase, picked up an iced coffee and some snacks, and left town.

The drive from Ypsilanti to Wellspring took about

three and a half hours. It was easy driving in the middle of the day and she'd had a chance to listen to her audiobook and enjoy the beauty that was Michigan.

Prior to her parents' deaths, and before starting her career, Kennedi had traveled far and often. It used to be one of her favorite things to do. She'd visited many states, but there were few destinations that could top the natural beauty of her home state. The beaches along the Great Lakes provided hours of entertainment for her as a child. Visiting Mackinac Island's Grand Hotel, one of America's top resorts, had been a highlight of her life. There was something to be said about immersing herself in a town that allowed no cars, and where carriage rides were the main source of transportation. She'd picked cherries in Traverse City, taken selfies at Pictured Rocks National Lakeshore, and ziplined on Boyne Mountain. And even after doing all of that, she still had many Michigan destinations on her bucket list.

Traveling by road, watching the landscape transform from the urban feel of Ann Arbor to the quaint town of Jackson to the hilly and green stretches of land on the western side of the state made Kennedi feel a peace she hadn't felt in a long time.

When Kennedi spotted the exit toward Wellspring, she smiled. She was home. Glancing to her left, then her right, Kennedi took in the new restaurants and shops that had popped up in the last few years. Her aunt had warned her that the small city had undergone significant changes as Wellspring Water

Corporation expanded. Yet, even though there were new businesses and more people, the feel of the town was the same. It was still the quaint little place she'd remembered. There were people walking down the street with their kids, dog walkers, elderly couples holding hands. On her left was the Bees Knees diner, which she would definitely pay a visit to as soon as possible. Dee Clark's Western omelets were to die for, but Kennedi preferred the catfish with lots of hot sauce and piping hot fried potatoes and onions. Her mouth watered in anticipation, and she fought down the urge to stop in right then.

The downtown area had definitely grown since her last visit a few years ago. There was a Panera Bread and a Jimmy John's on the strip. And she'd heard there was a new Walmart on the outskirts of town. But she was glad to see that the overall charm of the city hadn't changed.

Kennedi was ticking off all the things she'd like to do once she was settled. Distracted by the tranquility she'd felt as soon as she hit the city limits, she went to grab her second iced coffee and squeezed a bit too hard, spilling the drink on her brand new Chanel bag. The one she'd given herself as a divorce gift, the one that had cost a pretty penny. *Shit.*

She reached over and opened the glove compartment and pulled out several napkins. Dabbing her bag, she prayed it didn't leave a stain on the light-colored leather. Then, she was jolted forward as her car crashed into the one in front of her.

Oh no. Through her front window, she could see the luxury truck that she'd rammed into. *Oh my God.* While Kennedi was thankful that she wasn't going fast enough for her air bag to release, she was mortified that she'd officially become one of those distracted drivers she always railed against on her way to work.

Immediately, Kennedi jumped into action. The last thing she needed was to shell out another dime on a careless mistake. She put the car into park, then hopped out and rushed forward, checking for damage on the truck. Of course, since it was a truck and she was driving her Ford Taurus, she was the one with the huge dent in her grille.

Grumbling a curse, she resisted the urge to kick her tire. She heard the door of the truck open and footsteps heading her way.

"I'm so sorry," she said, still mentally cursing herself for distracted driving. How many times had she told people to avoid texting and driving, talking and driving . . . anything while driving? "I promise I'll pay for any damage to your truck. I was distracted." Kennedi rolled her eyes. She'd basically just told on herself. Another thing that she'd cautioned her clients against. *Way to incriminate yourself, Kennedi.*

"It's fine."

The voice was like butter, poured over fat, juicy crab legs—warm. When she finally looked up, she gasped. The man behind the voice was just as appealing, just as he'd always been. Parker Wells Jr.

Tongue tied, she pointed to his truck then her

car before finally finding her voice. "I'm so sorry," she repeated.

Parker smiled, bending low to assess the damage to her car. He smelled like musk and woods. Perfect.

"I have insurance," she blurted out. Embarrassed by her outburst, she grumbled a low curse and bit down on her lip. Hard. Okay, so not only was she guilty of distracted driving, she was a dork, too.

"That's good to know," he said.

Clearing her throat, she said, "Actually, I don't think we need to involve the police. I can cover any damages to your truck."

"There's no damage to my truck. It's yours that is in need of a mechanic."

And he didn't remember her. Well, she hadn't expected him to. She hadn't lived in Wellspring in years. Even when she did, he was older than her and traveled in a different crowd. And their families had a history of discord that spanned generations. "Yeah, I noticed that."

"Are you okay?"

Kennedi swallowed, rubbing her chest, which seemed to suddenly ache. "I-I'm good."

"Did you ram into the steering wheel?"

Shaking her head, she flinched when he reached out to touch her, nearly falling on her ass. Thankfully, her car was there to stop the further humiliation. "No," she answered once she was standing straight again.

She tugged on her shirt and smoothed her hair back. *I need a mirror.*

Parker frowned. "Do I know you?"

"No," she blurted out. *Get it together, Kennedi.* Clearing her throat, she muttered, softly this time, "No."

Parker's tongue peeked out to wet his lips. "Are you from Wellspring?"

"Yes, and no."

He searched her face, as if he was still trying to figure out how he knew her. "You look familiar."

Kennedi scratched her head and shrugged. "I must have that kind of face."

His gaze dropped to her mouth and she prayed her lip gloss hadn't failed her. "You're probably right. I don't know you. Because if I did, I'd remember."

Kennedi sank against her car and smiled. There were few things she remembered about sixth grade at Wellspring Middle School. The pizza was good and Parker Wells Jr. was fine as hell. But now she was faced with a grown-up Parker and she'd say time had been good to him. He'd removed his dark sunglasses to reveal his light brown eyes. He wore a tailored charcoal gray Armani suit, which accentuated his lean frame.

Her phone rang from inside her car, and she jumped. "Oh, it's probably my aunt. She's expecting me." She rushed to the door and pulled out her purse. After slipping a business card from her case, she handed it to him. "Again, I'm so sorry. If there is any damage, please call me. I have to go."

Parker peered down at her card. "Okay. I'll give you a call." He handed her one of his business cards. "If you need a recommendation on a mechanic, let me know. I have a friend."

Kennedi tucked her hair behind her ear. "Thanks."

When she was tucked safely in her car, she gripped her steering wheel and watched him hop in his truck and pull off. Sighing, she leaned back in her seat. Staring down at his card, she ran her finger over the embossed lettering of his name. *Parker Wells Jr.* Kennedi smiled at the masculine design and thought maybe her bad luck was running out.

Chapter 3

"Oh my goodness, you're here!" Angelia Hunt crooned when Kennedi stopped in front of the house she remembered so fondly. She'd taken the scenic route to her aunt's house, checking out some of her old haunts.

Kennedi smiled at her aunt as she barreled out of the house and rushed over to her car. Opening the door, Kennedi ran to her "Anny." The two women embraced fiercely, and Kennedi felt warm, safe in her aunt's arms.

Finally, Kennedi pulled back from her and peered into her aunt's teary brown eyes. "I missed you, Anny."

"Let me look at you," Anny whispered, brushing her thumbs over Kennedi's cheeks as she used to do when Kennedi was a small girl. "I'm so glad you're here. I have so much I want to tell you."

"I can't wait to catch up."

Anny pointed to her Taurus. "What happened to your car? Didn't you just get this?"

Kennedi sighed. "I had a little accident when I got to town."

"Oh Lord," Anny said, concern in her brown eyes. "Are you okay?"

"I'm fine, the other guy is fine. But car . . . yeah, not so much."

"Well, we can get you hooked up with my mechanic. He's good."

Kennedi smiled at her aunt. "You look marvelous, Anny." And so similar to Kennedi's mother that it made her ache sometimes.

Anny did a twirl for Kennedi and she couldn't help but giggle. Her aunt was fifty and fabulous. She wore a pair of capris and a sleeveless top. Anny's shoulder-length auburn hair was straight and accentuated her golden skin tone. "I try, babe," her aunt said. "Lord knows I get enough exercise taking care of all this." Anny motioned to the property behind her.

Kennedi took a moment to take in the surroundings. The Hunt land was breathtaking, if she said so herself. When her great grandparents settled in Wellspring over seventy years ago, they built the town's only greenhouse and started selling trees, shrubs, and perennials to the Wellspring community. That small greenhouse would later become Hunt Nursery. The nursery was one of the biggest on the western side of Michigan, complete with fifteen acres of quality nursing stock, several greenhouses, and a garden store. Hunt Nursery employees offered landscaping assistance and taught workshops to any interested in learning different crafts. And her aunt ran it all.

Standing in front of her was the house that her mother and aunt grew up in, the house that had held so many dear memories for her. Originally built in 1930, Hunt Manor as they called it, sat on the south side of Wells Lake. Immaculate grounds and gardens anchored the three-thousand-square-foot house, with a wraparound porch. There was a boathouse situated on the lake with a deck that overlooked the water. In the back of the main house was a sunroom, which had been a haven for Kennedi and her sister while they were growing up. The Hunt Nursery and store was a short drive from the house. It was timeless.

Kennedi sucked in a deep breath of fresh air. "The house looks great, Anny."

Anny shrugged. "It's a lot of work, babe." She motioned toward the house. "Let's go inside. I whipped up something for dinner. I'll ask Fred to bring in your bags."

"I've got them, Anny. No need to call Fred over here."

"It's no trouble. He is looking forward to seeing you."

Fred was Anny's right-hand man. He'd been working the land since they were kids, and he was one of her favorite people in the world. Kennedi suspected Fred stuck around as long as he did because he was secretly smitten with Anny, but Anny was stubborn and had refused to see it. Her aunt had been married once, but that relationship ended when her husband had tried to take the land out from under their family. Anny had promptly kicked him out and had been single since. That was twenty years ago. Kennedi still remembered what it was like when they all lived on the land, her mom and dad; Anny and her husband, Pete; and her grandparents. Those were good times.

Anny hooked an arm into Kennedi's. "Come on. Let's get ready for dinner."

Once inside the house, Kennedi kicked off her shoes and followed Anny into the kitchen. "Nice," Kennedi said, scanning the renovated space. "You've been busy."

Kennedi made it a point to talk to Anny often, and knew the older woman had recently finished renovating the kitchen and the sunroom. Dark brown cabinetry, granite countertops, and top-of-the-line stainless steel appliances replaced the white cabinets, countertops, and appliances that Kennedi remembered. Anny had preserved the original hardwood floors that stretched throughout the house.

Grabbing a seat on one of the bar stools off of the kitchen, Kennedi watched as her aunt tended to the food on the stove. It smelled like heaven with gravy. "Whipped up something" was code for tender short ribs, garlic mashed potatoes, hand-picked mustard and turnip greens with salt pork, and a peach cobbler. Kennedi gained twenty pounds just by being in the room.

"Anny, how did you get this ready on such short

notice?" Kennedi peeked in the slow cooker and closed her eyes when the delectable aroma seeped out.

"Girl, I was making these short ribs already. And you know I grow the greens in the garden. Everything else I had on hand anyway. The only thing I didn't have was the pie crust for the cobbler, so I hurried to the Walmart for that."

Kennedi shook her head. "I still can't believe there's a Walmart."

"You can thank Senior Wells for that," Anny murmured. "He was so hell-bent on bringing business here. Put ole Luther Mays out of business quick."

Kennedi remembered Mr. Mays's grocery store in town. She and her little sister, Tanya, spent every spare piece of change they earned buying candy from him when they were kids. "That's sad. So big business wins again."

Big business made Kennedi's career, but she hated to see people like Mr. Mays out of their life's work.

"Don't be too sad." Anny pulled the piping hot cobbler out of the oven. "Luther sold his storefront to Jimmy John's and retired to Tampa, Florida. He's doing just fine in the hot weather."

Surprised, Kennedi said, "That's pretty awesome, Anny. Glad to hear it."

Anny set the cobbler right in front of Kennedi, and she leaned down to inhale it. When she reached out to break a piece of the crust, Anny popped her hand lightly. "Nope. Too hot."

Barking out a laugh, Kennedi said, "Hey."

A few seconds later, Anny was next to her, wrapping an arm around her shoulder. "I've missed you, babe."

Kennedi saw her aunt's trembling chin. "You better not cry, Anny."

Anny waved a hand in dismissal. "Oh, please. We Hunt girls do not cry."

That was the understatement of the century. Kennedi definitely got that "no tears" thing from the Hunt side of the family. She hadn't shed a tear since her parents died, over six years ago. Observing her aunt's suspiciously bright eyes, she said, "This Hunt girl does not cry, but you look like you're on the verge, Anny." Kennedi brushed a finger under her aunt's left eye. "Are you okay?"

"I'm fine. Just happy to see you. I spoke to Tanya a couple days ago. She mentioned coming back for a visit as well."

Kennedi nodded. Her younger sister was busy finding herself in New York City. After their parents died, Tanya had a breakdown and refused to accept the devastating news. Kennedi had to take care of all the arrangements, handle all of her parents' affairs. It was amazing Kennedi didn't buckle under the pressure. Then again, she never buckled. Her father used to always tell her to never let anyone see you weak. And Kennedi had remembered that lesson through everything.

"I hope she does come back," Kennedi told Anny. "It's been a while. She has to deal with everything in order to live an effective life."

Anny locked her gaze on Kennedi. "And you? Have you dealt with everything?"

Kennedi tried to avoid her aunt's assessing stare. Tapping her thumbnail against the countertop, Kennedi shrugged. "Yes, I have. I had no choice."

Her words came out snappy, and Kennedi didn't mean to talk to her aunt in that tone. If it hadn't been for Anny, Kennedi would have been lost during the funeral planning and everything. Anny left everything in Wellspring behind to rush to her side.

"You're just like me, babe," Anny said. "You handle everybody's business, often to the detriment of yourself."

Kennedi guessed that was true. When her father accepted a job as an attorney near Detroit, they moved away from Wellspring, leaving Anny to care for her parents and take over a business she thought she'd run with her sister. And she'd done it all without complaining. Their stories mirrored each other so much, it was weird at times.

They both married for the wrong reasons and they both divorced for the right reasons. They both took care of their parents, even after death. And they both had chosen family obligation over their passion. For Kennedi, she'd chosen law because that's what her father wanted for her. For Anny, she'd taken over the family business because that was expected of her.

"Help me set the table," Anny said.

Kennedi hopped off the bar stool and went about setting the table as her aunt had requested.

As she gathered the plates, glasses, and flatware, she thought about how her life had changed after her parents died. It was difficult being in law school, reading case law, attending daily classes, studying mini torts, and attending student events. Wash, rinse, repeat. Add in the tragic death of both parents, a sister who wanted to die with them, and Kennedi was a ticking time bomb. But she'd made it, graduating with honors, then passing the bar on her first try.

"Where are you, babe?" Anny asked, approaching her from behind.

Kennedi blinked, her aunt's concerned question snapping her out of her head. "Just thinking about life. That's all."

"I wish I could be closer to you. I wanted to be there while you were . . ."

Kennedi set the three plates on the table. "Anny, there was nothing you could do for me."

"Still, that Quincy . . . I hate that he treated you the way he did."

It wasn't a surprise that Anny brought up her ex. Kennedi had prepared herself for the questions and had her answer all ready for her aunt. Except her prepared speech didn't come. Instead, Kennedi said, "It just wasn't meant to be, Anny. He wasn't the one."

"You loved him."

"Yeah, well . . . it wasn't enough." Kennedi finally took a seat at the table. Anny sat across from her and picked up her hand, squeezing it hard for support. "He wasn't right, Anny. I kept hearing things about him around town, seeing women who claimed they'd been with him. But I didn't want to see it. Then, he started talking about having kids. I didn't want to have a baby with him."

Quincy had denied that he was deceiving her, even after a woman came forward claiming that he'd fathered her child. The scandal, the lies had started to affect her career at the firm. Kennedi had worked too hard to let that man ruin her. Finally, realizing that there was nothing left to save, she filed for divorce. And Quincy had put her through hell. But she was free, and better off.

"But I'm fine, Anny. I . . ." Kennedi sighed. "I'd rather be alone than with a man who doesn't appreciate the woman that I am. I deserve to be respected."

"That's right." A tear streaked down Anny's cheek. She dashed it away quickly. "Damn, I let one sneak out."

Kennedi giggled. "Anny, stop. It's okay that you're becoming a crybaby in your old age."

"Oh shush." Her aunt jumped up and started to bring the food over to the table. "That wasn't a tear—that's called being tired. I work from sunup to sundown."

Kennedi narrowed her eyes on her aunt. "Okay, Anny. Whatever you say. But you do raise a good point. You work too hard. How often do you take a day off, go to the golf course and play?"

"I get as much time off as you do, babe."

Shrugging, Kennedi knew what that meant. Aside from this vacation to Wellspring, Kennedi hadn't taken time off in years. Even after her parents died, she had returned to work right after the funeral. Paula had implored her to take some additional time. Anny had told her she needed to decompress after everything, but Kennedi had refused. Instead, she'd thrown herself into work.

She'd met Quincy. He had turned into the distraction she thought she needed. He'd presented himself as a person whom she could depend on, which had been attractive to her during that time. She'd fallen for his charm and his good looks and his ambition, and married him on impulse one weekend. But that had all been a façade that she'd paid dearly for in the two years they were married.

"Anny, I'm serious. I want you to be around for years to come. I need you to be happy."

Anny sighed. "I know, babe. I am happy, trust that."

"Are you really?"

Kennedi knew that Anny had dreams of being an interior decorator, owning her own company that had nothing to do with the nursery. Her aunt was good at what she did, as evidenced by how she'd transformed the manor since she'd taken over. The kitchen and sunroom were the last of the complete transformation. Everything in the house was hand picked by Anny, from the colors to the furniture to the landscaping.

Picking up a vase that sat on the breakfast bar, Kennedi said, "You could make a pretty penny doing this for other people, Anny."

Anny smiled. "I've been doing some things, babe.

Making moves. But you know I could say the same thing to you. When are you going to follow your dream of opening a boutique hotel?"

Kennedi sighed. "Anny, you know that's not going to happen."

"I don't see why not. You're still young, you have plenty of money. Why not go for it?"

Losing her parents had left her with a lot of money, but Kennedi had yet to touch a dime of it. She lived off of only her earnings in her day job. In fact, that had been a bone of contention in her marriage. Quincy thought she should be spending her money on the extravagant lifestyle he wanted them to live. For some reason, she couldn't bring herself to spend her inheritance. "Why do you always do that, Anny?"

"What?" Anny batted her eyelashes innocently.

"Whenever we're talking about you, you steer the conversation to me."

"Because I'm your elder and I don't like being the topic of discussion."

Kennedi threw her head back in laughter. Anny was too much.

When the doorbell rang a few minutes later, Anny told Kennedi to answer it.

Fred Wyatt stood on the other side of the door when Kennedi opened it. "Fred!"

The six-foot-two man smiled at Kennedi and brought her bags in from outside. Once he'd set everything down, he turned to her. "Well, if it isn't my Kenni Bear."

Kennedi pulled Fred into a tight hug. "I'm so happy to see you."

"It's good to be seen." Fred shut the door behind him. At fifty-five, Fred was still devastatingly handsome, with his dark skin, salt-and-pepper hair and mustache, and worn jeans.

"Thanks for bringing my luggage in, but I told Anny I could get it. Come on back to the kitchen. Anny is finishing up dinner."

As he followed behind her, he said, "It was my pleasure. Besides, I know better than to pass up a plate of Angelia's short ribs."

When they entered the kitchen, Anny glanced up at Fred as she stirred the pot of greens. "Freddie," she said simply.

Kennedi didn't miss the look that passed between the two. Fred's love for Anny was as obvious as the sunset on a clear summer day. She wished Anny would let go and feel that love. While she was in town, Kennedi decided she would talk to Anny and get some answers.

Anny joined them at the table and motioned for Fred to say grace. Kennedi smiled at the quick, no nonsense blessing that Fred always said before every meal. Then, she scooped a hearty serving of short ribs onto her plate.

The three of them ate well and talked about everything. Kennedi learned that Fred was thinking of retiring soon, which made her happy. The man had worked hard all of his life and deserved to kick back and enjoy life. Anny didn't seem too happy about it, though. When Kennedi met her aunt's gaze across the table, Kennedi could have sworn she saw pain there and wondered what that was about.

After dinner, the three had dessert in the sunroom. The room had a rustic feel, with exposed gray beams and French doors that were open, allowing the fall breeze to fill the space. Kennedi sat on the comfortable furniture, pulling her legs up under her. The peach cobbler, vanilla ice cream, and sweet tea made the perfect nightcap, better than any wine on the market.

For a few minutes, the only sound in the room was the clink of spoons against plates. Until her aunt cleared her throat. "Kennedi, there's something I want to talk to you about."

Kennedi's phone buzzed on the table. Picking it up, she peered at the screen. She didn't recognize the number, but it was a Wellspring area code, which made her curious. "Hold that thought, Anny. Hello?"

"Hello, Kennedi."

Kennedi caught the voice immediately. It was Parker. "Hi. You called me. Please don't tell me there was hidden damage to your truck."

The low sound of his chuckle made her grin. "No. I realized that I didn't give you the name of my mechanic. You were in such a rush to leave."

"Oh. Well, there's no need. I found someone."

"That fast?"

Kennedi burrowed into the cushion. "I do like

the way my car looks without the huge dent in my fascia."

"Well, since you don't like to waste time, how about I just cut to the chase?"

"So you didn't call to check on my poor car?" It had been a long time since Kennedi felt attracted to someone, or even felt the desire to flirt. Because that was exactly what she was doing.

"Of course I did. But I also called to see if you'd have dinner with me."

"Wow, that fast?" she said, using his words on him. "You don't even know me."

"I want to know you," he said.

Kennedi glanced up and saw her aunt and Fred eyeing her curiously. Clearing her throat, she said, "Um, I don't know. I just got to town, and I had planned on spending time with my aunt tomorrow."

"It doesn't have to be tomorrow."

Kennedi thought about his offer. Could she really just accept his invitation just like that? She knew of Parker Wells Jr., but she didn't actually know him from Adam. He was a stranger. A *fine* stranger, yes, but still a stranger. "How about I play it by ear and call you tomorrow? Maybe we can grab coffee? Are you busy tomorrow morning?"

"Coffee is good," he told her. "I have to work, and I have an event in the afternoon. But I'll make it happen."

Kennedi nodded, as if he could see her. "Good. I'll call you in the morning?"

"I look forward to it," he said, his voice low.

"Bye, Parker."

"Bye, Kennedi."

Kennedi ended the call and set her cell phone on the table. When she met her aunt's amused eyes, she asked, "What?"

"You were grinning awfully hard."

Kennedi picked up her saucer and took a bite of her peach cobbler, moaning at the sweet taste. "It was harmless," she told Anny. "Remember I told you I hit someone? It just so happens I hit Parker Wells Jr."

Fred chuckled. "I saw the dent in your grille when I was bringing your luggage in. Meant to ask you about it earlier. I know a mechanic who could take a look."

Kennedi nodded. "So did he."

Anny laughed. "I can just imagine how mortified you were. I bet it was funny."

"Not really. But he was nice, kind."

"Did he know who you were?" Anny asked, an amused expression on her face.

"I don't think so. He said I looked familiar, but we didn't exactly know each other when I lived in town. And that was so long ago, I didn't expect him to remember me."

"He's handsome, isn't he?"

Kennedi's cheeks flamed. Her aunt obviously knew her well. "He's all right," she lied.

Anny flashed a knowing grin her way. "Whatever you say, babe. Anyway, Parker is one of the good guys," Anny crossed her legs. "Right, Fred?"

"He's good people," Fred agreed.

"Too bad you won't be able to go out for coffee in the morning," Anny added.

Frowning, Kennedi set her saucer back on the table. "Why? What did you want to talk to me about?"

Anny glanced over at Fred, who nodded his head in encouragement. "Fred and I are a thing now. And we're getting married Sunday."

Chapter 4

Parker walked into Brook's Pub later that evening, ready for a beer and a game of pool with his boys. He'd just left the office, after spending an hour on the phone with his attorney. Thursday nights at the pub were always poppin'. The crowd was thick on that evening. He stopped to greet several people on his way to the back, to the pool table the owner, Juke, held open for him and his crew on Thursdays.

His sister was standing over the pool table as he approached, her cue stick aimed and ready. She peered up at him and nodded before taking her shot, scattering the balls over the table.

Brooklyn grinned widely as three balls landed in the pockets, and winked at her husband, Carter Marshall, who stood on the other side of the table. Brooklyn was a talented billiards player and had successfully hustled all of them out of a few thousand dollars over the years. Carter was good, but he wasn't better than Brooklyn.

Parker laughed before he greeted Carter with a handshake. "You probably should give up," he teased his brother-in-law. "How many times does she have to beat you before you concede that she's the best?"

Carter clapped a hand on Parker's back. "That will absolutely never happen."

His sister and Carter were still in the newlywed phase of their relationship. To see his sister happy and in love made Parker feel proud. Carter had been good for her. He loved her for who she was and had been encouraged and supported her dream of opening the Wellspring Homeless Shelter.

Parker gave a similar handshake to his friend, Trent, before leaning down and placing a kiss to Brooklyn's forehead. "Hey, baby sis."

His little sister grinned up at him. "The witch is gone."

Snickering, Parker said, "I knew she would be. That's why I left her in your capable hands."

The waitress walked over to them and set a pitcher of beer in front of him with a frosted glass. "Thanks, Laura," he said, with a wink. The snap of her towel against his thigh made him flinch. "What was that for?"

Laura grinned. "That's for standing me up at our middle school homecoming dance. And you have the audacity to wink at me?"

Parker pulled Laura into an affectionate hug. "That's because I knew we were better as friends."

Laura had been his seventh-grade girlfriend for all of forty minutes. It lasted during recess, and over the lunch period. Once she'd told him she wasn't going to play Nintendo with him anymore since they were boyfriend and girlfriend, it was all over.

"You should have never threatened to take away his Super Mario Brothers fun, Laura," Trent added. "That was your downfall."

They all laughed. Laura had recently returned to town after a move to California to pursue her dream of acting. Things hadn't gone well for her in The Golden State, and she'd found herself struggling to make ends meet. Juke had offered to send for her and give her a job until she got back on her feet. He wondered when Juke would stop pretending he wasn't into Laura so the two could just ride off into the back room of the bar and make it official.

Parker poured his beer into his mug and took a sip before turning to Trent. "I can drop the truck off to you Saturday morning." Parker doubted there was damage to his truck, though. Kennedi drove a sleek, sporty American car, which was no match for his Range Rover in terms of ability to handle the impact.

Brooklyn rested her chin on her hands, which were perched atop her cue stick. "What's wrong with your truck?"

"He got rear-ended today," Trent answered for him. "By some beauty in a Ford."

Parker glared at Trent. Parker and Trent had grown up together. They were partners-in-crime in everything from little league baseball to building forts in the woods to having each other's backs on the football field to adulthood and everything that came with it. But, his best friend had always talked too much.

"She was just all right," Parker lied with a shrug. Kennedi was more than all right, and he was looking forward to seeing her tomorrow. "She may even call you. Her front grille was damaged."

Trent finished off the beer in his mug. "I'll let you know if I receive that call."

Parked nodded. Trent wasn't the only mechanic in town, but he'd made a name for himself as the *best* mechanic in Wellspring. In fact, his schedule was so jam packed, he'd had to start diverting business to a few of the other places in the city.

"And if you do, squeeze her in to your packed schedule."

Trent snorted. "You'd better be glad you're my boy. I do need a day off sometimes, man."

Carter poured beer into his empty mug. "So, she's someone you definitely want to see again?"

Shrugging, Parker told his brother-in-law, "Like I said, she's all right." There was no way he was telling them anything. Parker was private, and definitely didn't kiss and tell. Brooklyn had always accused him of being secretive, but some things were best kept close to the vest.

Brooklyn joined them, finally finished with her turn. Parker peeked behind Brooklyn and teased, "Carter, your turn. But you should just forfeit the game. You'll never catch up."

Carter turned, noting that she'd sunk all of her

balls except two. Pulling her into his arms, Carter kissed Brooklyn on her temple. "One of these days, I'm going to stop letting you get the first shot."

Brooklyn grinned up at her husband. "You're such a gentleman."

When Carter left them to start his turn, Parker smirked at his sister. "You really are my sister, huh?" He mussed her short hair. "You are ruthless."

"I'm your sister when it comes to competition in general, but not pool. You're not that great."

Trent barked out a laugh. "You told him, Brookie."

Brooklyn rolled her eyes at Trent. "And if you continue to call me Brookie, we're going to have to fight."

Parked laughed then. "She told you, Trent," he mocked.

"So, are you going to tell me what Patricia had up her sleeve?" Brooklyn asked.

Parker had failed to mention to his little sister that there was indeed another sister in the mix. That fact had just been confirmed by his attorney, who'd done some digging and discovered a paternity action filed years ago, but then dismissed. He supposed he couldn't keep it from her. She deserved to know, and so did Bryson. *If he ever answered his damn phone.*

Taking a deep breath, Parker told the story of the sister between them. By the time he was finished, Carter had rejoined the group.

"Wow, your father was a piece of work," Trent said with a shake of his head.

Parker couldn't really argue with that. "Tell me about it."

"To think he constantly turned his nose down at other people," Carter added.

Parker nodded, knowing that Carter had personally had a run-in with Senior when the old man found out Carter and Brooklyn were an item. "It's the hypocrisy of it all. The man was constantly judging others, making everyone else's life a living hell." Eyeing his sister, who had remained uncharacteristically quiet, Parker asked, "What's on your mind, Brooklyn?"

Brooklyn met his gaze. "I just can't believe I have a sister. Are we going to find her?"

Honestly, Parker wasn't sure how he was going to proceed. Adding another sister into the dysfunction that was his family wasn't ideal. But he supposed whoever she was had a right to be there. "I thought about hiring a private investigator to handle it. All we have is her name and hometown. There's no way to know if she's still there. I don't really have the time to do it."

"Well, that's why you have a brother-in-law who's practically a hacker," Brooklyn told him.

Carter owned a software company. He and his partner, Martin Sullivan, were contracted by Wellspring Water to implement a new Enterprise Resource Program.

"Hacking is not really my forte, but Martin can certainly help with it. He's actually coming here in a few weeks."

Parker considered that for a moment. It would

be helpful to have someone else do the legwork on this. After all, he had the big board meeting tomorrow, and other hot items that needed handling in the coming weeks. Then, there was Bryson. His brother had refused to show his face, or even call to see why Parker and Brooklyn had been blowing up his phone in the last several months. He'd tried to give his brother time, but he was close to hiring a private investigator to find Bryson.

Thinking aloud, Parker asked, "Maybe Martin can help us find Bryson?"

Brooklyn's eyes lit up. "I was going to ask him to do just that the other day, but I kept hearing your voice in my head telling me to give him time."

Parker had told Brooklyn that in the beginning, even as he'd continued trying to reach him. But it was time they connected with him. "I know. But Senior isn't getting any better, so Bryson should probably know that."

"Who knows, maybe that's why Senior is holding out. He wants all of us around him."

Parker shot Brooklyn an incredulous look. "He's never wanted us around before, so why would now be different?"

"I would have to agree with Parker on that one, baby," Carter said.

"I'm going to add my agreement to that, too," Trent said, before he rose from his seat. "And on that note, I just saw Madison walk into the pub. I'm going to head over and talk to her."

Madison was Trent's on-and-off-again girlfriend. The two had been circling each other for years.

"Tell Maddie I said what's up," Parker said as his friend walked off.

Brooklyn's arm came around his shoulder and he leaned his forehead against hers. "Brother, you look like you have the world on your shoulders."

That's because I do. "I'm fine, sis. There's so much to do."

"Well, I can help."

Parker appreciated Brooklyn's offer, but his sister had made it clear years ago that she was not about the family business, and he didn't blame her. Brooklyn was more about helping the community, which was why she'd pursued a social work degree instead of the business or law degree Senior wanted her to seek. "Thanks, but I'm good. Once I get a handle on the incomplete or unnecessary business, it should be smooth sailing."

Parker was up to the challenge. The overwhelmed feeling in his gut would pass soon enough. Then, he would show the company, the state, the world that he was no Parker Wells Sr. He was his own man, with his own agenda. And he would make it work.

Parker arrived at work early the next day, just as he had for the past five months. Sitting at his desk, he groaned at the new stack of files that was waiting for him that morning. The more he discovered about the way Senior conducted business, the more frustrated he became. Essentially, he'd inherited a mess of shady deals and a mire of potential lawsuits.

He picked up the business card he'd grabbed from the woman he couldn't stop thinking about since she'd rear-ended him less than twenty-four hours ago. *Kennedi A. Robinson, Attorney at Law.* As he studied her name, he thought about their encounter the day before. His mouth turned up as he recalled the way she'd practically sagged against her car. She'd reacted to him as if she was as attracted to him as he was to her, and the call he'd made to her last night had cemented that. Except, she hadn't called him.

There was something about her, something familiar. He knew the firm she worked for. But it was in Ann Arbor, over a hundred miles away on the southeastern side of the state. He tapped the edge of the black business card with his forefinger. It was simple, but it said something about her. She didn't go for a bold pink or purple, which he'd seen other women attorneys use. No, her card was sleek, bold.

Initially, he'd been irritated when she'd barreled into him, especially since he'd practically spilled his coffee on his Armani suit. But when he'd hopped out of the car, intent on giving the person who hit him the business, he'd paused when he'd seen her almost kick her tire. Immediately, his frustration had turned to amusement.

She'd been dressed comfortably, but she struck him as a city girl. Not like the women born and raised in Wellspring. He could be wrong, but he didn't think so. Kennedi had told him her aunt was expecting her. He wondered if he knew her family.

Was there some other reason she'd come to town?
A boyfriend?

Parker toyed with calling her, under the guise of
offering his mechanic's name again, just in case the
one she'd lined up didn't work out. He didn't doubt
she had her own connections, but Trent was damn
good at what he did. He would vouch for that.

His phone lit up with a text message, and he
picked it up, smirking at Kennedi's number. Unfortunately, the news wasn't good for him.

The text was simple: Can't do coffee today. Something important came up.

Parker wondered if that was text speak for "I'm
washing my hair" or "I'm just not that interested in
you." If she were any other woman, he'd . . . hell,
he'd never been in this position before. He wasn't
one to toot his own horn, but he'd never actually
been blown off before. Not by a woman, at least.
This one stung, because despite his hard rule to
never beg, he found himself wanting to persist,
to beat down her defenses.

Fuck it. He typed out his response: Is that your way
of telling me to back off?

Her response came back quickly: No. Never that.
I'm direct, if anything.

He smiled, typing furiously on his smartphone.
Good to know. Me too. Rain check?

Hope springs eternal, was her reply.

Parker relaxed into his chair. I'll leave the ball in
your court, then. Call me when you're ready.

Will do. Have a good day, Parker.

You too, Kennedi.

He set the phone back on his desk. *This is going to be fun.*

"Parker?" Sandra called over the speaker, pulling him from his thoughts. His administrative assistant had been with him for years, since he'd come into the company as an attorney. They were friends, not simply boss and employee.

"Yes, Sandy."

"Mr. Townsend is here."

Mr. Gary Townsend was his father's top attorney and a voting member of the board of directors, definitely someone Parker didn't trust. After he'd taken over, he'd encountered opposition from his father's closest allies in the company. Gary was one of them. Parker glanced at his clock, noted the time.

Grumbling a curse, Parker asked, "What does he need? Our meeting isn't until Monday morning."

"He says it's important," Sandy said, her voice tight and professional.

Parker told Sandy to see him in. Several seconds later, Gary entered his office and made himself right at home, taking the seat across from Parker after shaking his hand.

The older man was in his early sixties and had the look of a smarmy Billy Dee Williams knock off, with slick black hair and a thin mustache. It was well known around town that Gary Townsend was as corrupt as they come, and Parker had already spoken with his attorneys about terminating his contract. As far as Parker was concerned, he didn't need him. He'd brought in his own legal team and started the process of reviewing each employee and determining who he would keep on.

"What can I do for you, Gary?"

Gary set a file on the desk in front of Parker, obviously expecting Parker to immediately pick it up and read it. When Parker made no move to do so, Gary said, "This deal is something your father was working on prior to his health scare."

Health scare might be the understatement of the century. "And? My father was working on a lot of things prior to his heart attack. What makes this deal different from the others?"

"The Hunt property is prime real estate in this county. The deal would give Wellspring Water access to land that could potentially improve our hold on the natural springs in the area. It's a very important deal that needs to go through."

"Along with every other deal on my desk," Parker said. "But you still haven't answered my question. Why is this deal more important than the others?"

Parker had a guess as to why this deal had Gary salivating at the mouth. Angelia Hunt had yet to consider selling her land to Wellspring Water, or anyone else, for that matter. It surprised him that she'd willingly sign a contract with Senior.

"There's a time factor. We want the springs on the land, and we have a buyer who's interested in taking over the lucrative nursery business. The potential for profit is excellent. We're not talking small money, Parker."

Parker leaned back in his chair and assessed

Gary. In the grand scheme of things, the purchase of the Hunt land would be an amazing investment. Still, the fact that his father and Gary were involved gave him pause. And he was hesitant to purchase more land in Wellspring for the company. As it stood, the company and his father owned several plots. He wanted to encourage other business owners to come to Wellspring, and buying up all the land was counterproductive to that end.

"Actually, I know Angelia. In fact, I'll see her Sunday and will set up a meeting with her on Monday. I'd like to hear from her directly on this."

The ire in Gary's eyes was unmistakable. The man wasn't used to Parker asserting authority over him, which made Parker want to dig in his heels even more. It was time that everyone in the building knew he wasn't his father.

"Your father—"

"Is incapable of making decisions at the moment, Gary." Parker met his foe's hard glare with one of his own. "And chances are he won't be back at Wellspring Water in any capacity. Ever. As you know, I don't handle business like Senior. All deals started by him prior to his unfortunate 'health scare' will still need to be reviewed by me before we proceed. Are we clear?"

"Crystal. But let me tell you something you may not know, Parker."

Parker met his gaze directly. "And what would that be?"

"You're not as popular around here as you think you are. There are many people at Wellspring

Water who are not happy with your performance over the last several months. If you don't close this deal, the board may have no choice but to vote you out."

"And to those people I would say try it. I may not do business like my father, but I won't sit back and let you or anyone else pressure me into doing anything that is not going to benefit the company as a whole, and the community of Wellspring. If that means I have to weed out everyone in this company who does not have that same goal in mind, then I will."

"Fine."

Gary's response was curt, which made Parker smile. "Now, if we're finished, I have things I need to take care of."

Chapter 5

Kennedi didn't know what she had expected her visit to Wellspring to entail, but seeing Anny marrying Fred definitely wasn't it. And now she was in full-blown, last-minute maid of honor hell.

After her aunt and Fred shared their news, the three of them had talked about the wedding and their plans for the day. True to form, Anny had been stubborn and uncompromising. Fred had been gentle and accommodating. Normal, right?

Except Fred had one request. He'd told Kennedi that he wished Anny would wear a dress instead of that "damn pantsuit she wears to every single event in town."

Kennedi couldn't help but agree with Fred. Especially since Anny had been wearing that same "dressy" outfit since she'd graduated from undergrad. And that was over ten years ago. Fashion had changed during the last decade, and her aunt needed a makeover. That's where Kennedi came in.

They'd spent Friday morning at a small boutique

in town, and had eventually found Anny a dress. But that was after her aunt had murmured and complained about everything. Saturday had been spent running around making sure the house was set up for the ceremony. Kennedi had worked with the event coordinator at the nursery on the flowers and visited Hope's Bakery to order the cake.

It was all worth it, though, because staring at her gorgeous aunt dressed in full wedding attire made Kennedi's heart open up. "You look beautiful," she told Anny.

They were in front of the full mirror in Anny's bedroom, and her aunt was radiant in a white and silver knee-length dress with long sleeves. It was simple, yet classic. It was Anny.

"I agree with you," Anny said, turning to check out her butt in the mirror. "It definitely shows off my assets."

Kennedi giggled. "You're too much." She fixed Anny's hair, which was styled in barrel curls and pinned up on the side. "Fred is going to love it."

It was pure luck that they'd found the dress and were able to get Anny a Sunday appointment with Staycee, the best stylist in Wellspring. But the hairdresser, a longtime customer of the nursery, had opened her shop just for Anny.

"Fred is finally making an honest woman of me," Anny joked.

"I still can't believe it," Kennedi said. "You were going to get married and not tell me."

"I was going to send you a postcard," Anny said

with a shrug. "Just kidding. I didn't want to make a big deal of it. We're too old for that."

"Anny, you eloped before. You deserve to have a wedding. Every bride does."

Anny glanced over at her. "I'm glad you're here. It makes the day that much more special."

Kennedi hugged her aunt, overcome with emotion. "It's about damn time," she whispered.

Fred chimed in, stepping into the room, "Tell me about it. But you know how your aunt is. Stubborn and mouthy."

Kennedi jumped in front of her aunt. "Fred! You're not supposed to see her."

Anny stepped out from behind her. "Kennedi, I told you we're too old for that shit. And you shut up, Fred. I might be stubborn and mouthy, but I'm yours."

It warmed Kennedi's heart to see her aunt finally happy with Fred. She watched the way Fred pulled Anny into a tender hug, sealing it with a gentle kiss to her aunt's forehead.

"Are you ready to marry me, Angelia?" Fred asked.

Anny grinned up at Fred. "Ready and willing."

"The pastor is here," he announced.

Anny hooked her arm in Fred's. "Lead the way, love."

Instead of the traditional wedding march, Fred walked his lovely bride down the aisle. When the pastor asked who was giving the bride away, Fred said, "I'm not giving her away, I'm keeping her for myself."

The few guests in attendance laughed. Anny promised to cook for Fred when she wasn't tired, and love him with all of her heart forever. Fred promised to protect and keep and love Anny with everything in him. Then, on the mild September day, Pastor Locke pronounced Anny and Fred man and wife. The couple sealed their vows with a chaste kiss and strutted down the aisle of wildflowers.

Later, Kennedi stood off to the side watching her Anny and her Fred ballroom dance. Although they'd had a private ceremony, Anny and Fred opened up the house to a few guests. The back-yard was already beautiful, so it didn't take much decoration to turn it into a small reception. There was still daylight, but the party was in full swing.

"Beautiful bride."

Kennedi whirled around, surprised to find Parker standing behind her. "Parker? What are you doing here?"

"I don't know how I didn't put two and two to-gether," he said. "You're Angelia's niece."

Kennedi nodded. "I am. And she is the most beautiful bride I've ever seen."

Parker smiled, and glanced over at Fred and Anny. "It's about time they said I do."

"I know, right?" Kennedi's attention drifted back to the dance floor, and Parker stood next to her. "I had no idea you and Anny were close."

"Fred was my high school football coach. He means a lot to me, and I couldn't miss his big day."

Kennedi eyed Parker. The Parker she remem-bered was an all-around athlete, playing every sport. "That is very nice of you. I'm sure it means a lot to Fred that you're here."

"You're from Wellspring."

"I am," she admitted. "I haven't lived here for years."

Parker leaned in, giving her a whiff of his spicy scent. "I don't remember you in school."

Shrugging, Kennedi said, "You probably wouldn't, because you were older. We moved away when I was in middle school."

Wellspring Community Schools had a campus that housed the elementary schools, middle school, and high school. It wasn't uncommon for middle schoolers to see high schoolers during the day.

"We came back to visit often," she continued. "But it wasn't like we hung around in the same social circle. Probably because you're a Wells and I'm a Hunt." Kennedi bumped into him.

"But you knew who I was?"

Kennedi shot him an incredulous look. "You're not exactly low profile, Parker Wells Jr."

She had heard the news, heard about the scandal that had rocked Wellspring in recent months. Senior's heart attack had seemed to unearth a lot of secrets and thrown the town into a tailspin.

He tipped his head in her direction. "Touché."

They settled into a comfortable silence, while the guests mingled and laughed around them. Kennedi loved days like this. The breeze was soft, and there was a calm surrounding her. "Beautiful night."

"Dance with me."

Before she could answer, Parker grabbed her hand and led her out to the dance floor. He pulled her against him, and Kennedi melted into him as they swayed to an oldie but goodie.

His hand was low on the small of her back, and she felt its warmth against her, almost as if he was touching her bare skin. This man was too much, too virile. Everything about him called to her on a primitive level.

"You're beautiful," he whispered in her ear.

Kennedi sucked in a shaky breath. "Thanks. You too."

The rumble of laughter in his chest shot straight through her like a bolt of lightning. She leaned back, peered into his dark eyes. "What's funny?"

"I wasn't expecting that. I've been called a lot of things, but rarely beautiful. Handsome, fine, hot—"

"Okay, I get it." She laughed.

"I'm just kidding." He pulled her even closer. "Thank you."

As they swayed to the music, Kennedi tried to keep her wayward thoughts under control. But his scent, male and mint and woods, was enough to send her senses spiraling over the cliff.

This was easy, almost too easy. The way she seemed to fit into his arms, the way they moved together like they'd been perfecting this dance together for years, like they knew each other for longer than a day. It was kind of overwhelming, but at the same time, welcome. Kennedi wanted the distraction, but that wasn't the point. Did she need it? That was the question.

Still, it wasn't like they were going to run off and get married. No harm in getting to know Parker, spending time with him during her stay in Wellspring. The thought was appealing on many levels.

Experience had taught her well, though. And she knew better than to jump headfirst into temptation, even if the person was as tempting as Parker.

"What's on your mind?" he asked.

"Nothing much," she lied. "Just thinking about the clean-up. This will be winding down soon."

"Are they going on a honeymoon?"

"No, not right away." Kennedi had offered to step in at the nursery for Anny if they wanted to get away, but her aunt had turned her down, stating that they had planned a longer vacation over the Christmas holiday. "I tried to get them to take the weekend, go to Traverse City or something. They didn't want to leave."

"Well, they're both very stubborn," Parker whispered against her ear.

"That's an understatement," she croaked, trying not to think about the feel of his breath on her ear.

Kennedi heard the song change, but the thought of the dance ending made her feel cold. She wanted to stay where she was, in his arms, against his body. And the fact that he hadn't let her go either wasn't lost on her. When she finally pulled back, she gasped at the heat reflected in his orbs. So intense, so . . . *Damn.* He leaned forward, his eyes on her mouth. He was so close, so—

"Kennedi?"

Kennedi jumped at the sound of her name, pushing away from him as if he'd burned her. She wiped her palms on her dress, and turned toward the voice. Anny was waving her over to where she and the Clarks stood. Turning to Parker, she shrugged. "I should probably go."

"Thanks for the dance." His tongue darted out to wet his lips, and she followed the motion.

Nodding, she started to walk away, but his hand on her wrist stopped her. She turned to him. "Yes?"

"Coffee? Tomorrow morning?"

"Okay."

Parker watched Kennedi walk away and immediately wanted to go to her and pull her back into his arms. He'd never felt such an immediate connection to anyone. It was foreign territory for him, but not the least bit scary.

When he'd arrived that afternoon and spotted her standing next to Angelia and Fred, he'd considered it fate, like God had dropped her into his lap. She was dressed in a low-cut black dress. She wore little makeup and sported a pair of black flip-flops. And the simple fact that she didn't seem to care about what people thought of her made her all the more attractive to him.

Yes, he'd been wrong about her. Kennedi *was*

from Wellspring. He tried to recall what he knew about Angelia's sister, the only other child of Margaret and Bruce Hunt. Kennedi was right when she said they didn't travel the same circles. But he'd never bought into the story about the great Wells versus Hunt beef.

Parker knew of the history between their families, but he preferred to judge people based on his own personal relationship with them. Angelia had always been sweet to him, and he'd had a good relationship with her over the years. Just because their fathers had had a beef didn't mean they had to behave in a predetermined way toward each other.

"Parker," Fred said, walking over to him, pulling him into a hug. "I'm glad you came."

"I wouldn't have missed it, Fred." Parker grinned at the man who'd taken him under his wing in high school. "Congratulations. About time."

Fred stepped back and placed a hand on Parker's shoulder, squeezing it. It was something that used to give Parker a sense of normalcy, of security when he was a high school student. The gesture made him feel settled then, and now. "I'm just happy she finally said yes."

Parker knew that Angelia and Fred had been seeing each other for a while, in secret. At the weekly poker tournament they both attended, Fred used to tell him all about how Angelia didn't want to go public with their relationship until she'd told her nieces.

The night Fred announced his marriage was one

Parker would never forget. Fred had been the happiest Parker had ever seen him, and he would always be grateful to Angelia for making it happen. As far as Parker was concerned, Fred was one of the best men he knew. The older man had never hesitated to be there for Parker, even though he couldn't stand Senior.

"I heard that Kenni Bear rear-ended you the other day," Fred said.

Kenni Bear? So, that's Kenni Bear? In hindsight, Parker realized that he'd heard a lot about Kennedi from Fred, who seemed to be genuinely fond of her.

Parker nodded. "Yeah, she did."

"I saw the two of you over here dancing. Looked pretty close."

What was he supposed to say to that? "Well—"

"She's a good girl," Fred interrupted. "Been through a lot. But always comes out kicking. Just like her aunt. I'm proud of her."

Parker frowned, listening to Fred babble on about short ribs, trees, and boxing. Laughing, he realized that his mentor had had a little too much to drink. "Fred, you all right?"

Fred waved him off. "I'm fine. Just happy."

"I can tell," Parker said, unable to hide his amusement.

Soon, Angelia was at his side. "Hi, Parker."

Parker kissed Angelia on the cheek. "Hello. You look beautiful."

"My wife is gorgeous." Fred wrapped his arm around his new wife and kissed her full on. A little uncomfortable at the sight of his old coach kissing Angelia as if Parker weren't standing right there, Parker turned, but stopped in his tracks when he spotted Kennedi cleaning up.

He started to head over to her and give the newlyweds some time alone when Angelia said, "She doesn't know yet."

Confused, Parker asked, "Who doesn't know what?"

Angelia motioned backward to where Kennedi was. "My niece, Kennedi. You two looked to be very cozy over here earlier."

"It was a dance," Parker said, not wanting to say anything more than that.

"I just wanted to let you know that she doesn't know about the sale."

"Ah." Parker looked at Fred, then back at Angelia. "Why?"

Angelia glanced back, but Kennedi was no longer there. "I didn't expect her to come to town. I hadn't seen her in so long, I didn't want to throw a damper on the visit, ya know?"

Parker was surprised that Angelia had been less than forthcoming with Kennedi. The older woman was always direct and straight to the point. No bullshit, no chaser.

"I'll tell her before our meeting Monday. In the meantime, can you not say anything?"

"Okay," Parker agreed. "But to be honest, I'm not very familiar with the offer. It just landed on my desk Friday."

Angelia nodded. "I understand. There has been

a lot going on. I've been dealing mostly with Gary Townsend."

Parker shook his head. "In the future, I'd appreciate it if you would come straight to me if you have any questions or concerns, especially if we move forward with this. I plan to review the proposed contract before our meeting Monday."

Angelia squeezed Fred's arm. "Thanks, Parker. I'm happy you're taking over Wellspring Water. It makes me feel better."

"Thanks. Can I ask you a question, though?"

"What is it?"

"Why sell? I mean, I imagine you're doing good business at the nursery. You can still take a step back, but maintain ownership."

"We are doing well, but I'm just ready for a change. And with the rising taxes, and these old bones, I'm ready to retire."

Running a business was tough, and time consuming. After a certain point, Parker understood the desire to step away. And he knew that Angelia had given a lot of time to the business.

Parker was aware of the problems many of the older business owners in Wellspring and other cities had encountered trying to stay relevant. In recent years, he'd heard from countless owners that the property tax increases were negatively impacting their bottom line. Many were selling, and moving away from the town as a result.

"Well, only you know what's best for you," Parker told her. "You know I wish you the best, and if

Wellspring is the company you choose, then I'll make sure everything goes smoothly."

Angelia gave him a tight hug. "Thanks, again. And thanks for coming."

Parker nodded, and gave Fred another quick embrace. "You're welcome. Congrats, again."

Angelia led Fred away, and Parker glanced at his watch. He scanned the area. No Kennedi. Deciding to just head out, he turned, then pulled out his phone and typed a text to Trent.

From behind him, he felt someone lean close, brushing up against his back. Her scent washed over him, and he smirked. "You want to go get that coffee now?" she whispered against his ear.

Chapter 6

It wasn't a five-star restaurant, an art gallery opening, or even a concert. It wasn't even coffee in a quiet café, like she'd originally envisioned. But it was the best time she'd had in months—no, years.

"I won!" Kennedi jumped out of the go-cart and jumped up and down, a la Rocky at the Philadelphia Museum of Art. She was even humming the theme song to the movie she'd watched with her dad growing up. All was right with the world.

Parker was staring at her, a grin on his face. "You're a sore winner."

Kennedi danced around him. "There is no such thing as a sore winner. You just can't stand the fact that I beat you." She poked her finger in his face.

He grabbed her finger and yanked her forward. "Once. You beat me one time out of three."

"It doesn't matter. I won!"

After Kennedi had asked Parker to take her for coffee, she'd been surprised when he'd told her to change clothes and not ask any questions. It had taken her all of twenty minutes to discard her dress and flip flops for a pair of tennis shoes, a sweater, and jeans.

Kennedi yanked her finger away and continued to do her victory dance around him. She'd always been a competitive person, so she'd been frustrated when he'd beat her easily the first two times. She blamed those losses on her being distracted by him. But that last time, she'd put on her game face and peeled out while he was talking shit at the start point.

Sports-o-Rama was a sports complex located on the south side of Wellspring. It offered a huge go-cart track, miniature golf, and an arcade. The thought of spending Sunday night doing things that she'd done as a kid was refreshing, and she'd enjoyed every bit of it.

"Ice cream?" he asked. "Or drinks?"

Inside the complex, there was a sweet spot counter that had everything from ice cream to Lemonheads to cheesecake to funnel cake to cotton candy. There were also a bar and booths on the other side of the complex for adults.

"Cotton candy," she said.

After he'd ordered her a blue cotton candy, they walked around the place as she ripped off pieces of her cotton candy bouquet. "This is pretty awesome. When did this get built?"

"About a year ago." Parker tore a piece of his funnel cake and popped it in his mouth.

Kennedi was ashamed to say she hadn't been to see her aunt in a year. Her life had been hectic, but it was no excuse not to make the short drive to see Anny more. "I haven't had this much fun in a while."

They exited the building and Parker gestured to a courtyard that had benches. They sat on the far edge of the courtyard, away from the hub of activity.

He offered her some of his funnel cake, and she took a piece. The taste of the soft dough and sugar elicited a low moan. "Yum. That's excellent. Reminds me of Cedar Point."

Cedar Point was an amusement park located in Sandusky, Ohio. When Kennedi and Tanya were kids, her mom would often surprise them with trips to the second oldest amusement park in America. She'd ridden her first roller coaster there, The Blue Streak. It was an ideal little getaway, being a mere hour and a half drive from Ann Arbor.

"Right," Parker agreed. "We went there a few times with the football team."

"I haven't been in years, but I love roller coasters."

Lost in her cotton candy, Kennedi suddenly realized Parker hadn't responded to her. When she looked up at him, he was staring at her intently.

Kennedi was used to eyes on her, people studying her to get a read. But she'd never felt as unsettled as she did at that very moment. Even as a child, she'd never been forthcoming and she'd already shared a memory of her childhood with him. Her life was not an open book, and she didn't make friends quickly, like her sister. She was the shy Robinson girl, preferring to play alone as a kid.

In fact, Kennedi could count her friends on one hand—one finger, really.

Sure, Kennedi had many acquaintances, people with whom she could go have dinner, see a concert, or go to the gym. But those were surface relationships. She wouldn't trust them with her personal business or even her hopes and dreams. She was a firm believer in that old saying that people came into her life for reasons, seasons, or lifetimes. Every relationship had a purpose, and she was fortunate to have one really good lifetime friend in Paula.

Kennedi swallowed, unable to turn away from Parker. It wasn't creepy or anything. No, it was . . . *hot*. He wasn't touching her, but the intensity of his gaze, the way his eyes traveled down her body, made her feel like his hands were all over her, brushing against her skin. For a minute, she allowed her mind to travel to the what-ifs. *What if he did touch me? What if I let him do more than touch me? What if I throw caution to the wind and let myself go there? What if he is as intense in bed as he is—*

"Did you hear me?"

Kennedi blinked, her cheeks warming at the knowing look on Parker's face, almost like he'd been reading her mind. "No, I zoned out for a minute. Cotton candy, and all."

"I asked when you'd last visited Cedar Point. I thought about visiting during Halloweekends this year."

"Oh, I haven't been in years. No time. But I hear Halloweekends is fun."

Cedar Point had an annual Halloween event. During that time, the park added haunted houses and scare zones, and other attractions geared to pull people in during the off season.

Over the next few hours, Kennedi lost to Parker at miniature golf and celebrated as she beat him on the ice hockey table. They talked about movies and food and sports. Before she knew it, the place was closing and it was time for them to go.

He drove her home, through the city, pointing out everything new since she'd last visited. When they made it back to Hunt Manor, he walked her to the door. Once on the porch, she turned to him. "Thanks, Parker. I had fun."

"I'm glad I could show you a good time."

"I should have bought that little trophy in the gift shop," she teased. "I fought hard for that ice hockey win."

"You're funny," he said. "But you can't really consider yourself the champion if you didn't win all the games, or even two out of three."

"Whatever. Don't steal my thunder."

Parker stepped forward, his eyes on her mouth. "I know this wasn't coffee, but we can do that, too, another day."

Kennedi sucked in a deep breath. She felt his fingers brush against her hand and slowly up her arm. "Sounds good."

Parker leaned in, and Kennedi braced herself for the touch, the feel of his lips on hers. When his lips touched hers, all of that shit talking seemed to fade into oblivion. His mouth, the way his tongue swept against her bottom lip, unraveled something in her. "Open up," he murmured.

Kennedi did as she was told, opening for him, deepening the kiss. He tasted like dough and powdered sugar. Soon—too soon—he pulled back. "I'd better get going before your aunt comes out here shooting."

She giggled. "Oh yeah. She's a beast with the shotgun."

"I'll call you," he said, stepping backward down the stairs. "Good night, Kennedi."

Kennedi waved at him. "Bye, Parker."

Once inside the house, Kennedi leaned against the door. She'd never been one to sleep with someone on the first date, but she was definitely tempted to invite Parker in. Good thing he was a gentleman and didn't ask or even insinuate that he'd wanted to come in, because she would have definitely let him.

"Hey, babe."

Kennedi jumped, hitting her back against the door and nearly toppling over. Soon, the dark room was bright, revealing Anny sitting on a chair. Frowning, she dropped her key on the table next to the door. "Anny, what are you doing up? Shouldn't you be enjoying your wedding night with Fred?"

Anny shrugged. "We're old. He's asleep."

"Okay." Kennedi joined her aunt in the sitting room, plopping down on the chair next to hers.

"You had a good time?" Anny asked, a grin on her face.

Kennedi told Anny about her night out with

Parker, leaving out the kiss on the porch. "I had so much fun. It's been a while."

She looked at her aunt, tilting her head to observe her. "Is something on your mind, Anny?"

Anny met her gaze and gave her a wobbly smile. "I don't know how to say this. Well, I've made a decision that will affect you and Tanya."

Kennedi's heart tightened, and she said a quick prayer that the decision didn't involve estate planning and a terminal illness. That was the last thing she needed right now. "What is it?" She leaned forward, grasping Anny's hand in hers. "Just tell me. Are you sick?"

"No. It's nothing like that."

"What is it? You're scaring me."

Anny sighed. "I'm selling Hunt Nursery."

"You're what?" Kennedi asked, sitting up in her seat.

Anny smiled sadly. "I'm selling, babe."

"You can't sell, Anny. The land has been in the family for years. The business is your—our—legacy."

Anny's gaze dropped to the floor and her shoulders sagged. "Kennedi, babe, this business has been my life for so long. I'm ready to explore, to live. I can't do that as long as I own the business. Hunt Nursery takes up every minute of my day. I want to travel with Fred. I want to open my own business, take on interior design projects like we discussed."

"So, hire someone you can groom to watch over the business while you're doing those things."

"You know that's not how it works, Kenni Bear,"

Fred said, walking into the sitting room. He squeezed Anny's hand. "As long as the business is in her name, she'll want to run it. That's just how she's wired."

"But I can help. I'll come to town more. I just don't think it's a good idea to let it go."

"Kennedi, I've put my blood, sweat, and tears into this land, into this business. I'm tired. You weren't here." Kennedi opened her mouth to speak, but her aunt held up a hand. "No, let me talk. You weren't here, and I know that's not your fault. Your mom left Wellspring to go with her husband and I've never begrudged that. But when she left, I was in charge of everything. I took care of Mom and Dad, I grew the business, got my hands dirty every single day. By myself. I'm proud of the work, but I'm ready for a change. Fred is retiring, and we want to move to Florida. Together."

Kennedi's shoulders fell. Anny was right. She'd given her life to the business and deserved to retire and travel with the man she loved. "Do you have a buyer?"

Another glance passed between Anny and Fred before Anny said, "Yes. There's a nursery in Grand Rapids looking to expand. And Wellspring Water Corporation."

Kennedi gasped. "What?"

Suddenly, the butterflies that Parker had left in her stomach had disappeared, and she was left feeling cold.

"As you know, Senior has tried to buy our land for years," Anny said.

It was no secret that Hunt land was prime real estate, and many developers had tried to get their hands on the acreage over the years. And Anny had always said no. Wellspring Water was no exception. "And you've turned him down every time he's asked. Why even consider Wellspring Water?"

Parker Wells Sr. was a tyrant in the community of Wellspring. He'd used threats and fear to get the people of the town to sell their land over the years, often pulling strings with county officials to foreclose on certain properties so he could buy the land out from under the good people of the community. So far, there was only a small contingent of residents who had managed to keep Senior at bay. Anny had been one of the most vocal people against Senior, but that hadn't stopped him. The Hunt family owned the biggest piece of Wellspring land, second to the Wells family. Will and Dee Clark, owners of the Bees Knees, were next in terms of acreage.

"Honestly," Anny said, "I was leaning toward the company in Grand Rapids—until Senior had his heart attack. Now that Senior is incapacitated, and Parker is running the company, I feel like it might be a good move to sell to Wellspring Water."

"But the company, the people running it are still as corrupt as they come. Senior's most trusted advisers," Kennedi argued. "Parker is only one man. I don't trust them to do right by the land."

"Well, that would be their choice, but they can't touch the greenhouse, and I'm not selling Hunt Manor," Anny said.

In order to protect the family legacy, Anny had made sure to have the original greenhouse on the property designated a historical landmark, which limited development on the land and ensured that the structure could not be demolished.

"Which begs the question, why does he even want it? The greenhouse is in the middle of the land. He can't tear it down. What is he going to do? Build around it?" Kennedi asked.

"My guess is for the water on the far end of the property, closest to their own land. He can gain access to the springs," Fred mused. "Senior had been attempting to purchase land all over Michigan for this purpose. Hunt land's proximity to the lake and the Grand River makes it very appealing to Senior."

"Knowing everything that Senior has done, why give in?"

"Like I said, because Parker Jr. is running the company now," Anny said, as if it was the most logical answer in the world.

Kennedi thought back on her interactions with Parker. He was nice, a gentleman even. But the fact that he'd taken her out and hadn't even mentioned they were trying to buy her aunt's property didn't sit well with her. And the fact that her aunt was entertaining an offer from another company made her think that he was possibly cozying up to her to get the deal. *But he didn't know who I was before today.* And he wasn't Quincy, who'd pursued her after he'd heard she had money. Even though she wanted to believe that, she couldn't stop herself from believing the worst. He could have been pretending to be oblivious. He could have planned the whole thing. *But he didn't plan on me hitting his truck.*

The niggling doubt in her mind was enough to make her put the brakes on every feeling, everything that would have allowed her to enjoy his company while she was in town. For all she knew, Parker could be just like his father in the board room. People were different in business, after all.

After grumbling a low curse, Kennedi said, "I don't know, Anny."

Anny stood and walked over to a desk on the far side of the room. She pulled out a large manila envelope and handed it to Kennedi. "These are the offers. I figured you'd be wary and I wanted you to look at them. I haven't signed anything yet, because this is partly your and Tanya's business."

Part of her inheritance was owning a 50 percent share in the Hunt land and nursery. Anny owned the house outright, as it was left to her in Kennedi's grandparents' will. After opening the envelope, Kennedi scanned the first page of the document.

"I'll read them over."

Anny smiled down at her. "That's all I ask. Once you've had a chance to review it, we can discuss the sale further. I have a meeting scheduled with Parker tomorrow. I'd like you to go. He's a good guy, nothing like his father."

"I thought he was, but now, I'm not so sure. He spent hours with me and didn't even mention this."

"That's my fault. I told him not to say anything,

because I wanted to tell you. Knowing Parker, he'd do anything to put your mind at ease. Many of the residents are ecstatic that he's taking over the company. He's already done some pretty amazing things in the community. Things that Senior never would have done."

"And what would that be?"

Anny explained how Parker and his sister, Brooklyn, were opening a homeless shelter and were in talks with the county to build a Mercy Health Campus in Wellspring. Kennedi thought those things admirable. But she still wasn't ready to fly a banner in support of Parker and Wellspring Water Corporation.

Standing to her feet, Kennedi yawned. "I'll review the contract. But even with everything you told me, I'm not sold. Truth is, the Wells family has never done anything to deserve this land."

"But you like Parker."

"I don't know him, Anny. One date, a meaningless flirtation does not constitute a relationship. And you have worked too long and too hard to just sell it to someone who won't appreciate its beauty."

Anny shifted, placing a hand on her hip. "I get it. You are worried. But I'm going to ask you to consider one last thing before you head to bed. It's been a long day, so you should get some rest."

"Okay. What should I consider?"

"The fact that you don't live here. You aren't involved in the day-to-day operations of the nursery. Neither is Tanya. For years, it's just been me and Fred keeping things afloat around here. Now, I know that your mother left you her shares of the business, but you've always trusted me to do what I think is best. Just like she did."

Kennedi nodded. There was never a doubt in her mind that Anny could run the business. Until now, Kennedi hadn't questioned her aunt's choices. And she wasn't sure why she was doing it now. Perhaps it was because the land, the business, Anny herself were her last connection to her mother and her past. With them gone, and the land in someone else's hands, what would she have left of her mother?

"I'm asking you to take that into consideration." Anny stepped forward, leaned up, and placed a tender kiss on Kennedi's cheek before pulling her into a hug. "It's time," she whispered in Kennedi's ear.

Closing her eyes, Kennedi let herself relax in her aunt's arms, then finally brought her arms up to hug Anny back. "I love you, Anny. I just want to be sure everything is right."

"I know. I love you too, babe."

Kennedi felt Fred's warm hand on hers and looked up at him. "Thanks, Fred. For being here for Anny, for taking care of her."

He nodded his acknowledgment. "I wouldn't have it any other way."

After a few moments, Kennedi pulled back and gave Fred and Anny another smile before excusing herself and heading to her room.

Chapter 7

Kennedi sat in a corner booth at the Bees Knees, nursing a cup of coffee and reviewing the contract in front of her. She'd fallen asleep while trying to review it the night before. She'd even used her secure password to study the financials for Hunt Nursery for the past year. Her aunt had given her remote access years ago. There was much cause for concern, but she didn't feel comfortable talking to Anny about it until she knew more.

When she'd awakened that morning, Fred had given her the name of his mechanic, Trent Lawson, who owned Lawson Garage off of Maynard Street.

Instead of joining Anny at the nursery that morning like she'd planned, she'd told her aunt that she was going to head into town and stop by the garage for an estimate of the damages. After the news Anny had dropped on her last night, she felt like she needed time to process it alone.

Although she lived in a different city, she'd

always felt comforted by the knowledge that she had somewhere to go. As long as Anny and Hunt Nursery and the manor were still there, she had a home. Now, that stability was threatened, and it had brought out her fangs. Before she left the house that morning, she'd barely said two words to Anny. It was the first time that had ever happened.

After her parents died, Anny and Kennedi were still able to communicate. There was little her aunt didn't know about her. Anny was the cool adult in her life, the one person whom Kennedi never had to censor herself with. She was able to chat with her about sex, about love, about food, about the price of tea in China. Anything and everything.

Kennedi felt selfish about projecting her insecurities onto Anny. Lord knew the woman deserved happiness in her life. She'd given of herself so freely to everyone around her. Guilt settled over Kennedi, and she wanted to make it right. The truth was, knowing that her aunt was a few short hours away from her had always felt like a warm blanket that she could pull out anytime the temperature of her life dipped to freezing. Without that safety net, without that security blanket, Kennedi felt lost. For the first time in years, she wanted to cry. At the same time, she prayed the tears wouldn't come because they would make it worse.

She pulled out her phone, then typed a text to Anny, asking her to meet her at the restaurant so they could talk. Fifteen minutes later, Anny walked through the door, greeting the hostess with a kind smile. Once Anny spotted Kennedi, she headed over to the table.

"Wow, you made it here in record time," Kennedi said, watching her aunt as she took a seat in the booth across from her.

"I was already in town," Anny explained. "Had some business to take care of at the county building."

"I wanted to chat with you about the sale of the land and business."

Anny's gaze dropped before meeting hers again. "Kennedi, I know you're upset with me, but I have to do what's best for me. I've spent my life giving to this company. I've sacrificed so much for the good of the family."

"I know, Anny. I wanted to apologize to you for the way I behaved. I just . . . I don't even know why I acted like that."

It was a lie. Kennedi knew exactly why she'd behaved that way. Judging by the look on Anny's face, her aunt did, too. Anny picked up her hand and squeezed. "It's scary, I know."

Closing her eyes, Kennedi willed the tears that threatened to fall away. She had to be strong, or her aunt would never leave. "It is. But it's a good scary feeling. And if this is what you really want to do, I'll support you."

Anny breathed a sigh of relief. "Great, because I need your support."

Kennedi swallowed past the knot in her throat. "Always."

Anny glanced at the contract on the table. "Did you have a chance to look it over?"

"I did. Which is another reason why I wanted to

talk to you. I understand wanting, or even needing, to sell, but I just don't have a good feeling about selling to Wellspring Water. What if, by some miraculous medicine, Senior survives his heart attack? Then the Hunt land and everything Grandpa and Grandma stood for is tarnished. I think it might be wise to try to sell to the other company. The offer isn't as good, but they will do right by the land, keep the nursery open and the land untouched. Or you can always shop it around to another company."

Anny seemed to consider that for a moment. "That could take months, or even years. Wellspring Water has offered market value for the land, and given me a fair offer for the business."

"That's no guarantee they'll keep the business open. Think about your employees. You're the second top employer in Wellspring. If they close the nursery, where would that leave your employees?"

Kennedi really wasn't trying to play hardball with her aunt. But she wanted to make sure Anny was thinking about this move logically, from all sides of the equation. She knew her aunt cared about her employees, had been a wonderful boss to them through the years. It was the reason why she had one of the lowest turnover rates she'd ever seen.

"What if Parker assures us that he won't close the nursery?" Anny asked.

"That's only a part of the problem with this offer," Kennedi said. "After reviewing some of the provisions, it appears they want to use the land for the water reserves mostly and are not opposed to selling parcels to outside corporations. Aside from the original greenhouse, there is no protection for the majority of the land with the historical designation. I just worry they are going to build a pumping station or something that will destroy the natural resources on the land, the green."

"I hadn't thought about that, babe."

"I definitely think you should take some more time to consider this before you sign on the dotted line."

"Well, as the family attorney, I trust you to represent our interests."

Kennedi sat back, frowning at her aunt. "I'm not the family attorney, Anny. You already have one of those."

Mr. Ronald Levine had been the Hunt family attorney for years. He'd overseen the transfer of ownership after the death of Kennedi's grandparents and had successfully seen Anny through the expansion ten years ago.

"Yeah, Ron is getting older. He's been pulling back some in recent years, not as sharp as he once was. I think he'd be okay if you handled this deal. I know you're on vacation, but I trust you. Besides, you have a personal stake in this as well."

"Anny, I hope you know that I would never block the sale if you thought it was best."

"Babe, I get it. You're just looking out for your Anny." She finally flagged the waitress over to the table and ordered a coffee. Once her cup was topped off, Anny said, "Whether we sell to Wellspring Water or not is irrelevant. I just want to move on to the next Chapter of my life."

Dee Clark poked her head out of the kitchen.

"Anny, hey." The short, curvy woman strolled over to their table. When she made it to the table, she glanced at Kennedi. "Hey, Kennedi—looking like a mixture between Yo-Yo and Anny." Yo-Yo was Kennedi's mother's nickname during high school.

Kennedi stood and embraced Dee. "Good to see you again," she told the older woman. "I'm sorry we didn't get a chance to talk much at the wedding."

"Oh, I know it was a busy day. I saw you sitting out here earlier, but you looked to be deep in thought and I didn't want to intrude. This gal here"—Dee pointed to Anny—"kept your visit under wraps this time. Usually, she's in here bragging about her beautiful nieces. But I'm glad you were able to make the wedding. You missed catfish and potatoes on Friday."

"Oh, trust me, I will not leave town without getting my catfish and potatoes, Dee." Kennedi grinned up at the kind woman in front of her.

Dee and her husband, Will, had been friends of her family for years. Their son had grown up really close to Kennedi's mom and Anny and they were the best of friends. But he had moved away years ago, due to his military career. Kennedi didn't remember Jackson Clark much, because she was a small child when he left Wellspring. But she did remember that the Clarks raised their only granddaughter, Jordan, while their son was deployed. "My visit wasn't planned this time, Dee. I just stumbled on the wedding." Kennedi shot her aunt a pointed look, then smiled. "But I'm glad I did."

Dee gave her a sad smile, and Kennedi knew

what was coming next. "Your aunt told us about your divorce, sweetie."

Kennedi met her aunt's guilty gaze across the table before turning to Dee. "Yeah, it was tough. But it's over."

"And to think a grown man would ask for spousal support. And the judge ordered it? That is awful."

Shooting another side eye her aunt's way, Kennedi said, "Well, unfortunately, he wasn't really a man, Dee."

Kennedi's answer seemed to placate the older woman because the subject was dropped. "Well, in your honor, I'll put the catfish on the menu as the special tonight. Okay?"

Grinning, Kennedi replied, "Yes, please. I'll be here."

The three women spent a few minutes catching up before Dee had to get back to work in the kitchen. Anny stood and dropped her napkin on the table. "I'd better get back to work, too. Coming by the nursery today?"

Kennedi slid out of the booth. "After I visit WWCH to speak with Parker. You don't have to come to the meeting. I'll handle it."

Anny gave her the once-over, and a slow grin spread across her face. "And you look hot today."

"Anny!" Kennedi glanced down at her attire. She'd chosen to wear a pair of black wide-leg trousers that she'd packed on a whim, and a white blouse. She'd topped of her look with a pair of black pumps that she had in her trunk.

Anny stepped closer, tucking a strand of Kennedi's brown hair behind her ear. Kennedi hadn't planned to have to work, so she was ill prepared for a meeting of this magnitude, but she'd pulled it together. If need be, she'd head to the Woodland Mall in Grand Rapids to buy a suit. Hopefully, it wouldn't come to that.

Parker slammed his office door and stalked over to his desk, setting his laptop down on the surface. He went to the window and peered out at the property. The board meeting that morning had been a disaster, with Gary Townsend leading the charge against Parker and his authority.

The man had gone behind his back, speaking with board members to get them to vote against a proposed collective bargaining agreement with the employees' union. Parker had been working with the union to come to terms and allow much needed raises for the workers. Senior had put a freeze on pay increases over the last three years, citing changing economic factors and the rising cost of health care. Parker was livid and had made his discontent known in the meeting.

It was clear to him that the only way he could do what he needed to do was to get rid of every single one of his father's cronies as soon as possible.

A few minutes later, Sandy entered with her tablet and took a seat in the chair in front of his desk. Sighing, Parker walked over to the desk in front of her and leaned against it. "Thanks for cutting your lunch short, Sandy," he said.

Sandy crossed her legs and peered up at him, her eyes soft. "Not a problem, Parker. Before you came back from the board meeting, the phones lit up. Several board members have expressed interest in meeting with you as soon as possible."

"Do you have my calendar open?" Parker asked.

"I do," she said. "How would you like me to schedule the meetings?"

Parker grit his teeth together, still upset about the meeting. "Don't schedule any meetings with the board this week."

Sandy's eyes widened, and her mouth fell open. A few seconds later, she must have realized that she was staring at him in shock, and averted her gaze. "Okay," she mumbled, straightening her posture. "When do you want me to schedule the meetings? You have a few meetings later this week, but I could work some time in to meet with them."

"I meant what I said, Sandy. No meetings with any board members. And if Gary Townsend comes calling, tell him my schedule is full. I will not be meeting with him anytime soon."

It was a tactic that he'd actually learned from Senior. He would avoid meeting with the board members until he had everything lined up, and then he would pounce. He needed receipts.

"I'll handle it, Parker," Sandy said.

"But I do want you to block off several hours this afternoon after the Hunt meeting." He planned to spend the rest of his day strategizing. Although he'd planned to woo Kennedi, he felt he had to get ahead of his work. Parker still hadn't had a chance to go over the Hunt Nursery offer Gary had left Friday, and had considered moving the meeting that afternoon, but he still wanted to see where Angelia was coming from.

Parker spent the next half hour going over his schedule with Sandy and giving her a few things to take care of next week. No sense in letting one thing ruin his day. He would get the board to concede and approve the agreement. He just had to bide his time.

A buzz from his cell phone interrupted the conversation, and he glanced down at the screen. Bryson. He dismissed Sandy and picked up the phone. "Bryson? Where the hell have you been?"

There was static on the line, but his brother's voice came over the receiver. "I've been overseas for work. I didn't bring my personal cell phone with me. What's going on?"

"For five months, Bryson?"

When Bryson didn't answer his question, Parker dropped it. Bryson was an environmental engineer, and Parker thought he would be a great addition to Wellspring Water since he worked in water resources. "I didn't want to tell you this over the phone," Parker said, "but Senior has had a heart attack."

"I heard," Bryson said simply. "My mother told me."

"And you didn't think to call home?"

"Not sure why you expected me to call, or why I should even care?"

Parker had asked himself that question too many times to count. "They don't expect him to regain consciousness."

"I'm sorry for you and Brooklyn."

"He's your father, too." Even as Parker said the words, he felt the bile rise in his throat. Senior hadn't been a good father to any of them. "Look, it would be nice if you came home to see us. Brooklyn thinks he's holding out for you."

There was silence on the other end, prompting Parker to glance at his phone to see if he was still connected.

"I don't know, Parker," Bryson said finally. "I love you and Brooklyn more than anything. But . . . I can't come back there. It's not healthy for me. Too many bad memories."

Parker knew that Bryson resented their father for basically stealing him away from his mother, forcing him to come live with them and restricting his access to her. "I understand that, you know I do."

"Do you? Because it doesn't sound like you do."

"I just don't want you to have any regrets, Bryson."

"I won't."

His brother's voice was hard, firm. And as frustrated as he was, he couldn't begrudge it. Bryson had a right to feel the way he did about Senior, just like all of them did. Senior had never been particularly kind to Bryson. He'd basically snatched him away from everything he loved when he won sole custody of him.

The experience had skewed Bryson's worldview and made him bitter but determined to distance himself from the Wells family and name, and the drama that came along with it.

"Parker, I'm happy where I am. I have a job that I

enjoy, and people who love me for me, not because I'm a Wells."

"Well, you have two people here who love you for you."

Bryson sighed. "I know. And I love you and Brooklyn, too."

"I won't push you," Parker said. "But I'd love for you to come see us."

"I'll think about it," Bryson said. "I have to go."

Seconds later, the phone call was disconnected. Parker plopped into his chair. For the first time in his life he actually envied his brother for stepping out there, for getting away from Senior and the business. Part of him wished he had done the same. In the end, though, he couldn't see himself leaving Brooklyn or the town of Wellspring behind. God help him, he loved his town and wanted to see it remain the haven that it was to so many people.

Parker opened his laptop to check his e-mail, then closed it. It was only Monday, and he already needed a break from the office.

"Parker?" Sandy called over the intercom.

"Yes, Sandy."

"You have a visitor."

Frowning, Parker asked, "Who is it?"

"A representative from Hunt Nursery."

Parker glanced at his watch. She was very early. He pulled the offer for Hunt Nursery. "Send her in, Sandy. And hold my calls."

Parker stood, ready to greet Angelia Hunt, but when the door opened and Kennedi A. Robinson stepped in, Parker was rendered speechless. After his conversation with Angelia at the reception, he hadn't expected to see Kennedi.

"Parker." Kennedi held out a hand toward him.

It wasn't a question, and he was jarred by the ice in Kennedi's tone. Especially after the night they'd had, and that kiss. He'd woken up with her on his mind—her golden skin, big brown eyes, and deepset dimples . . . her lips.

Frowning, he said, "Kennedi? I wasn't expecting you. I thought I would be meeting with Angelia."

Parker allowed himself a glance at her. She was wearing black slacks and a simple white blouse. Somehow she'd managed to make a plain work outfit look sexy as hell.

When he met her gaze again, she was eyeing him with a little bit of curiosity. "Can I have my hand back?" she asked.

Parker dropped her hand as if she'd been holding a hot coal in her palm. "Sure. I'm sorry, come on in." He motioned to the chair Sandy had vacated earlier. "Have a seat."

"No, thank you."

Parker paused, thrown off by the formality, but decided to roll with it. Maybe Kennedi preferred to conduct business in this way. He walked over to his chair and sat down.

"I'm representing my aunt in the sale of Hunt Nursery." Her tone was brisk. It was a big change from the night before.

Parker thought back to the conversation he'd had with Gary, about how Angelia was on board with the terms. "I was told this was practically a done deal. Is there a problem with the offer?"

With narrowed eyes zeroed in on him, Kennedi said, "Oh, there are many problems with this offer."

"Like what?" Parker knew he was stalling. He hadn't even looked at the contract. "I'd like to hear what provisions you have an objection to."

Kennedi pulled the contract from her briefcase and dropped it on his desk. "I've taken the liberty of highlighting several things that I find objectionable. If you could take a look, we can possibly schedule a meeting next week to discuss?"

Parker sighed. He wasn't prepared to deal with Kennedi and the Hunt deal. He'd planned to study the contract before meeting with *Angelia Hunt* later in the afternoon. He picked up the contract and scanned it quickly, noting the red pen marks throughout the document. Sighing, he said, "Can you just give me the quick version? This deal just landed on my desk Friday, and I haven't had a chance to review it yet."

"Oh, that's easy," Kennedi said, a smile across her full lips. "I've looked at the terms and found them to be outrageously unfair to my family. But what I'm trying to figure out is if your legal team tried to push this through assuming that sweet Mr. Levine wouldn't catch some of the contradictory language, or if your team thinks that we're stupid . . . or both."

Parker tried hard not to take offense. It was one thing for Kennedi to come in there and act like he hadn't been kissing her less than twenty-four hours ago, and quite another for her to accuse him of doing bad business. "Again, can you be a little more specific, Kennedi?"

"I know you recently took over for your father," she said, sidestepping his question.

"That's hardly news. Everyone in the state, even the country, knows that."

"My aunt seems to think that you're above board, that you're nothing like your father."

"Your aunt would be right."

"I'm not sure about that, though. I've read up on some of the things Senior has done to steal land from well-respected members of the Wellspring community and surrounding areas."

"My father is not a factor, and we're not stealing Hunt land. It's an offer that Angelia can feel free to take or leave."

"You should know that we're also reviewing another offer. I've advised my aunt to tread carefully with your company. Wellspring Water's reputation isn't one that would inspire a lot of faith."

Parker stood, ignoring the sweet scent of her perfume that wafted to him. Kennedi had cut straight to the bone on that one. He'd worked hard to distance himself from his father's reputation. Fine or not, Kennedi was not going to stand there and accuse him of doing anything that would damage the Hunt family—or any family, for that matter. "Be careful. I'm not my father, and I would never allow an agreement that would hurt Angelia. And I won't allow you to come in here and spew unfounded accusations about my agenda."

"Well, I suggest you talk to your legal team because it will be a cold day in hell before I let your company rake my aunt over the coals."

Chapter 8

Kennedi stood, toe to toe, with Parker. He smelled clean, like fresh rain and wood. And Kennedi had to fight her body's natural response to his nearness. She hadn't planned to come in like a bulldog, but the clueless game Parker was playing wasn't sitting well with her.

There was no way a man as perceptive as Parker hadn't looked over the proposed contract yet. No, he knew exactly what he was doing, and she wasn't falling for his charm and his good looks. She'd done it once, fallen for a beautiful smile and kind eyes, but Quincy had proved to be the opposite of what he'd portrayed when they'd first met. Everything about Parker screamed danger to her. The attraction she'd felt to him was palpable, made her senses sing from the moment they met. But Kennedi wasn't going to be that girl again—she wasn't going to ignore the warning bells for anyone.

"Kennedi." His voice was low, tempered. "Maybe

you need to leave before this conversation gets out of hand."

Kennedi blinked, surprised by his solution to the problem. "So, you have nothing else to say?"

"Obviously, you came here believing something about me that is preventing you from looking at this clearly, which is a shame. We don't know each other well, but I thought you would at least give me the benefit of the doubt. So I'm going to help you out."

Crossing her arms over her breasts, she tilted her head, indicating that he could continue.

"If this deal is going to be a problem for you and Angelia, then we can just cut our losses. It's not that serious for me at this point."

"Is that your way of telling me that you've never had a serious interest in my property?"

Parker stared into her eyes, pinning her with his intensity. Kennedi felt naked, exposed. It was almost like he was reaching inside her and pulling her apart, like he could see to her very core. "What I said was I needed time to review the offer before I could speak intelligently to your concerns. *You* said that you weren't going to let me rake your aunt over the coals. At this point, I believe we're at an impasse. And since I don't make it a point to work with people who are intent on seeing the worst in me, I suggest we end this discussion now."

Parker turned and walked away from her, stood with his back to her as he peered out the huge window overlooking the Wellspring Water factory.

Kennedi was left standing there in her place. She'd been effectively dismissed, and it infuriated her. The frown on his face was evident, reflected in the glass of the window. For the first time since she arrived at his office, Kennedi felt bad, guilty for barging in and confronting him the way she did. But this was also business, and she couldn't be distracted.

Stepping toward him, she said, "Mr. Wells, I—"

"Parker," he said curtly.

"Mr. Wells," she repeated.

With a deep sigh, Parker turned, giving her his profile. "Ms. Robinson, perhaps I didn't make myself clear. I'm done with this conversation."

Kennedi swallowed. *Whoa. He's serious.* "I don't think you understand." Dammit, she was backtracking and that wasn't her style. Clearing her throat, she forged ahead. "Maybe I came on a little strong."

He raised a brow but didn't speak.

"I just care about what happens to this land."

"And you think I don't."

"I don't know what you're—"

The sound of his phone ringing interrupted her attempt to put the conversation back on track. She could admit when she was wrong, when she was off base. She'd projected her feelings about Quincy onto Parker and that wasn't fair. That didn't mean that she wasn't still wary about the sale transaction, but she could try to give him the benefit of the doubt.

Parker picked up his phone and spoke in a hushed tone, while Kennedi picked at invisible lint on her blouse. The slam of his phone against the base startled her and she took a step back.

When his eyes met hers, there was fire burning in them. "Ms. Robinson, if there's nothing else?"

Taken aback at his dismissive tone, Kennedi bit down on her rising temper. "I thought we were in the middle of a conversation."

"I think it's pretty clear where this is heading. To nowhere. Now, if you'll excuse me, I have to take care of something important."

Kennedi took a measured breath. She wanted to kick herself for even considering giving him the benefit of the doubt. "Thanks for your time. I think it's safe to say this deal is dead. There is no way we're selling now."

"That's good because the deal is off the table," he retorted. "Have a good day, Ms. Robinson."

Kennedi wanted to tell him to go to hell, but she was a professional. Instead, she nodded and then walked out of the office without looking back.

After that disastrous meeting, Kennedi didn't feel like visiting a mechanic and talking about dents, auto parts, and paint jobs. She needed to burn off some steam, and she knew just the thing. The manor had a small workout room, and she would put it to use that day.

Back at her aunt's house, Kennedi made quick work changing into her workout gear and jogged over to the gym, which was located in the pool house. Hanging in the middle of the room was the black seventy-pound punching bag. It wasn't the same heavy bag she'd learned to punch on all those years ago, but it was the same brand, same height, same weight.

Kennedi did a quick warm-up, then got right to it, wrapping her wrists and pulling a set of boxing gloves on. The first smack of her fist against the bag was a jab with her left hand, followed by a cross with her right fist. She threw her entire body into several one-two combinations to get the feel of the bag before graduating to power punches and uppercuts.

She lost herself in the movements, putting her all into the workout. Boxing was her favorite form of exercise because it allowed her to burn calories while sculpting her body. When she was finished, she felt it in her legs, her abdomen, her arms, her entire body. Taking a deep breath, she picked up the towel she'd brought with her and wiped her brow.

"That bad, huh?"

Kennedi whirled around, fists in the air. Fred was standing in the doorway, leaning against the jamb. "Fred, what are you doing here?"

"I came to check on you. Angelia has been trying to call you. I saw your car and figured I'd try to find you."

He handed her a cold bottle of water. Kennedi took the offered bottle, scoffing at the Wellspring Water label before gulping it down. When she was done, she glanced at Fred, who was watching her. "I'm fine, Fred. You can tell Anny I'm here."

"I'm guessing your meeting with Parker didn't go too well."

Kennedi didn't want to think about how that

meeting went earlier. She'd let her emotions rule her common sense. It was a business deal, plain and simple. There should be no feelings in business, and she'd been all in her feelings that afternoon. She'd come at him like a bulldozer, loud and bossy. But Parker . . . he'd called her on it and dismissed her like she didn't even matter.

After plopping down on a bench, Kennedi leaned her head against the wall. "The deal's off the table, Fred."

A few seconds later, Fred was sliding onto the bench next to her. She glanced at him out of the corner of her eye. He was the same man he'd always been. Even as a child, Fred had proven himself to be someone she could count on. He was a protector, strong and fierce. He'd chased bullies away, helped her with her science projects, and taught her how to use the bag she'd just pummeled. There wasn't much that Kennedi had thought Fred was incapable of when she was a child. He'd told her tall stories of him going to battle with things like gorillas or tornadoes, and she'd believed every single tale. It only added to the security she felt when she was with Fred. Not that Kennedi's father didn't mean the world to her. He did, in a different way.

Kenneth Robinson was the brains, hired by her grandfather when Kenneth was fresh out of law school. He'd spent years working for Hunt Nursery, helping build it into the business it was, but he rarely got dirt in his nails. Fred, on the other hand, was just like her grandfather. He didn't pull any punches and thought women should be able to do whatever men could do. When her father had refused to give her boxing lessons, Fred had stepped up and done it. He was family. Being away all those years hadn't changed that, and it never would.

"So you'll fix it," Fred said simply.

"I'm not doing business with that man." Funny how business could take Parker from being *that* man to that man. Although there was a part of her that felt bad for behaving the way she had, she still didn't trust the deal. Everything that had concerned her was in black and white, on paper. And she had a right to be wary, to question Wellspring Water's intentions. Then, there was the other information she'd unearthed that she still hadn't told her aunt about. But she didn't want to let her aunt down. She realized how important it was for Anny to sell. "I'll find another buyer."

Fred shrugged. "If you think that's best."

"I do."

Kennedi accepted her role in the mess, but it was too late. She made it a point not to react, but Parker had thrown her equilibrium off and it was best she stayed far away from him.

"Kennedi?" Anny walked into the gym. "You're here."

"I'm here." Kennedi stood. "I'm sorry I didn't answer your phone calls. I was working out."

"It's okay. There's someone here to see you."

Kennedi frowned. "Who is it?"

Parker walked into the gym at that moment, ducking under the low entryway, and Kennedi sucked in a breath. Parker scanned the small room before meeting her gaze, and she swore she saw a smirk play across his lips. It was gone as quickly as it had appeared.

In the small room, Parker seemed too big for the space. His navy blue suit and azure top fit him well. He'd removed his tie, though, and left the top button unfastened. He still looked professional, but good enough to eat.

"I wanted to apologize," he said, flashing the smile that she was sure made women fall all over themselves just to see. "Today wasn't a good day for me. I didn't mean to take it out on you."

Kennedi looked at Fred, then Anny, before turning to Parker. "No need to apologize."

"Can we start over?"

"Actually, no," Kennedi said.

Anny's gasp was loud from the other side of the room. "Kennedi?"

Holding her hand up, she told her aunt, "Let me handle this, Anny. Please?" Her aunt covered her mouth and took a step back. Kennedi eyed Parker. She had to hand it to him. He didn't react to her words. *He is good.* "I've thought about it. The entire deal doesn't sit well with me. And if you had bothered to hear me out when I came to you, we wouldn't be going through this."

"Maybe if you had approached me like you were open to an actual conversation—you know, where two people talk and listen to each other—we wouldn't be in this situation."

Touché. "I have to hand it to you, though." Kennedi

paced the floor. "What you're doing is noble and all, with the company, but I just don't trust you. Well, I don't trust Wellspring Water. I don't really know you."

"And here we are again. You're making sweeping accusations without being specific."

Kennedi hadn't been able to bring up what she'd discovered during their meeting earlier. "I've studied my aunt's business records. There's been some trouble—she's been targeted by the state. They've even gone so far as to try to say she's behind on her taxes. Upon further research, it didn't take long to put two and two together. Your father has been in cahoots with Senator King of Michigan to grab local land and water. It just seems very odd that the property taxes are increasing so astronomically, forcing a lot of good people to sell their business. It's also not a coincidence that Wellspring Water has purchased a lot of that land."

Parker frowned. "Where's your proof?"

"I don't need it at this point because we're not selling to Wellspring. It doesn't matter what your company does to screw with Hunt Nursery, I'll block it at every turn."

"I can assure you Wellspring Water's interest in your land is above board. Yes, there is interest in the natural springs under the southern plot of the land, but that is not a secret. Everything else is hearsay."

"Even if what you say is true, I would be a fool to sell to Wellspring Water at this time."

"Parker," Anny said, stepping forward. "Maybe we

can discuss this later. I need to talk to my niece. Do you mind if we set up another meeting next week?"

"I don't need a meeting, Anny," Kennedi said through clenched teeth. "I've said all I needed to say."

"Kennedi, I said it would be best if we table this discussion right now." Anny's eyes were flashing with anger, and Kennedi couldn't figure out why. She'd been acting in her aunt's best interests. There was no reason for her aunt to be upset with her. Anny turned back to Parker. "I'll give your secretary a call."

Parker met Kennedi's gaze, then nodded before leaving the room.

Anny whirled around on Kennedi. "What are you doing?"

"I'm helping you, Anny."

"Is that what you call it?"

Fred stepped between them. "Let's talk calmly, ladies. Both of you are strong willed women, so it's important to listen to each other."

"Fred, I need a moment alone with Kennedi," Anny ground out.

Sighing, Fred kissed Anny on her forehead and patted Kennedi on her shoulder before leaving them alone.

"Anny, there are other options out there that don't involve Wellspring Water purchasing our land."

"Don't you think I've thought about this, Kennedi? I've heard the rumors of land grabbing for years, but I don't think Parker would let that happen."

"Why didn't you tell me about the taxes?"

"Because I took care of it, Kennedi. Just like I've

taken care of everything that has happened with this business for the last fifteen years. Listen, we've already had this conversation. I thought you understood where I was coming from."

"I do, Anny. I want you to be able to retire and travel the world with Fred. But it has to be right."

"Have you ever considered working with Parker to make it right?"

Kennedi shook her head. "Parker isn't the only buyer in the world, Anny."

"And he isn't Quincy either."

The words felt like a smack in the face, and Kennedi stumbled backward. "I know he's not Quincy, Anny."

"For years, I denied what was in my heart because of my first marriage. I let my experience with my ex-husband prevent me from feeling Fred's love for so long. I know you say you're okay, that you're better off. Yet, from where I'm standing, it doesn't look like you are. Watching you just now with Parker, after seeing how well you two got along yesterday, reminded me of myself when dealing with Fred about business. You were closed off, unyielding. You weren't even trying to hear him out."

Anny had her number and Kennedi couldn't even deny it. Basically, she'd treated Parker as if she hadn't spent any personal time with him, like he was a transaction. She'd ignored the simmering attraction. She'd discounted the fact that she'd considered a mild flirtation with him, a fling to top off her vacation.

Up close and personal, though, he scared her.

He'd brought out something in her that she'd never felt before. She'd let her guard down quickly with him, opened herself up to him. Yes, there was the overwhelming attraction to him, but there was something else she couldn't put her finger on.

"You're attracted to him, babe," Anny said softly. "And that's okay. Feel it."

"Anny, we just met. Yes, we had a good time, but there's nothing there," she lied. "He looks good in a suit, yes, but that's it. We're fundamentally different people who live in different parts of the state."

"Maybe you're not so different?" Anny suggested as she walked to the pool house entrance. Stopping at the door, she turned to Kennedi. "Get it together, girl. Don't let your past dictate your choices or your future."

Then, Anny was gone.

Brooklyn opened her front door, her smile fading when she peered up in Parker's face. "Come in," she said.

Parker stepped into his sister's home, took one look at the candles lit on the pool table and a shirtless Carter sitting on the sofa, and turned back to the door. "I'm going to go."

His sister's hand on his arm stopped him in his tracks. "No, stay."

"Obviously, you two had plans tonight," Parker argued.

"Nothing important, Parker," Carter said, standing up. "You're always welcome here."

His brother-in-law disappeared in the back and came back a few seconds later with a shirt on. Brooklyn motioned Parker toward the couch. "Have a seat."

Parker fell back on the soft cushion, rubbed his head. "I always knew Senior was reprehensible, but it's always a shock when I hear the lengths he's gone through to conduct business."

Brooklyn wrapped her arms around her knees, perching her chin on top of them. "What did he do now?"

"Hunt Nursery. Gary Townsend offered to buy the land and the business for Wellspring Water with Senior's blessing."

"Yeah? I'm surprised Angelia would consider selling to Senior."

"That's what I said. But apparently she did."

"Wow," was Brooklyn's response.

"Her niece is the woman who rear-ended me. She is representing Angelia's interests."

"Really?" Brooklyn grinned. "Small world."

Parker grumbled, "Too small. Anyway, Kennedi came to see me this afternoon. She had some issues with the offer. And I hadn't had a chance to look it over yet, so I asked if we could discuss it later after I'd reviewed it. She then insinuated that I was running the business like Senior was, like I would purposefully do some sneaky shit to Angelia to get the land. Needless to say, I shut down."

Brooklyn nodded. "That's what you do."

"Exactly," Parker agreed before he realized what

his sister was really implying. When he did, though, he shot her a side eye. "Brooklyn."

His sister held up her hands. "Sorry. Go ahead."

"I felt bad about the way the conversation ended, so I went to her, to apologize. Then she leveled even more accusations about Senior and land grabbing and unscrupulous business practices. She even implied that Senior has been working with Senator King to drive up property taxes so that business owners will be forced to sell."

Brooklyn stared at him.

"What?" he asked.

"You can't tell me you didn't know that was going on, Parker. She does have a point."

Parker had suspected that his father was doing it, but he hadn't found any proof of it. "Can you let me finish?"

He explained how he'd left Hunt Manor and immediately called his attorneys. They made quick work of gathering several files of recent sales transactions. Parker had spent the last few hours combing through documents, contracts, and financial statements. Kennedi had been right. His father had done the unthinkable. He'd stolen parcels of land from several Wellspring citizens.

"The deal with Hunt Nursery?" Parker continued. "As far as I can tell, the parcel of land closest to Wellspring land is crucial to our water reserves. If we don't get access to the land, it would be bad for the company."

Kennedi had been right. The contract wasn't favorable to the Hunt family. Considering the potential of those springs, Senior had underbid on his offer and padded the contract with language that would eventually destroy the land. They wouldn't be able to tear down the greenhouse, but they'd be able to divvy up the land, develop it, and sell it to the highest bidder while still maintaining access to the springs.

"So, what are you going to do?" Carter asked.

Parker shrugged. "Nothing. I'm not going to pursue the land."

Brooklyn gasped. "But you just said that it's crucial to your water reserves."

"I'll figure out something else," Parker said. "There has to be a way around this."

"What if there isn't?" Carter leaned forward, elbows on his knees. "It doesn't sound like there's a lot of time."

"There's not," Parker agreed. "But there's more."

Brooklyn muttered a curse. "Oh Lord. What else is there?"

Parker closed his eyes, shook his head, and finished. "I'm complicit in Senior's deeds."

"What?!" Brooklyn roared. "That's impossible."

"Not a willing or even knowing participant, but I am." Parker explained the paper trail. E-mails that he was on, documents that had his signature. "On the surface, the e-mails were a standard business type. But if this is leaked, and there is an investigation, I'd be hard pressed to prove that I wasn't involved. I am his son, after all. I'm the freakin' interim CEO of the company."

A surge of pent-up energy filled Parker, and he

stood to pace the room. It was just like Senior to do something that would implicate him in a crime. The old man would have known that Parker would be forced to defend himself, and, in turn, Senior. It was a betrayal, one of many over the years.

"I shouldn't be surprised," Parker said. "It's not like this is out of the realm of possibility where Senior is concerned, but it's just one more thing on a long list that I have to clean up. Senior, man." Parker rubbed his head in frustration. "The man is lying in a coma, and has been for months. Yet, his actions are reverberating in the company and the community."

"You're going to need a top-notch legal team to fight this, Parker." Brooklyn's voice was soft, small in the open space of her great room. "Do you have any ideas how you're going to handle this?"

Parker had a plan, but he wouldn't bore Brooklyn and Carter with the details. Instead, he simply said, "First things first. I have to get rid of Gary Townsend and the other members of the staff still loyal to Senior and conducting his business."

"That's simple," Carter said. "Fire them."

In Carter's world, where he was the owner of a company controlled solely by him and his partner, firing him was the easy choice. But simply firing Gary wouldn't terminate his role as a member of the board of directors, so Parker couldn't move that fast. The company bylaws allowed Gary to serve on the board and maintain a position in the company, which was a conflict of interest that his father overlooked for nefarious reasons for sure.

Parker would have to work on this on his own, build a case against Gary, cement his hold with the board, cultivate the relationships, and gain their trust. Gary had successfully blocked him with the labor deal, but Parker wouldn't be swayed.

"It's not that simple," Parker told Carter. "But I'll handle it."

The room descended into silence for a few moments. Parker didn't know how he was going to tell Brooklyn the next hurdle they'd have to jump through. When Kennedi was at the office earlier, he'd received a call that would undoubtedly throw his sister into a fit.

"Brooklyn?" Parker turned to his sister. "Patricia has filed a motion with the court to reopen the divorce case. She's basically accused us of forcing her hand, and is claiming that she signed under duress out of fear for her life."

Parker watched his sister suck in a deep breath, saw the sadness in her eyes be replaced with disgust. Then, she blew. "What the hell?" Brooklyn bolted upright from the couch. She murmured a few long curses, seemed to reason with herself about her next words, and stalked over to her laptop. "This is ridiculous. No, this is some bullshit. Her attorneys were present when she signed the divorce papers."

Parker and Carter exchanged looks while Brooklyn continued to grumble under her breath. She was now typing something on her laptop, tapping each letter on the keyboard furiously.

When she was done, she looked up at them. "I'm fed up, Parker. If this woman doesn't scurry away into the dark like the night critter she is, I will bury her and she won't get a dime."

Another look passed between him and Carter. Brooklyn was a firecracker, the one thing she probably got from the Wells side of their family. If he didn't despise Patricia, he would feel sorry for her.

"In light of this new situation with Wellspring Water, I—"

"I'll handle this," Brooklyn said, closing her laptop. Hard. "You concentrate on the company, I'll handle Patricia. And I'll take the lead on finding our sister as well."

"I talked to Bryson."

Hope bloomed in Brooklyn's eyes. "Really? Is he coming home?"

"No, he isn't."

Lowering her head, Brooklyn said, "I can't even be mad at him, Parker. I'm not sure I would come home either, if I were him."

After he spent a few more minutes with his sister and brother-in-law, Parker felt a little better about his path. Now that Brooklyn had offered to take a few things off his plate, he would go forth with his plan for the company. It was the only way he would be able to save himself and the company.

Chapter 9

Parker had been sitting there for twenty minutes and still hadn't been able to say anything. When he'd arrived at the long-term-care wing of the hospital where his father was a patient, he'd planned to say everything that needed to be said. He'd planned to confront his father about the news of a new sister, about the land grabbing. He'd wanted to tell his father what he'd always thought of him. But the words hadn't come yet.

With Senior lying so still, Parker had to wonder if he would even hear him. The doctors had told him and Brooklyn that comatose patients often hear what is going on around them. The medical staff had encouraged them to talk to him, to let him know that he wasn't alone. Brooklyn was better than Parker, though.

At least his sister had managed to visit on a somewhat regular basis, if only for a few minutes. Parker, on the other hand, couldn't bring himself to come. There was too much past between him and Senior, too much damage done by his father.

Leaning forward, his elbows on his knees, he rubbed his face. When his mother, Marie, died, Parker had been distraught. Without Marie, it was up to him to protect his siblings, who were four and six years younger than him.

Despite the fact that Bryson was Senior's son from another relationship, a by-product of his father's long-term mistress, Marie had accepted Parker's youngest sibling. She'd treated him like one of her own, bringing him in for weekend visits, even though he'd been a constant reminder of Senior's infidelity. That was a testament to how wonderful his mother was. Losing her was life changing and had almost destroyed him.

"I guess I shouldn't be surprised," Parker said finally. "Patricia told me about your long-lost daughter. Well, I guess she's not really lost because you knew about her. You knew you had another daughter. You knew there was someone with the Wells name who existed and chose to keep her a secret. For what? So you could pull her out of your ass at some point in the future to keep us in line?"

According to the birth certificate faxed over to him, his sister's name was Veronica. She was a year younger than him, three older than Brooklyn. Veronica was born in Hammond, Indiana, which was about thirty miles south of Chicago.

"Brooklyn told me I need to talk to you," Parker said. "She told me I should tell you exactly how I feel. Before, I hesitated because I wasn't sure how that would help the situation. I asked myself what difference would this one-sided conversation make. It won't change anything because you're lying there, not reacting, not defending yourself."

Parker swallowed past a lump that had formed in his throat. The sounds of the hospital machines and the whoosh of the ventilator breathing for his father filled the room. When Senior had been rushed to the hospital all those months ago, Parker had been told that his father wanted extraordinary measures taken, meaning Senior wanted to be kept alive at all costs. Unlike Parker's mother, who had requested not to be resuscitated in the event her heart stopped, the hospital staff had been bound to save Senior's life even though he'd nearly died several times those first few days in the hospital.

Once Senior had stabilized, the doctors had announced that Senior slipped into a coma and they were doubtful his father would ever regain consciousness. Parker couldn't imagine choosing to live his last days out in that state of being, but he never did understand Senior's motive for doing anything.

"Yet, I'm here," Parker continued. "Knowing you, being your son, makes this even harder to say because I know you don't care. You've spent your life proving that we are nothing more than a means to an end for you. Despite trying, I can't remember one time that I actually believed you loved me as a father should love his son. You wanted to control me—you used manipulation and fear to do that for so many years. I guess that's what a narcissist does, and I fully believe that's what you are. Or were."

Everything was about Senior. Every person in his father's life served a purpose that furthered Senior's agenda. Even Parker's grandfather hadn't been exempt, especially in his later years of life when Senior was supposedly handling his affairs.

His father had made some bad deals, used his grandfather's money to finance those deals, which resulted in the company going through financial trouble when Senior took over as CEO. Parker and Brooklyn had recently learned the details once they found out that it was their mother, Marie, who'd bailed Senior out by investing a large part of her own inheritance to help save the company. Instead of being grateful, and treating her better, Senior had treated her worse. Parker suspected it was part of a plan concocted by his father to drive his mother crazy so he could control her money and shares. Yes, Senior was a master manipulator, a tyrant, an asshole. There were no redeeming qualities in his father, and Parker had tried to find them.

Parker shook his head, remembering the physical and emotional abuse he'd suffered at the hands of his father. Brooklyn had good memories of their father, because she was younger and the only girl, but Parker was hard pressed to remember anything good about growing up in that house, with that man.

He had the memories of being banished to the empty wing of the house by himself, of feeling hungry for days, of feeling like his sanity was hanging on a thin string. Then, he'd be called back, cleaned up, and brought out for show at an event or a fund-raiser.

It was cruel and not-that-unusual punishment for Senior. Before his mother died, there were little things, the way he'd be held to a different standard, the way his father rode him about his schoolwork and sports. It steadily got worse after Parker's mother died and the carousel of new wives were introduced into the home. That's when Brooklyn's eyes were finally opened to the true beast under her father's skin.

Parker had often stood in and taken that abuse so that Brooklyn and Bryson didn't have to, and he had the scars to prove it. Until one day, he'd had enough. Until that day that Senior realized that Parker was bigger than him, stronger than him. Until the moment Parker knew he could knock the shit out of his father in a heartbeat and not bat an eyelash. That was the day Senior kicked him out of the house.

For years, Parker lived on the outside, sneaking to stay in touch with his sister and brother, forced to fund his college education on his own. Luckily, he'd been stellar in school and was able to receive scholarship money. He'd worked long hours, studied when he wasn't working, but he managed to make it. He credited that time as molding him into the man he was today. It was during that time that he'd also come up with the plan to work his way back into his father's graces, for the sole reason of cementing his role in Wellspring Water Corporation.

And it worked. Senior eventually brought him in, as a member of the legal staff initially. It had sickened Parker to play nice for a while, but he'd reasoned with himself that it was what he had to do. Wellspring Water was a multi-billion-dollar corporation, a top employer in the world. There was no way he would allow the company to end up in the hands of a stranger, or, heaven forbid, one of Senior's wives, should something happen to the old man.

Wellspring Water was founded by Parker's great-grandfather Harry Wells back in 1955, who'd been one of the original settlers to a plot of land that would later become Wellspring, Michigan. The company distributed the first bottled water in 1956. The natural springs in Wellspring became a selling point, and Harry marketed the water as having healing properties. Local hospitals and smaller communities in the area were the first to purchase the bottles.

But it wasn't until 1976 when Parker's grandfather Patrick took over the company that the company started growing, diversifying, and purchasing other brands of water. In the 1980s, Patrick made Wellspring Water a household name, when the country was looking for healthy hydration. Back then, bottled water was considered a commodity and mostly purchased by people who had money to spare. Now, families from all walks of life purchased bottled water for their homes, for their jobs.

"I plan to take Wellspring Water into the future, Senior. But I want to do it with the respect and the support of the community. Not the fear and loathing that you seemed to thrill in. I want to do right by Grandpa Patrick's legacy. And I will."

Parker stood finally, stepped closer to the hospital bed where Senior lay. Still. Too still. Peering down at his father, he bent low until he was right in his ear. "I just want you to know that you didn't break me. All those beatings, the lies, the scandal, even this new sister . . . I'll still handle it with a grace you have never possessed. The birthright you tried to steal from us, we're fixing that. The company you used to terrorize the people of this town, I'm in charge now. You hear that, Senior? Me. I'm going to right every wrong you made in the name of Wellspring Water."

Standing to his full height, he sucked in a strong breath. There was no movement from his father, no spike in his blood pressure. Only silence. Only stillness. And Parker was done. Without another word, he exited the room.

Kennedi entered Lawson Garage first thing Tuesday morning. Approaching the counter, she said to the cashier, "Good morning. I'm here to see Trent Lawson."

The man behind the counter grinned wide at her. "Sure thing, ma'am. I can grab him for you."

When the man disappeared, Kennedi scanned the garage. It was tidy, unlike any shop she'd been to. Not that she'd been to many garages. She normally handled her car business directly with her dealership. The couches in the waiting area were clean, and there was a coffee station on the far wall, which immediately made her salivate with the need for a cup. There was an older gentleman reading a newspaper over by the flat screen television hung on the wall.

Getting up that morning had been a struggle. She'd been tempted to laze around in bed for the day, but figured there was no use hiding from the world. Unable to deny the lure of hot coffee any longer, she walked over to the counter to make herself a cup.

Kennedi grabbed a K-cup and set it in the Keurig. Grabbing a paper cup, she glanced up at the pictures on the wall. In one, Trent Lawson stood, arms outstretched in front of the building. Tilting her head, Kennedi wondered if the picture was taken on the grand opening of the garage. He certainly looked proud of his accomplishment. Next, there was a picture of the same man with an older gentleman, same build, same height. *Probably his father.* When her eyes gazed at the next picture, she dropped her cup on the floor.

"Shit," she murmured, bending to pick the paper cup up off the floor. "Thank God that was empty." She tossed the cup into a nearby wastebasket, then looked up at the picture. It was Trent again, standing with the same wide smile, next to Parker Wells Jr.

The two were happy, shaking hands in front of the building. Parker wore a pair of jeans and a button-down shirt. He looked relaxed, comfortable.

She wondered what the story was in the picture. There appeared to be a genuine fondness between the two, almost like brothers. Or very good friends.

"Good morning."

Kennedi jumped at the greeting and whirled around, finding herself face-to-face with the man in the pictures. Stepping forward, hand outstretched, she asked, "You must be Trent?"

Trent grabbed her hand and shook it. "I am. What can I do for you?"

The pictures behind her didn't do Trent Lawson any justice. Sure, he was handsome in them, but in person, he was gorgeous. His eyes were a startling green, and he was tall. His hair was cut low, and he wore a pair of dark denim pants and a black T-shirt. Trent was a hottie. *Not as fine as Parker, but . . .* Kennedi shook her mind free from that last thought. What the hell was she thinking about Parker for? "Um, I got your name from a family friend. Fred Wyatt?"

Trent grinned then. "Ah, Fred. He's a good man."

Kennedi nodded her agreement. "Yes. I was in an accident the other day that damaged the front grille of my car. I was wondering if you could take a look?"

Trent's eyebrows furrowed, then released. A slow smile spread across his lips. "An accident?"

Frowning, Kennedi answered, "Yes. I hit a car from behind." Suddenly nervous, she tucked a strand of hair behind her ear. Trent was gazing back at her with focus, almost like he knew her, or knew of her, or wanted to know her. Swallowing, she retreated back a step. "As far as I can tell, his car wasn't damaged. I wasn't going fast, but the truck was pretty big. And I drive a car, a nice car," she babbled.

Trent nodded slowly. "A nice car?" he asked, amusement in his eyes.

Embarrassed, Kennedi corrected her earlier statement. "I meant a newer car. Actually, I just purchased it a few months ago. It's a custom color and grille. I'm sure there will be an upcharge to order the correct parts."

With raised eyebrows, he said, "You talk like you know cars."

Kennedi grinned. "I know a little bit. My father liked to restore cars. He and my grandfather liked to restore cars. He owned several, and I was his helper."

"Nice," Trent said. "I own a few myself."

A jingle signaling someone entering the shop interrupted the conversation. Kennedi turned, surprised to see Parker walking in.

Shit.

Trent waved Parker over. "What's up?"

The two greeted each other with a handshake-hug, and Kennedi forced herself to stay put. *Maybe if I'm quiet he won't notice me.*

Unfortunately, that was wishful thinking. Parker turned to her, a tight smile on his lips. "Kennedi."

"Mr. Wells." She lowered her head, pretended to pick at her nails.

"Ouch," Trent said. "What brings you out this way?"

When Kennedi looked up, Parker was looking at

her. With disgust, if she had to wager a bet. "Thought I'd catch you before your day started, maybe get you to look at my truck. Like I told you the other day, someone rammed into me." Parker told Trent, never taking his eyes off Kennedi.

She rolled her eyes. "Oh please. I didn't ram into you. It was a light bump."

"You never can be sure with a rear-end collision," Parker said.

"Whoa! Neutral corners, people." Trent's gaze flitted back and forth between Kennedi and Parker. "Parker, you also told me you were going to bring the truck by Saturday. Today is a busy Tuesday. I'll take a look, but I have a few cars in front of you. Been here since six this morning. One of my mechanics quit last week. I'm picking up the slack. It might be better for you to bring it back another day, man."

Parker finally turned to Trent, and Kennedi had to force herself to not react to the loss of his heated gaze. That thought had her tugging on her jacket. Hard. *What the hell is wrong with me?* As she watched the men converse, she wondered what their story was, how the two became friends.

Clearing her throat, she asked Trent, "I don't mean to be rude, but do you think you could take a look at my car?" Soon, two pairs of eyes were on her, making her a little uncomfortable. Kennedi scratched her neck. "It's just . . . I have something to take care of this morning, Mr. Lawson."

Trent smiled. "Oh, it's cool. And call me Trent."

Kennedi nodded. "Thanks, Trent." She started toward her car, parked out front.

Outside, Trent jotted notes on a tablet he'd grabbed on their way out. As the man circled her car, inspecting the damages, Kennedi struggled to focus on Trent and her car, rather than Parker, who was also standing there. Watching her.

Once Trent was done, he walked over to her. "I'm sure a woman with your expertise could guess that I'm going to have to replace that fascia." Kennedi glanced at Parker in time to see the curious raise of his eyebrows. "But I can get the part in within the week," Trent continued.

"That's actually expected. They don't make cars like they used to." Kennedi walked around to the front of her car and peered down, running a hand over a small scratch on the hood. "The grille?"

"You're good there," Trent said. "I'm guessing the car runs smoothly?"

"It does. I don't think there's any damage to the transmission or anything. After all, I didn't hit the truck hard." She shot Parker a pointed look. "The paint color is custom, though." Kennedi had splurged on a white metallic color that appeared more like a pearl color than plain white. When she'd decided to go light with her new car, as opposed to the black she'd always bought before, she didn't want the vehicle to resemble a rental car. And white cars always made her think of Avis or Hertz.

"No problem. I am one of the best in this area for paint. I can match it easily."

"Great. I can call my insurance company and give them your information." Michigan was a no-fault state. It wasn't necessary for an accident to be reported to the police in order for her to file a claim. And since it was her fault, she'd just pay her deductible and get the car fixed. "Once you check out Mr. Wells's truck, will you give me the bill if there is any damage to his vehicle?"

Trent turned an amused glance toward Parker. "Parker?"

Parker nodded, his eyes on her. "You heard her."

Kennedi eyed Parker as he and Trent made arrangements for Parker to bring his truck back tomorrow afternoon. *I should just walk away.* But she wanted to look at him for one more minute. All of the resolve she'd had to stay away from him evaporated like water on a hot day. Everything about him was classic, almost iconic like a 1965 Mustang or a rare jewel. From his looks to the way he radiated calm. He was powerful, cool, but he wasn't afraid to laugh loud and often.

"Kennedi?" Trent called.

Kennedi blinked. *Oh God.* "Huh?"

The smirk that played across Parker's lips made her want to kick him. He knew what he was doing, and he was damn good at it.

Posture straight, Kennedi. She held her chin high, turning away from Parker to face Trent. She smiled, hoping to convey a confidence and comfort she didn't quite feel. "You were saying?"

Trent grinned. "You can leave the car here with me, and I'll work on it as soon as I get the part. Or I can call you back when it comes in. Up to you."

Kennedi looked at her car, then back at Trent.

"Um, I guess I can leave it. I can walk over to the nursery and use my aunt's car."

"Or I can have someone drop you over there," Trent said. "It's kind of chilly out this morning."

It was pretty nippy outside. She'd attempted to go for a run that morning, but ended up putting in a few miles on the treadmill in the home gym. "Oh, that would be—"

"I'll drop her off," Parker offered.

Kennedi's head whipped over toward him. "No," she said, a little too forcefully. Lowering her voice, she added, "I mean, I wouldn't want to put you out."

Parker shrugged. "You're not. I'm going toward the nursery anyway."

For some reason, Kennedi didn't believe Parker, but she couldn't actually prove he was lying. "But . . ." *Oh hell.* "Fine. That would be nice."

Parker looked at Trent. "I'll be back later, Trent. After work. Maybe we can get into something tonight."

"Poker?" Trent suggested.

"I'm good with it," Parker said, a smile on his face. "Are you sure you're okay with losing your money again?"

"Whatever, man," Trent said. "Juke already called about a game tonight."

Kennedi wondered what a "Juke" was. "Is Juke a person?" she asked. When the men looked at her, she regretted her choice to butt into their conversation.

"Juke is the owner of Brook's Pub," Trent explained. "He has a poker room in the back of the pub. We play sometimes on Tuesdays and Saturdays."

"Sounds like fun," Kennedi said, with a grin. "I know Brook's Pub. I've been there before, during a visit about a year ago. Didn't know the owner's name was Juke, though."

"Don't tell me . . . you know cars and you play poker?" Trent asked.

Kennedi shook her head. "Nah, I don't like losing money."

Trent barked out a laugh. "Tell me about it."

"Maybe you should stop playing, then, Trent," Parker teased. "I can keep taking your money, but since you don't like to lose it . . ."

"My aunt plays," Kennedi offered, for no apparent reason. She had no idea what possessed her to keep talking. "I do remember there were good cheese fries." *Shut up, Kennedi.*

"That is the truth. You're welcome to join us. I can teach you."

"Not if she has any hope of keeping her money," Parker deadpanned.

Trent waved a hand of dismissal. "Seriously, you should come on out."

Kennedi considered the offer. It wouldn't be a bad thing to get out and have some fun. But there was the added inconvenience of Parker being there that gave her pause. "Can women join the game?"

"We're an equal opportunity group," Trent assured her.

Shrugging, Kennedi said," Maybe. I'll think about it."

"We need to get going," Parker said, his voice low. "I have some errands to run."

Sighing, Kennedi shook Trent's hand again. "Thanks again." She handed him her business card. "Please call me when you complete the quote. I want to get it over to my insurance agent."

Trent and Parker shared their own good-bye that consisted of them giving each other dap. Kennedi strolled over to the truck and reached out to open the door, but Parker was there pulling it open for her.

"Thanks." She climbed in and buckled her seat belt.

Once he was in the driver's seat and had started the truck, she waited for him to put it in reverse. But that never came.

"What's wrong?" she asked, frowning.

Parker turned to her. "It's high time we had a conversation, Kennedi."

Chapter 10

Parker couldn't describe what was happening to him. All he knew was it was strange, and it had everything to do with the woman sitting in his passenger seat staring at him like he had grown another head.

It wasn't like she was his girl. She didn't belong to him, but Parker had been possessive, jealous even. Of Trent. Because she'd called Trent by his first name, while referring to him as Mr. Wells. She couldn't know that it drove Parker crazy to be called Mr. Wells because that was his father, that was Senior. And he didn't want to be anything like Senior. That wasn't the only reason, though. Somehow, the fact that she didn't call him by his first name made him feel inadequate. That wasn't something he was used to feeling with a woman.

And now . . . What? Was he going to force her to talk to him, to have a conversation she obviously didn't want to have?

"Why would we need to talk about anything?" she asked, with a raised brow.

"I came to you, yesterday. I apologized to you, and you basically told me to go to hell."

"I didn't say that," Kennedi argued.

"You did."

Kennedi sighed. "Look, I was out of line. You just pissed me off."

Parker smiled. This woman was refreshing. Honest, confident. "I pissed you off?"

"Yes, you did." She hunched her shoulders. "What can I say? I don't like being blown off. Especially when I'm right."

"Hence, the apology."

"Mr. Wells, I—"

"Please." Parker gripped the steering wheel. "Don't call me Mr. Wells."

When he turned to Kennedi, she was observing him, her head tilted. It was a long moment before she spoke. "Parker, I'm sorry. That was below the belt."

Damn, she is beautiful. And his name on her lips was soft, sexy. When he'd gone to Hunt Manor to see her, he'd had to fight to not stare at her in her workout gear. The yoga pants she wore fit her like a second skin. And she wore one of those little sports bras, too, showing off her toned stomach. Even now, just being near her made him want to do all kinds of things to her.

Arriving at the shop and seeing her car outside had felt like a windfall, like God had just dropped her into his lap. Now, she was in his truck, looking at him like he was crazy.

Parker shook his head in an attempt to clear the haze from his mind. "Join me for coffee?"

She pulled at her ear, the same ear he wanted to lean forward and take in his mouth. "I don't know. I told my aunt that I would meet her at the nursery."

"Angelia would be happy we're having coffee. We do have business to discuss."

"About that?" She wrinkled her nose. "Aside from this little bit of a truce we have going on, I meant what I said. Until I can see important changes, we're not signing."

"That's fair. I know Angelia wants to sell. I'm confident that we can come to terms."

"It has to be right for her. She's already sacrificed a lot for the business. She's ready to retire and she deserves to leave on her own terms."

Parker wanted to ask her what she meant but knew it wasn't the right time. "Can I ask you a question?"

She leaned back, angling away from him. He wanted to pull her back. "What?" she asked.

"Earlier, I got the impression that you didn't really agree with the decision to sell. Can I ask why?"

The car descended into silence and he wondered if he'd hit a nerve or if she would even answer the question. Finally, she said, "Good question."

"Okay. And?"

"I'm just not going to answer it. Where are we going for coffee?"

* * *

At the Bees Knees, Parker watched Kennedi stir the cream in her coffee. They'd arrived about ten minutes earlier, after a short ride. Parker couldn't figure Kennedi out, but . . . *Oh, how I want to.* She'd clammed up after she agreed to come have coffee with him, and he figured it had something to do with the question he'd asked her.

Before he could ask her why she was so quiet, Dee Clark came over to their table. "Hey, Parker," the older woman said. "Hey, Kennedi."

The smile that appeared on Kennedi's face at Dee's presence made Parker smile. It was obvious Kennedi was fond of the owner of his favorite Wellspring restaurant. It was a busy Tuesday morning at the diner, as it always was. People came from miles around to get a sample of the famous Denver omelet that was Dee's specialty.

"What can I get for you two? Are you eating today?"

Kennedi shook her head. "I'm not really hungry."

Dee waved her off. "Girl, please. You didn't come in for your catfish Friday night. Just so happens my catfish and grits is a winner as well."

Kennedi flashed Dee a wicked grin. "Oh, Dee, you tempt me."

"How about I bring you a plate?" Dee asked.

"You twisted my arm," Kennedi told her with a laugh. "Extra hot sauce, please."

Dee turned to him then. "And you? Your usual?"

Nodding, he told her, "With an extra side of bacon. Crispy."

Dee walked off, chatting with a couple of the

customers before she disappeared in the back. Kennedi turned to him. "What's your usual?" she asked.

"The Denver omelet, of course." It was a no-brainer for him. He'd been eating them since he was a kid.

Kennedi frowned. "But you ordered a side of bacon. Doesn't the omelet already have ham and bacon in it?"

"Just ham. And you can't go wrong with a side of bacon."

"You do have a point there," Kennedi said with a chuckle. She picked up her mug of coffee and took a sip. "So what does Parker Wells Jr. do when he's not kicking corporate ass at Wellspring Water?"

Parker rubbed his brow. "Sleep."

"One of my favorite things to do." She set her mug down on the table.

"Yours, too?"

"There is nothing in the world like a warm blanket and a firm mattress. Those two things make the harsh reality of the world a much better place."

"True story." He held his fist out to her and she bumped it with hers.

"The question is . . . how often do you sleep?"

Talking about sleep was not how he envisioned a conversation with Kennedi. He'd expected her to steer him right to the matter at hand—the potential sales transaction. She was serious about her business. But she was also not afraid to laugh.

"I cannot tell a lie," he answered. "I can fall asleep at any time. My friends used to tease me in high school because I can pretty much sleep through anything."

With wide eyes, she asked, "Anything?"

"Pretty much," he repeated.

She laughed. "Now, that's surprising."

When Kennedi smiled it was like her soul was shining, offering him a glimpse inside her. She was saying something, but he had no idea what it was. He couldn't stop staring at her mouth, her dimples, her smooth skin.

"Why?" he asked, finally picking up his black coffee and taking a sip.

"You're running a huge corporation. I can't imagine you being able to turn it off and fall asleep."

"I will admit that the last several months have been hard, but I still find a way."

"I wish it was that easy for me to sleep," she murmured. "It takes me at least an hour to fall asleep once I lie down."

Dee walked over to the table with their plates before Parker could tell her that *he* could put her to sleep. "Here you go, Parker and Kennedi," Dee said. "Enjoy."

Kennedi leaned over her plate and hummed softly. "I can't wait to dig in."

"Have you ever been fishing?" he asked.

She flinched. "I'll pass. That's disgusting."

Her reaction surprised him. Angelia was a woman who loved to fish, and he'd often seen her and Fred on the riverbank, poles in the water. "You should try it. I see Angelia at the bank all the time."

"You fish?"

"Sure do." Parker's grandfather took him out fishing a lot when he was a kid. It was their personal time together, and Parker had considered that time invaluable. It was on the riverbank that Grandpa had told him the secret to life: God and family. Parker had often wondered how a man like Grandpa Patrick could have fathered Senior. Grandpa was all about family and legacy, and Senior was about himself. It was no wonder the two didn't really get along.

"My grandfather used to take me, before he died."

"I'm sorry." Her voice was soft, soothing.

Parker knew that Angelia's sister had died, so he knew Kennedi had experienced loss in her life as well. "It's okay. I'm just glad I had him for the time I did. My sister and brother don't really remember him. But I do."

With a heavy nod, she said, "That helps."

Parker wanted to ask about her parents but sensed it would be uncharted territory. When he lost his mother, he'd closed himself off for a while. Eventually, he'd allowed himself to grieve with his siblings. Being able to talk about her with his friends had also helped. He wondered if Kennedi had ever had that opportunity.

They ate silently for a few minutes before she said, "My father used to like to fish." She admitted softly, "I never wanted to go with him, but my sister used to go."

"There's something about the river, the sound of the water that is peaceful. You should try it."

"I can't imagine holding a fish that wasn't fried in cornmeal with hot sauce."

Parker chuckled and pointed to her plate. "I see."

Once they were done eating, Kennedi leaned back. "So, I don't have to tell you I have reservations about doing business with Wellspring Water."

"I kind of figured that out."

"But since this is something Anny wants, I'm willing to come to the table with you."

"Attorney speak," he muttered.

"Is that a problem?" she countered.

He shook his head. "Not really. I am an attorney myself."

Kennedi eyed him thoughtfully. "I can see that. Did you start out at a firm, or have you always worked for Wellspring Water?"

"I was courted by several firms, but I ended up coming back here and working for the company after I graduated from law school."

"That's devotion. I'm sure your father was proud."

The mention of his father made him toss his napkin down on the table. "I wouldn't know," he admitted, unable to help the bitter tone in his voice. "Senior isn't exactly full of compliments."

"Anny told me Senior had a heart attack."

"He did," Parker confirmed. "He's comatose, in a long-term-care facility in Grand Rapids. The doctors don't expect him to ever wake up."

Kennedi turned her attention to her coffee. "That's tough."

You don't know the half of it.

When her gaze met his again, she said, "But I hear you're doing good things with the company."

"I'm trying," he said. Needing a change of subject, he asked, "So, are you just here to handle the sale?"

Kennedi snickered. "Actually, I didn't come here to handle the sale. That was kind of just thrust upon me when I got here. I'm supposed to be on vacation."

"For how long?"

"A month. I'm taking an extended leave."

Curious, Parker asked, "Are you okay?"

"Yes," she replied. "Just needed some time away."

Parker fought the urge to ask her why. He wanted to know more about her. "It's healthy to take breaks from work . . . or people."

"I definitely agree with that," she said.

"Okay, I have to ask. Are—?"

"I think I know what you're going to ask. And to answer your question, I'm not running from a person, although I'm sure my ex-husband would love it if I left because I'm so heartbroken over our divorce. I'm here because I really needed a vacation. I haven't had one in years, and it was long overdue."

Parker wasn't surprised that she'd read him. She seemed to do that often. "Okay. I'm glad you decided to get away to Wellspring. Too bad you rammed into my truck on your first day back in town."

Kennedi giggled and swatted at him with her napkin. "Oh, stop. Your truck is fine."

He barked out a laugh. "You hope so. Seriously, though? I'm glad you did."

Kennedi was enjoying her impromptu breakfast with Parker, which was a pleasant surprise. He was a surprise, unlike what she thought. Parker Wells Jr. seemed to be a man with integrity. She'd secretly given him high marks for that "God and family" reference earlier. And his smile, his laugh, that voice . . . She'd spent the bulk of breakfast trying to rein in her treacherous body, which had been flooded with warmth the entire time.

"You're divorced?" he asked, after the waitress came and topped off their coffee mugs again.

"I am. For a year now," she grumbled. Kennedi wasn't sure what it was about Parker that made her want to talk so much, share things with him.

"How long were you married?" he asked.

Kennedi traced the rim of her mug with her finger. "Couple of years."

"Hm. Why the divorce?"

"You sure do ask a lot of questions."

He smiled then. "I'm sorry." Parker took a sip of his coffee. "Occupational hazard. You know how it is."

Kennedi did know. She was the same way. Relentless when it came to getting the story on someone. "I can definitely relate. But we just weren't a good fit. My husband and I."

"I'm sorry to hear that."

She shrugged. "I'm not. Quincy wasn't the man for me. I realize that now."

"Quincy, huh? He sounds like a punk."

Kennedi couldn't help it. She laughed, and it felt good. That fact that Parker made her laugh made him even more attractive, and she found herself hoping he would ask her out again. Because aside from the whole land transaction, she enjoyed his company immensely. What was the harm in a little vacation fling?

"I'm kidding," Parker said. "Don't tell my boy Q I said that."

Giggling, Kennedi whispered, "Don't worry. Your secret is safe with me."

"I can honestly say that your Quincy is a punk. And a fool." His gaze slid over her like a caress. The heat in his eyes was electric, made her want to lean in and bask in his warmth.

She drew in a shaky breath. "I'm glad you agree with me."

He barked out a laugh. "Have dinner with me?"

Finally. "When?"

She knew from his earlier conversation with Trent that he had plans that evening, so she wasn't expecting him to say, "Tonight."

Shifting in her seat, she crossed her legs. "Don't you have something with Trent planned?"

"Trent will understand."

Kennedi smiled. "I'm sure he would, but I don't want to ruin your plans. As we've already established, I'll be here for a while. Besides, I was kind of leaning toward going to Brook's Pub tonight."

"Fine," he said. "Then, I'll see you tonight?"

She nodded. "Hopefully."

Parker paid for breakfast and they made their

way outside the restaurant. His hand on the small of her back was firm, as he led her to his truck. "I'll drop you at the nursery," he said, opening her door for her and waiting for her to climb in before he closed it.

It was refreshing to be with a man who opened doors for her without prompting. Kennedi found herself wanting to know more about the man who was sliding into the driver's seat. "Thanks for breakfast," she said. "And the conversation."

"You're welcome. What do you say we table any and all contract conversation until later in the week?"

Kennedi nodded her agreement. "Sounds good."

The drive to the nursery was fast. Once again, Parker hopped out of the car and opened her door for her. He grabbed her hand and helped her out. They stood there for a moment, him with his hands in his pockets and her with her stomach in knots. It wasn't like they'd just gone on a date and it was the awkward moment before the first kiss. *We've already had our first kiss.* A perfect first kiss. Still, it felt like something more should happen. Not a kiss necessarily, but . . . something.

Then, Parker pulled her to him, hugging her tightly. Kennedi closed her eyes and melted into his embrace, inhaling his scent. *That's it.*

When he pulled back, he said, "I'll see you later?"

She smiled. "Maybe."

He shook his head. "Whatever. Bye, Kennedi."

"Bye, Parker."

Chapter 11

Brook's Pub was off the chain when Kennedi arrived Thursday evening, standing room only. It shocked her because it was a Thursday and a workday. But the crowd was lively, full of cheer. She scanned the bar, looking for Parker. Tuesday hadn't worked out for them, because he'd ended up being stuck at the office. So, they'd agreed to meet at the pub for five-dollar pitchers and pool.

Kennedi liked to play different games, but she admittedly didn't know anything about billiards. She would give it a try, though. Walking closer to the bar, she spotted a big, buff man with arms full of tattoos. He wore a T-shirt that said Brook's Pub, and she took that as a sign that he worked there. She leaned forward, catching his eye. "Hi, I'm looking for the pool tables?"

In direct contrast to the scowl he wore a few seconds earlier, he grinned, showing off pretty white teeth and a dimple in his left cheek. "All the way in the back."

Kennedi smiled. "Thanks."

"Can I get you something to drink?" he asked. Well, more like yelled.

Shaking her head, Kennedi said, "Not right now. You have a nice place here."

His chest poked out a little bit at her compliment and he thanked her. "For that, your first drink is on the house. Just come back when you're ready."

Kennedi headed toward the back, sliding between bodies and smiling at the patrons. When she finally reached the back, she spotted the pool tables. There was a couple playing on one of the tables. A short woman with spiky hair and a wicked grin. And a man, dark skinned, nice looking. To the right of the table, she noticed Parker sitting on a stool, chatting with Trent.

When he glanced up, their eyes met and he grinned. Standing, he approached her. "You made it."

Kennedi nodded. "I told you I was going to come."

Parker stepped aside and gestured over to his table. Kennedi grinned at Trent. "Hi, Trent," she said with a wave.

Standing, Trent pulled her into a hug. "We don't wave around here, we hug."

Kennedi froze, but eventually relented and hugged the man back. "Okay," she said when he pulled away and took his seat again.

Parker pulled out a seat and she sat. "Want a drink?"

Kennedi shook her head. "This place is busy. I

don't remember it being like this last time I was here."

"Juke has done a good job of marketing, having daily specials, and the remodel helped."

"Brooklyn!" Parker shouted, waving at the woman at the pool table.

Kennedi held her breath as the woman walked over to the table. She knew Brooklyn was Parker's sister. She remembered her in school, although Brooklyn was a couple years younger than her.

"Hi," Brooklyn said, approaching the table. "You must be Kennedi?"

Kennedi held out her hand, but Brooklyn hugged her. *Wellspring is full of huggers.* "Nice to meet you."

"I think I remember you," Brooklyn said. "From Walker Elementary."

Kennedi nodded. "Yes, I went there. We must have seen each other walking the halls."

Walker Elementary was named for another resident, Emeline Walker. She was the first person to open a schoolhouse in Wellspring, back in 1945. Up until that point, school was conducted in the First Baptist Church of Wellspring. The Walker family had a history as long as the Hunt family and Wells family in Wellspring. Last Kennedi remembered, the sheriff was a Walker.

The man who'd been playing pool with Brooklyn walked over to the table. Brooklyn introduced him as her husband, Carter, and Kennedi greeted him with a handshake.

"I hear you're from Ann Arbor."

Kennedi nodded. "I actually live in Ypsilanti."

"Oh yeah. I'm very familiar with Ypsi," he said. "I'm from Detroit and went to school in Ann Arbor."

"Hail!" Kennedi held out a fist and he bumped it. *Hail* was a term University of Michigan alumni used when referring to the school. It was short for "Hail to the Victors."

"Did you go to undergrad there?" Carter asked.

Kennedi shook her head. "No, I went to Howard. I came back and went to U of M for law school."

With raised eyebrows, Carter said, "Nice."

"I didn't know you went to Howard," Parker said.

"You didn't ask," Kennedi countered.

The slow smile that spread over his face filled her with a warmth that made her forget where she was for a minute. Her mind was cloudy with only visions of him. Everything around her seemed to melt away when he leaned forward and said, "I'm going to have to ask more questions then. You're beautiful."

Once again, Kennedi felt a blush creep up her neck. Parker was worth millions. She knew he didn't say things he didn't mean. He didn't show his hand before he had to. She was the same way. Perhaps that's what fueled the need that shot through her whenever they were near each other.

Kennedi ducked her head, averting his gaze. "Thanks."

She'd dressed casually, rocking a pair of black skinny jeans and a cold shoulder sweater. And it was the third outfit she'd tried on that evening. Kennedi had never been so concerned with how she looked. She'd never had low self-esteem. Even Quincy's attempts to break her, comparing her to other women or trying to make her feel like she would never find anyone else, hadn't changed that.

What did end up affecting her was the way he'd used her, the fact that he never really loved her. He just loved what she could do for him and his career, what her money might have allowed him to do. She suspected Parker may have had similar experiences with women, being the heir to the Wells family fortune.

"You play?" Brooklyn asked, pointing to the pool table. "Carter is losing, so he probably won't mind if you get on the table."

Parker laughed. "Damn, Carter."

"Ah, shut up," Carter replied, yanking Brooklyn to him and placing a kiss on her.

Kennedi saw the genuine affection Carter had for his wife, the way his eyes followed her across the room. The same way Fred watched Anny.

Forcing herself to turn away, Kennedi glanced over at Parker and found him watching her. "What?" she asked.

"Nothing. Just looking at you." He leaned forward, brushed his lips against her temple. "I like to look at you."

Kennedi trembled in anticipation. What was she supposed to say to that? Thanks? "Oh," was all she got out. And even that sounded like a breathy moan.

Trent bent low, over her back, breaking the

spell Parker had her under. "You know, we are in a public bar. Get a room."

Kennedi laughed and swatted at Trent. "Stop."

Parker shot Trent a mock glare. "How about you go talk to Maddie? She's standing over there glaring at you."

That got Brooklyn's attention. "What did you do now, Trent?" she asked, hand on her hip. "It's time for you to get off your ass and make it official and stop playing around."

Kennedi leaned forward, hands on the table. "Who's Maddie?"

Parker leaned forward, hands on hers. "She's the one woman Trent can't live without. He just doesn't know it yet."

"I am standing right here," Trent said.

"You should be standing over there, man," Carter added with a laugh.

Trent waved them all off, muttered a curse, and said his good-byes.

Kennedi spent the rest of the evening watching Brooklyn take turns at beating Parker and Carter. When Parker lost the last game, he turned to Kennedi and asked her if she wanted him to teach her to play. Laughing, she pointed at Brooklyn. "I wouldn't mind learning, but I want *her* to teach me."

Brooklyn barked out a laugh. "See, she already knows what's up," she teased, pinching Parker's nose.

Parker wrapped an arm around Brooklyn's neck and gave her a soft noogie, which made her dissolve into a fit of giggles. Kennedi enjoyed watching

Parker with his sister. The affection and tenderness he showed Brooklyn made Kennedi think of her aunt's and Fred's words. *He's a good guy.*

Soon, Brooklyn yawned. "We'd better get going. I have an early day tomorrow." She gave Parker a hug, then turned to Kennedi, embracing her. "It was so good to meet you. How long will you be in town?"

Kennedi glanced at Parker, who was watching her intently. "I'm on leave for one month. So I'll be going home in a few weeks."

"What type of law do you practice?" Carter asked.

"Corporate."

"Ah." Carter gave Parker some dap. "Lots of money, but not a lot of time off."

Kennedi had to agree with Carter's assessment. She'd found out that Carter ran a software company, and she'd found his passion for his work inspiring. For as long as Kennedi had been practicing law, she'd never felt passion for the job. She didn't hate it, but she didn't miss it. In fact, she hadn't even thought about the office. Perhaps, that was the Wellspring effect.

After Brooklyn and Carter left, Parker stood up and reached out for Kennedi's hand. "Ready?"

"Sure."

Kennedi let Parker lead her out of the bar. When she stepped out into the chilly night air, Parker twirled her around and pulled her to him. "I'm glad you made it," he said.

Grinning, she said, "I'm glad I did, too. Your sister is lovely. And so are Carter and Trent."

"I don't think I like hearing you say Trent is lovely."

Kennedi giggled. "Jealous?"

Parker leaned in, brushing his nose against hers. "Very," he murmured.

Kiss me. "I think I like that you're jealous."

They were a breath apart, and Kennedi found herself staring at his lips. She wanted him to pull her to him, to taste him.

"Where's your car?" Parker asked. The faint smell of beer wafted to her nose. "I'll walk you to it."

Disappointed, Kennedi pointed toward Anny's car, which was parked on the street, a little way down from the pub. As they strolled leisurely, she told him, "Wellspring has quite the little nightlife."

"Yeah, we like to turn up." He bumped into her softly, as they neared the car. "I love my town."

"I can see that," she said. "Listen, I'm sorry about how I reacted about the whole sale thing. I really am."

"You already apologized. No need to do it again." Next to Anny's car now, Kennedi turned to Parker and relaxed into the car. Parker caged her in. "So, we've raced go-carts, ate cotton candy, had drinks—even though you didn't drink—and had breakfast together. When are you going to let me take you to dinner?"

"I don't think that's necessary, Parker. I've had fun with you, and I don't need to go to a fancy restaurant or dress up to have a good time."

"You are amazing," he said, eyes on her mouth again.

"Well, I can only be me."

"And I want to know you."

Kennedi felt unhinged, like at any moment the desire she felt for him would take her over and render her a pile of goo on the floor. *If this man doesn't kiss me, I'm going to die.*

Then, Parker said, "Well, I'd better go." He started to pull away.

Kennedi gripped the lapel of his jacket. "Boy, if you don't stop playing with me . . ."

"You want me to kiss you?" He chuckled.

"What do you think?" Kennedi asked.

"I want to kiss you," he whispered against her ear.

"Do it," Kennedi whispered.

Parker cupped her face in his hands. "Did I tell you how beautiful you are?"

She gripped his wrists. "Yes, you did."

He leaned forward, brushing his lips against hers lightly, stealing her breath away, before he pulled back. "Where do you want it?"

Parker's body was on fire, every nerve ending alive. She was like art in motion, always moving with confidence, like she would have no trouble kicking it with the fellas, rocking it in a board room, or cooking a full-course dinner. And he suspected that fire bled into the bedroom.

And shit he wanted to find out.

He'd issued a challenge. He wanted her to tell him where she wanted him to kiss her. She eyed him hesitantly. "Where do I want it?"

"Yes, you can pick where I kiss you."

She seemed to think about it for a few seconds

before her mouth turned up in a grin. She hummed. "How about right here?" She tapped her forehead.

He leaned forward, placed a lingering kiss on her forehead. When he pulled back, he raised a brow. "That it?"

"How about . . . here?" She pointed to her cheek.

He followed suit, kissing her cheek softly. She then pointed to her other cheek and he kissed it. Her finger then went to her ear, and he bent forward, tugged her earlobe in his mouth, and sucked.

Her sharp intake of breath egged him on and he traced his tongue down her neck.

She pushed him back. "Hey," she said. "I didn't tell you to kiss me there."

He pinned her with his gaze. Every time their eyes met, his emotions overwhelmed him. It was almost more than he could take. She was amazing. And it blew him away that he could be the man she wanted.

He raised his hands at his side. "Okay, I cheated."

They stood like that for what seemed like an eternity. Her staring at him, and him wishing she would just say the word. All he needed was a yes. Then, she took that finger and tapped her full lips, and Parker sent up a silent *Yes, Lawd* before capturing her lips with his.

Parker wouldn't call himself a kisser. In fact, he usually avoided it at all costs. For some reason, it always felt too close, too intimate. But Kennedi . . . *Damn.* One kiss, one peck wasn't enough. He tilted his head, deepening the kiss, trying to steal every bit of her because that's how he felt—like she was systematically taking him apart and putting him back together with her mouth.

She was pouring her soul into the kiss, nipping, licking, and it was driving Parker crazy. It was playful, gentle, and a little aggressive, just like Kennedi. He felt her, learned a little more about her with each brush of her lips to his. She was intoxicating.

He was drowning in her, submerged in her scent, the sound of her voice, the feel of her breath against his mouth, the taste of her kiss. . . . She surrounded him, touched him in places that he didn't know could be touched.

He stopped only to breathe before he pulled her back to him again, closing his mouth over hers, drawing a low moan from her. The kiss was wild, hard. It was tongue and teeth, hot and heavy. He molded her body to his and squeezed her behind, pulling her closer still.

It sounded close, but far away, but he registered the buzz of her cell phone in her purse and heard someone drop their keys. But it wasn't enough to make him pull away. Because all that mattered in that moment was Kennedi's mouth on his, her body pressed against his.

If anyone were to happen upon them, he knew he'd draw more than a few curious stares. Parker was well known in Wellspring and had purposefully kept his personal life private. Sure, there were the stray reporters who would come to town if there was a breaking news story about Wellspring Corp., and he'd been a topic of quite a few blogs. But save for a picture here and there of him having dinner with a woman or attending a fund-raising gala with a colleague, he'd done a pretty good job of staying out of the spotlight.

After all, he wasn't a celebrity. He was just plain Parker. And he was kissing Kennedi Robinson senseless right in the middle of Main Street.

When he couldn't take it anymore, he pulled away, leaning his forehead against hers. "I want you," he whispered. Her breath was warm against his skin. "Come home with me."

Chapter 12

Lips, hands, teeth, arms, Parker, hot, sex. Those were all the words running through Kennedi's mind when Parker asked her to come home with him. She hadn't hesitated either, didn't feel the need to play the typical game of playing hard to get.

The fire in his eyes when he'd pulled back from that kiss, coupled with the demand of her own desire, made her feel weak and strong at the same time. God help her, she wanted him. She needed this. She was going to have it.

Taking matters into her own hands, she suggested she follow him to his house in Anny's car. That gave her plenty of time to think about her approach. *Will he want to get right to it? Or will he want to slow it down a bit before we get busy?*

Kennedi got her answer soon enough, because as soon as he opened the door, he pulled her into his house and eased her back until she was pressed against the wall. *That's good, that's perfect.*

Anticipation for what was to come made her giddy with excitement. Kennedi wanted to be drenched in him, filled to the brim with Parker. In a way she'd never been with anyone else.

"Beautiful, you're shaking," he said, pulling back to peer at her.

Kennedi hadn't realized she was trembling, but now that he'd brought it to her attention, she realized that it wasn't a new thing where he was concerned. "That always seems to happen with you."

"If you want me to stop, or take it slow, just say the word."

Good guy.

Kennedi smiled. "No. Parker, I don't want you to stop. And if we take it any slower, I'm going to scream."

Parker barked out a loud laugh. "In that case . . ."

He scooped her up in his arms and she squealed in delight. "Parker, put me down."

As he walked her through the house to his bedroom, kissing her along the way, Kennedi clung to him, wrapping her arms tight around his neck. Parker kicked his bedroom door open and stepped inside. Once he stopped moving, he dropped her to the bed. She climbed on her knees and scooted to the edge of the bed. With a quirk of her brow, she tugged her shirt off and tossed it behind him.

"God, you're beautiful," he murmured.

Parker trailed his fingers over her shoulders, over the tops of her breasts, down her sides, across her stomach, and lower to the edge of her jeans. It was almost like he was etching her into his memory. His touch was warm, electric and she was tingling with need before long.

Before she could think better of it, she pulled him to her, crushing his hard body to hers. His mouth was on hers in an instant, kissing her long and hard. Kennedi pulled away, gasping, her hands firm on his chest.

"What's wrong?" he asked, concern in his brown eyes.

"Nothing." Eyes on his eyes, Kennedi gripped the bottom of his shirt and pulled it over his head. "Now we're even."

His hand slid down over her hip, then slowly up her inner thigh until his fingers brushed against her core, through her jeans. Kennedi let out a low curse and started to unbutton her jeans to give him better access. But his hand on hers made her pause.

When she met his gaze, he smirked. "Let me," he said.

She fell back on the mattress and he climbed over her. He undressed her, pulling her jeans and her panties off so slow she was writhing on the bed with need by the time he was done. He pressed his mouth against her stomach, then lower, lower still—until his tongue stroked her core and he sucked her clit into his mouth. Her orgasm was swift and stole her breath.

Once her breathing was back to normal, he was over her again, kissing her deeply. She fumbled with his belt but finally got it unbuckled, then slid it off of him and threw it somewhere over his shoulder. She unbuttoned his pants and pushed them down over his hips.

He licked the tops of her breasts, but when she went to remove her bra, he once again stopped her. "Leave it on."

Parker pulled a condom out of his drawer and pulled it on, then lowered himself on top of her. The hard press of his body against hers, the brush of his skin against hers, made her feel alive. "Please," she muttered against his lips.

With one smooth thrust, he was inside her. He moved slowly at first, leisurely, kissing her thoroughly in time with his thrusts. As their pace increased, pleasure built inside her and desire pooled low in her belly. She was so close, so ready.

"Now, Kennedi. Come for me." When he buried his face in her neck, biting her sensitive skin lightly, she was done, exploding around him. And he was right with her, groaning her name.

Later, Kennedi opened the front door of the manor and tiptoed in. The house was dark, and still. *Thank God.* Slowly, she set her keys on the table. It didn't take much to wake Anny up, and she didn't want to take the chance of her aunt watching her take the walk of shame.

Parker had made love to her three times that night, and Kennedi felt sated and relaxed. But she had no intention of waking up in his house. She didn't want the perfect night to be ruined by an awkward morning. And she knew herself—she'd be awkward. It was just her way. So, once he'd fallen asleep, she'd snuck out. Much like the way she was sneaking into Anny's house.

"Um-hmm."

Kennedi squealed. "Anny! I wish you would stop doing that." The light clicked on, and Anny was sitting there in the same spot she'd been in when she'd told Kennedi she was selling the business. Kennedi squinted against the bright light. "Do you just like sitting in the dark, or something?"

Anny laughed. "All you have to do is call, and I won't feel the need to wait up for you."

"It's pretty early," Kennedi countered. "You should be in wedded bliss with Fred, ya know."

"Where were you? Brook's has been closed for hours."

Kennedi hesitated. Anny had always been easy to talk to, understanding. She'd told her aunt things that she wouldn't tell anyone else. But she couldn't tell her aunt that she was doing Parker. She drew the line at that.

"Seriously, Kennedi. The only thing you could have been doing at his house is getting that back blew out or committing a crime. And since you're an officer of the court, and all . . ."

Kennedi covered her face. "Oh my God, Anny! Stop."

Anny shrugged as if she'd said something as

innocent as she was going to the store to buy sugar. "Hey, you know I call it like I see it."

"We're not having this conversation, Anny."

Her aunt looked at her, no humor on her face. Only seriousness. "Kennedi, you're a grown woman. You're attractive, and it's okay to explore another attractive person. But you need to call me, so I won't worry."

"Okay," Kennedi conceded. No sense in arguing with Anny. Her aunt was a stubborn woman. "I'll call next time."

Anny burrowed into her favorite chair. "So, tell me . . . change your mind about Parker?"

Kennedi massaged her temples with her fingers. Finally, drawing in a deep breath, Kennedi collapsed onto a chair. "I don't know what to say to that."

"Start with the truth."

"I didn't expect this, Anny. I thought I would come to Wellspring, get some R&R, and leave. Unscathed and untouched. Parker is unexpected, Anny. Who knew I'd come to town and hit his car. After all these years, our paths have crossed and I actually like him." Because Kennedi *did* like Parker. She liked him a lot.

"I figured you liked him. I mean, we haven't actually talked a lot about your relationships in recent years, but I know you're not one to sleep around."

Kennedi nodded. Anny was right. Although she wasn't shy when it came to sex, she was very discriminating when deciding to take any relationship to that level. And what scared her the most about Parker was that she'd let him in so fast. She'd basically disregarded every single rule when it came to him. She'd been caught off guard by Parker.

"What's holding you back?" Anny asked.

Kennedi shrugged. "Nothing really. There's nothing concrete here. I feel like it's premature to think tonight was anything more than two people enjoying one another's company."

"Want to know what I think?"

Meeting her aunt's gaze, she urged her on, "What do you think, Anny?"

"I think you know that this is more than two people kicking it." Anny threw up air quotes when she said "kicking it."

Kennedi couldn't help but laugh at Anny's antics. The older woman had always kept her on her toes.

"What?" Anny said with a shrug. "Anyway, it's very rare to meet someone who speaks to something inside you."

Kennedi thought about her aunt's words. Anny had a point. Parker did make her feel things she'd never felt before. Not with Quincy, not with any man before him. They hadn't known each other long at all, but she felt connected to him. And she wasn't used to feeling that way around anyone.

Rubbing her forehead, Kennedi stood. It was obvious to her that Anny was on to something. But it was something Kennedi couldn't talk about anymore. She needed to sleep. And then she needed to keep it moving. That's what she did. She kept it moving. In a few weeks, she'd be leaving Wellspring and going back to her job, her life. It wasn't like Parker could go with her. So she decided to just enjoy the little time they had and not look too deep into anything. Because instinctively she knew that was the only way she'd be able to walk away sane.

Kennedi bent low, placing a soft kiss to Anny's head. "I'm going to go to bed, Anny."

"I worry about you, ya know?" Anny said, halting Kennedi's retreat.

"Why, Anny? I'm fine."

"But you're not fine," Anny said.

"Why do you say that?"

"Because I know what tomorrow is. Because you haven't dealt with everything. Your way of dealing with things is to just push past it. Doesn't mean that you've actually processed them. My sister and my brother-in-law died, and you discovered them."

Kennedi closed her eyes. Tomorrow was the anniversary of her parents' deaths. "Anny, please."

When her parents were killed, Kennedi had been the one to find them. She'd been calling them and when they didn't answer she'd gone to their house to check on them.

It had taken Kennedi years to get the image of her dead parents out of her mind, to be able to remember them when they were beautiful and vibrant and alive, instead of lifeless and bloody. She didn't want to go to that place again.

Anny shot her a sad look. "Fine. I won't say any more about it. But I will say, the same thing is true for your relationship with Quincy."

Kennedi had met Quincy and gone out on a few dates with him shortly before her parents were killed. He had supported her during her time of grief. Kennedi had fallen for him and impulsively married him at a courthouse in Toledo, Ohio.

It had been just her, Quincy, the judge, and a random witness. After they married, Kennedi knew she'd made a mistake but tried to make it work. She'd put her all into the relationship, but ultimately it didn't last. Quincy had shown his true colors early, and she paid dearly for her choices.

Her aunt had always told her she was the sensible one, but her decision to marry Quincy had not made any sense. It was a low point in her life, and now that she was out of the relationship, she didn't want to spend any time reflecting on the lessons she'd learned. Just like everything in her life, she was determined to push through it. That was how she operated. She didn't expect Anny or anyone else to understand.

"I just worry that one day everything that you've been holding back will come out and take the wind out of you," Anny said. "I just hope someone is around to catch you."

"I'll be fine, Anny," Kennedi repeated. "I'm going to head to bed. Love you."

"Love you, too."

* * *

Parker had a problem, and her name was Kennedi. He'd spent hours making love to her, exploring her body. He'd invited her into his home, which wasn't something he did often. His home was his haven, a private oasis that he'd been content to keep to himself. But he'd let her in, just as he'd let her into his thoughts.

He'd woken up that morning ready to pull her into his arms. Except he couldn't do that because she wasn't there. She'd left like a thief in the night. There was no kiss good-bye, no note. She was just gone.

After the night they'd had, he'd expected her to be so tired she couldn't move. But, no, she'd moved all right. Right out of his house like what they'd shared hadn't meant anything to her, like he was nothing more than a meaningless fuck.

And instead of going to work—like he knew he should—he was pulling into the driveway at Hunt Manor, ready to go to battle with Kennedi. Because, dammit, Parker was not going out like that.

Fred walked over to his truck, nodding at him when he hopped out. "Parker? What brings you out this way?"

"Here to see Kennedi," Parker said, scanning the area as if she'd just appear. He didn't see Angelia's car, so he wondered if she'd gone out.

"She's at the gym."

"Thanks, Fred."

"Oh, Parker?" Fred called.

"Yes?" Parker met Fred's firm stare directly. "Is something wrong?"

"I don't have to tell you that it would be a bad thing if you hurt Kenni Bear, right?"

Parker chuckled. "No, I think that's pretty clear."

"She's been through a lot. I want to see her happy."

It wasn't hard to see that Kennedi had her share of trauma in her life. Aside from her parents' deaths, she'd mentioned she had an ex-husband, but he didn't push for more information. She was strong, but it was impossible to go through the things she had without it shaping her as a person. "I understand," Parker told Fred. "I don't plan on hurting Kennedi."

Fred observed him under the brim of his hat. "I know you don't plan on hurting her. But sometimes things happen when you jump headfirst into a situation without considering all the factors."

Parker didn't want to get into his . . . Well, he couldn't call it a relationship, yet. He knew what Fred was referring to. There were many variables at play. Number one on the list, she didn't live in Wellspring. "I hear you, Fred," he said.

Without another word, he walked toward the pool house. He knocked on the door and tried the knob. It was unlocked, so he let himself in. He could hear water running in the bathroom.

"Kennedi?"

"Come in," she shouted from inside.

Parker frowned, unsure if he heard her right.

Did she want him to come into the bathroom? Into the shower with her? Deciding not to question it, he toed off his shoes and unloosened his tie, before unbuttoning the top of his shirt. Slowly, he pushed the door open.

He expected to find Kennedi soaped up beckoning him into the shower with her forefinger, like the siren she was. Instead he found her on her knees, her hair in a messy bun, scrubbing the shower floor. When she turned to face him, she burst out in a fit of laughter. He knew she'd figured him out.

"Parker, oh my God!" Her eyes traveled the length of his body. "You're pretty comfortable," she teased. "What did you think I was doing in here?"

Shrugging, he said, "I knew what you were doing."

She turned the faucet off and stood. "Sure, you did."

Cutting right to the chase, Parker said, "You left."

Kennedi averted her gaze. At least she looked ashamed of her action. "I know."

No apology, though. He narrowed his gaze on her. "I didn't like it."

"Well, I had things I needed to take care of this morning."

"Like cleaning the bathroom?"

"I-I . . . yes," Kennedi stuttered.

He moved forward, pleased when she retreated back a step. Easing her backward into the shower stall, he caged her in, planting his hands against the shower wall. Would there ever be a moment he saw her that he wouldn't want to have her? Even in a sweatshirt and sweats, she was the most beautiful woman he'd laid eyes on.

"You can't deny it," he said, running his finger down her cheek.

"Deny what?" she asked.

Kennedi had tried to hide it, but he'd caught it. It was in the way her breath hitched in her chest, the way her eyes darkened, the heat emanating from her body.

"Tell me," he demanded, ignoring her question.

"Tell you what?"

He pinned her hands above her head and leaned in. "Tell me you want this as much as I do," he whispered against her ear.

"Oh God," she breathed.

Parker trailed a line of kisses down her neck, nipping at her skin before soothing the spot with his tongue. He pushed into her, wanting nothing more than to take her against the shower wall. He was pretty sure she'd let him. But that's not what he came there for. He had a plan, and Kennedi wasn't going to distract him from it.

"Kennedi?" Angelia's voice sliced through the heat of the moment.

"Hold on, Anny," Kennedi said, ducking under his arms. "I'm coming."

Parker gripped her wrist and tugged her to him. "We're not done."

Kennedi left him standing in the bathroom—hard as hell.

After a few minutes, Parker joined Kennedi and Angelia in the main room. "Hello, Angelia."

Angelia blinked, obviously surprised to see him. "Parker?" She frowned. "What were you two doing in there?"

"Anny, we were just talking," Kennedi said.

"I'm glad you're here, Parker." Angelia took a seat on one of the benches. "I wanted us to discuss the sale."

Parker sighed. "I'm not sure that's a good idea, Angelia." The last thing he wanted was the sale of the nursery to come between him and Kennedi again. Not when he'd had the chance to be with her, to experience the woman she was.

"It's okay," Kennedi said. "We should probably discuss it. I behaved badly about the offer, Parker." She turned to Angelia and picked up her hand. "If this is what you want, we can move forward."

Angelia grinned. "It is what I want."

Kennedi glanced at him. "The contract has to be fair, though, Parker."

"It will be," Parker assured them. "I'm on your side, and I'll make sure you're taken care of. Kennedi, why don't you stop by my office tomorrow, and we can discuss the changes you want made. I'll get it approved by the board."

Angelia smiled. "Thank you." She pulled him into a hug, and he met Kennedi's gaze over her shoulder.

Kennedi made a face, sticking out her tongue, then mouthed, "Suck-up."

Parker chuckled and mouthed, "You like it."

When Angelia pulled back, her gaze flitted back and forth between him and Kennedi. "Are you going to work today, Parker?"

Kennedi folded her arms over her chest and pinned him with a heated gaze. "Yeah, Parker. Are you going to work?"

"Actually, I'm not," he told them. "Kennedi, if you can get your stuff? I'm taking you out."

Chapter 13

When Parker whisked her away to a hidden destination, Kennedi wasn't sure what to think. Especially when he'd told her to wear clothes she wouldn't mind getting dirty. And now, sitting on the Grand River in a motorboat with him, fishing pole in hand, she knew what he meant.

To prepare for the fishing excursion, he'd taken her to get a fishing license, which is required in Michigan for anyone over the age of seventeen. Then they'd gone to buy a fishing pole. He'd taught her all about fishing lines, hooks, fishing lures, and the different types of bait. Parker had purchased live bait and plugs. The plugs looked like little fish, and Kennedi had thought it better to use those than the red earthworms he'd purchased.

It had taken about an hour to get everything they needed. Then they had loaded everything on his boat and he had driven them out to his favorite spot on the river. The trees were turning, so the view on the river was gorgeous. Kennedi had taken in the sights and smells and felt at peace.

For someone who'd never gone fishing, never even thought she'd like to fish, Kennedi was pleasantly surprised that she'd caught on to the process of getting her spinning reel ready so quickly. Casting the line was another story. It had taken several tries for her to cast her reel, and Kennedi had been tempted to just throw the damn thing in the river. Parker had been patient, holding her hand in place and guiding her motion. Finally, her line was cast and she'd taken a seat to wait.

"I cannot believe I'm out here fishing like this," Kennedi said.

Parker glanced at her out of the corner of his eye. "It's nice, huh?"

"It's . . . different. But I can see why you like to do it."

"Me and my grandfather used to sit out on the river for hours. It didn't matter if we caught a fish or not. It was quality time, the unknown, and just being on the water made the trip for me."

Kennedi watched Parker for a minute. It was obvious he loved being outside. He was dressed casually, in old jeans and a T-shirt. He wore a Detroit Tigers baseball cap. His muscular arms were loose, but she could tell he was still alert, watching for any sign that they'd caught something.

"How often do you come out here?"

"Any chance I get," he said honestly. "It's been a little harder since taking over Wellspring Corp., but I've been able to carve out time here and there. It's stress relief."

"Did you always know you wanted to take over the company?"

It took Parker so long to respond, Kennedi had wondered if he'd even heard the question. "No. When I was growing up, I wanted to do anything that was opposite of what Senior wanted."

Kennedi wasn't surprised. Over the past week, Parker had made it very clear that he was nothing like his father. "But you ended up there?"

"Once I realized that I could effect change, once I realized that Senior wouldn't be around forever. It then became about making my grandfather proud, helping the Wellspring community at large."

"When did you realize that?"

Kennedi wasn't fooling herself. She wasn't naïve enough to believe that just because they had shared some things, found some common ground, he'd magically feel comfortable sharing his secrets with her. But she couldn't help it. She wanted to know.

"Right around the time Senior kicked me out of the house and cut me off."

Turning slightly to the left to face Parker, she eyed him. The more he revealed about himself, the more she wanted to know. "He kicked you out?"

Parker nodded slowly. "At first, I thought it was a blessing. I had the chance to be free, to do my own thing. But then . . . I couldn't leave Brooklyn and Bryson."

"Bryson is your younger brother?"

"Yeah."

"Where is he?"

Parker glanced at her, his eyes flickering with what looked like regret. "He's off, living his life."

"And you wish you were?"

"Sometimes. But then I remember my mission, I

think about what I've worked so hard to do. And it's okay."

"If you could do anything else, what would it be?"

Parker stared out at the water. "Before I went to college, I wanted to work in environmental law."

Impressed, Kennedi said, "Wow! So you've always wanted to be a lawyer, just not necessarily work for Senior?"

"True."

Kennedi looked out at the river. It was a still day, but she enjoyed the sounds of the water hitting the boat, the calls of the birds above. She wished she could say the same thing. Law had never been something she'd dreamed of pursuing. But it was something she could do. She was good at what she did.

"What's on your mind?"

"Nothing," she lied. "Just taking this all in."

"And you? What does Kennedi want to do with her life?"

Kennedi expected he'd turn the questions on her at some point. Turnabout was fair play. She giggled. "I knew that was coming."

"Well, then answer the question," he retorted.

"I guess I haven't really allowed myself to think about it much. I chose law."

"So I take it that's not what you're passionate about?"

"I like it—don't get me wrong—but . . ." She didn't finish that thought, unsure if she was ready to tell him her hopes and dreams, no matter how far off they were.

"Go on," he urged softly.

Kennedi sucked in a deep breath. It seemed that despite her intention to not say much, she always wanted to say more to him. "If I could do anything else, it would probably be to open a boutique hotel."

Parker stilled, his eyes boring into her. "So why don't you?"

"Why don't I?" She asked with a frown. "It's not like I can just drop everything, buy some land, and open up a hotel. I have obligations, a career."

"Why not? You own sixteen acres of land that can be developed."

Kennedi would be lying if she said that thought had never crossed her mind. In fact, she'd even written up a business plan that she'd planned to present to her mother and Anny during undergrad. "Parker, life isn't like that. You of all people should know that sometimes we make decisions that take us far away from our dreams."

"I do know. But you also have an aunt who's pretty damn supportive."

"I have an aunt who runs a huge company," she said.

"Why not take over the nursery? That way the land stays in your control and you can choose to develop it at some point."

Kennedi had never really thought about taking over Hunt Nursery. Logically, she knew that Anny would retire at some point, but running the nursery had never been on her agenda. Yes, she loved going to visit. It was beautiful, and she'd always thought it would be good if it were eventually turned into a botanical garden, something that people could visit when in Wellspring.

In college, she'd once broached the subject with her parents and Anny. Her mom was on board, but Anny had never said anything one way or the other. At the time, Kennedi guessed it was because Anny was the type of person who dealt in the present. She didn't really spend a lot of time thinking about the future because she was so busy preserving their way of life.

With that in mind, Kennedi couldn't help but be proud of her aunt's decision to finally sell. Even though she'd been resistant to it initially, she knew it had taken a lot of courage for Anny to make the decision. Especially since she'd always been the one working so hard to maintain the company.

"Kennedi?" Parker's voice snapped her out of her thoughts.

"Yes?"

"Where did you go?"

She sighed. "Just thinking about Anny."

"You're pretty close, huh?"

Kennedi smiled. Anny had been her best friend for most of her life. It sounded cliché, but she'd learned from the beginning that her aunt was someone she could count on, someone she could share just about anything with. They'd talked about everything, from sex to food to politics. They rarely argued, and viewed life in similar ways.

It made Kennedi feel stronger to know that, no matter what, Anny had her back. Even after she'd moved away, even after her parents died, even now. "Yeah," she finally answered. "Admittedly, we haven't been as close over the past few years, but I love that woman with everything in me."

"I know that feeling," he said. "I feel the same way about my siblings."

"I can see that. You and Brooklyn are pretty close."

The corner of Parker's mouth lifted. "That's an understatement. That's my heart, always on ten for me. I've never had to wonder about her. She keeps it real, and is one hundred percent TeamParker."

"That's funny."

"What about your sister?" he asked.

Kennedi and Tanya had grown up close, but once Tanya realized that she was a woman who liked men, that had all changed. Her sister was always searching for Mr. Right, and she'd do that in myriad ways, from changing her major in college to quitting whatever job she had to even pretending to be someone else in order to land a man.

They'd clashed a lot before and after her parents died. And Kennedi couldn't help but feel regret at not having a closer relationship with her sister. That's why she was grateful that she'd enrolled in law school, because if she hadn't she never would have met Paula.

"Tanya is doing her own thing," Kennedi answered simply.

"Like Bryson," Parker said. "And you're left dealing with everything."

It wasn't a question. It was a statement, likely stemming from his own experience being the oldest sibling. "Exactly."

Kennedi didn't say anything more, and Parker seemed to get the hint because he'd grown silent. A bell sounded, and Kennedi's eyes snapped to her line. "I think I caught one."

Parker stood and walked up behind her. "You caught something."

As Kennedi pulled at the line, she was hit with a surge of adrenaline. He'd gone over what to do if she caught a fish, but to actually catch one and try to pull it up was quite another story. After several minutes, and a lot of help from Parker, Kennedi had a squirming catfish on her line. Unable to hold it in, she jumped up and down shouting that she caught a fish. Once she was done with her victory dance, Parker helped her unhook the fish, which was something she never wanted to do again.

Staring down at dinner on the floor of the boat, she thought about the fun week she'd had. And it was all because of Parker. When she peered up at him, he was watching her, a soft smile on his face. Suddenly hit with white-hot need for him, she reached up and pulled him into a kiss.

"Is this good?"

Parker peered at the table, groaning at the cards Kennedi had just laid on the table: three aces. "Are you hustling me, Kennedi?"

Her eyes widened. "No. I've never played poker in my life."

Shaking his head, he tossed his cards on the table and slid his money over to her. "For someone who has never played before, you definitely took my money."

Kennedi did a cute little fist pump at her victory, and Parker felt his heart open up. A week ago, if someone told him he'd meet a woman who made him want to be with her, he would have laughed in the person's face.

Parker had never believed in "once upon a time" love. He didn't exactly have the best role model either. After his mother died, Senior had burned through women and wives at the speed of light.

When Brooklyn had fallen in love and married Carter within a few months, he'd considered them an outlier of sort. Something that happened occasionally, but the probability was small. Not that he didn't know beyond the shadow of a doubt that Carter and Brooklyn were happy, but he didn't expect his story to be the same. But with Kennedi . . . He didn't think he was in love with her, but he knew that he was more than just infatuated with her. He knew that he wanted to explore more with her.

After she'd caught her fish, they'd returned to his house, where he cleaned and fried the fish while she made a caprese salad and homemade balsamic vinaigrette. Over dinner, they'd talked about *Law and Order* and baseball games. He was happy to learn she was a Tigers fan.

She'd told him that her mother had taken her to the ballpark to watch them play as a kid because that's what her grandfather had done for her. Then, she'd changed the subject and asked him to "teach" her how to play poker.

"Game over," he said, standing up.

She grinned as she scooped up her winnings and stuffed the bills in her pocket. She slid out of her chair and walked over to him. "Thanks for teaching me how to play. I like the game."

"I'm sure you do. But you forget, my sister is

Brooklyn. She's been hustling men at pool for years. I'm still not sure you didn't just hustle me out of my money."

Her mouth fell open, but her smirk was clear. "I'm not lying to you. This is my first time. And I'm kind of offended that you're basically accusing me of cheating."

Parker had met his fair share of women, but none of them held a candle to the one standing in front of him, a mock glare in her eyes and a flirty pout on her full lips. He hooked a finger in the waistband of her sweatpants and tugged her forward, wrapping an arm around her when she crashed against his chest.

"What do you think you're doing?" she asked.

"Taking what I want." He bent low, kissing her until she moaned his name.

Parker wanted all of her. He wanted everything—her thoughts, her body, her heart. That he'd even thought that last word—*heart*—was a shock to him. But he was done questioning it. He wanted what he wanted.

"I'm going to make love to you. Right here." He tugged on her shirt. "Take this off."

Doing as she was told, she yanked her shirt off, wrapped it around his neck, and pulled him into a kiss. What started out as slow and tender quickly turned to fast and passionate. She tugged his shirt off and pushed his pants off, freeing his hard erection.

Then, she was on her knees, licking him slowly before taking him in her mouth. Parker's head fell back as she tasted, teased him with her wicked mouth. He struggled to maintain control, she felt so good, so warm. His control snapped and he yanked her upright, pushed her pants down, lifted her up, and pinned her to the wall. With his eyes on hers, he entered her.

"Shit."

"Damn."

Their words came out at the same time, but he couldn't even be sure who said what. And he didn't care. He just wanted her. He pulled out slightly before pounding into her again. Her low groan kicked his heartbeat up a notch.

Parker wanted to lie at her feet, worship her. *Thy will be done.* But there was another side to Kennedi, one hidden behind a locked door. And he wanted to find the key, he wanted to open the door to her heart. And he wanted her to let him in.

"Parker," she breathed. "Now."

That one word pushed him forward. He thrust into her, in and out, until she exploded around him, groaning his name over and over again. The force of her orgasm was enough to trip him over the edge and he came so long and hard that his knees gave out and he slid to the floor, with her still in his arms.

Several minutes later, Parker was finally able to move again and he stood, cradling Kennedi against his chest, and headed to his bedroom. He set her on the bed and slid in behind her, wrapping his arms around her.

"I have to go," she murmured, her eyes half closed.

"No, you don't." He kissed her neck, behind her ear.

She turned to him, tucked her hand under her head. "This has the potential to be very hard if we keep this up."

Parker traced the line of her nose with his finger. "I say we just let it flow, for now."

Worry lined her forehead, and he smoothed the creases with two of his fingers. "You don't understand."

"Trust me, I do."

"I don't do this. I mean, I haven't done this in years. And it's been even longer than that since I've felt this way."

Her honesty took him by surprise. "I would say that's mutual."

She sat up, ran her hands through her hair. "There's a lot you don't know."

He smoothed his thumb down her spine. "And I don't need to know everything now, Kennedi. I just want to enjoy you."

She smiled at him, over her shoulder. It was a sad smile, and Parker wanted to pull her into his arms and assure her that everything would be okay.

"You know you can talk to me," he told her. "What's on your mind?"

"I don't think you realize what you've done for me today. It was a hard day, but you helped by keeping my mind off of it."

Parker didn't know what she was referring to, but he could take a guess. He didn't push her to reveal more, but he suspected that whatever was going on with her stemmed from her parents' deaths. He recognized the pain in her eyes, because he'd felt a similar loss when his mom died. The difference is, he had been able to talk about it. He wasn't sure she had been able to do that.

"When my mom died," he said, "I was devastated. I didn't know why God allowed it to happen. I was angry, withdrawn." Parker was older than Brooklyn, but he'd been ill equipped to handle the barrage of emotions that came with his mother's sudden death. The thought that he hadn't been able to say goodbye or even tell her he loved her still haunted him. But he'd made peace with the knowledge that she knew, just like all mothers knew. "It's still hard, and it's been over fifteen years."

"I have to go," Kennedi said, jumping out of the bed and bolting out of the room.

"Wait," Parker said, following her into the living room, where she was hastily pulling on her clothes. "Where are you going?"

"I have to get out of here. I can't do this right now."

"You didn't drive. The manor is too far of a walk. Give me a second. I'll drive you where you need to go."

She gripped her jacket in her hands like it was her lifeline, and Parker fought the urge to pull her into his arms. "Thanks."

Parker drove Kennedi back to the manor. Once he stopped the car, he turned to her. "Let me come in with you. We don't have to do anything. We can just talk."

She clenched her fists, then released them. "I'm fine. I have to go."

Kennedi was out of his car and running toward the door before he could stop her. And he let her go.

Chapter 14

Parker walked into Brook's Pub the next afternoon and spotted Kennedi sitting at the bar. He'd called her to check on her, but the call had gone straight to voice mail. So, he'd gone into work, since he'd skipped yesterday. It had been quiet in the office, with only a few people in the building on that chilly Saturday morning.

But he hadn't been able to get any work done. Instead, he'd spent his time there thinking about Kennedi, about the day they'd had together. It was just as he suspected. A quick Google search revealed that yesterday was the anniversary of her parents' deaths.

He'd just given up on getting any work done when he'd received a call from Juke, who'd told him that Kennedi was there at the bar. When he'd asked if she was drunk, Juke had told him that she was stone-cold sober, had been nursing the same drink for hours. Parker had dropped everything and headed straight to town.

As he approached the bar, he nodded at Juke.

His longtime friend, who was drying a glass with a white towel while keeping an eye on Kennedi, met him at the end of the bar.

Parker noticed the empty glass in front of her. "I thought you said she didn't drink anything?"

Juke lifted his shoulder in a half shrug. "And right after I said that, she gulped the drink down, and asked for another one."

"And you gave it to her?" Parker asked incredulously.

"This is a bar," Juke said unapologetically. "She's not drunk. She's just drinking. I only called you because I saw you here with her the other night. Figured you could come keep her company because she looks like she needs some."

Parker shook his head. "Thanks." He didn't bother to hide the sarcasm in his voice.

"Hey, I do what I can." Juke strolled over to another customer at the bar, leaving Parker to contemplate his next action.

Sighing, Parker approached Kennedi and slid onto the bar stool next to her. "What are you doing here, Kennedi?"

She inclined her head, assessing him for a minute, before turning her attention back to her empty glass. "What are *you* doing here? If you've come here to try to get me to talk, it's not going to happen. I told you that last night."

"I'm here because Juke called me."

"Traitor," she muttered under her breath.

"Let me take you home, Kennedi. The lunch crowd will be here soon, and you probably don't want anyone seeing you like this."

Kennedi was a wreck, dressed in a brown sweater and pink leggings. Her hair was pulled back in a ponytail and her eyes looked tired, haunted. "I don't care what people think of me. I never have."

"Okay, but wouldn't you rather wallow in the comfort of your own home?"

Kennedi laughed then. "Parker." His name was so soft on her lips, he wondered if she'd really said it. Then, she turned her brown eyes on his. They were like tiny pools of milk chocolate, so rich, so beautiful. He knew he could get lost in those orbs.

"Come on, beautiful." She closed her eyes, her chin trembling. "Come with me."

Finally, she stood. He put a fifty-dollar bill on the bar and led her out, waving at Juke.

Back at Hunt Manor, he opened the car door for Kennedi and she stepped out. Wrapping an arm around her, he eased her toward the porch, but she stopped. "The pool house," she said.

Changing course, he walked her over to the pool house. Once inside, she kicked her shoes off and headed straight to the outdoor patio. He followed her, watched her curl up on a chaise lounge.

"Need anything?" he asked her, sitting next to her.

"No." Parker started to get up, but she stopped him. "But can you stay?"

Kennedi felt like she was wrapped in a tight glove. Parker's arms around her made her feel protected, cherished, and she burrowed into him.

"You're up, sleepyhead." His voice was soft, and

so was the kiss he placed to the back of her neck, sending shivers straight to her toes.

"Thanks for coming to get me," she told him. "I really appreciate it."

"No worries. I wasn't going to let you go out like that."

Kennedi chuckled. "I have no idea why you make me laugh so much. I haven't laughed like this in years."

"Well, then I'm glad I could help with that."

Overcome with emotion, Kennedi bit her lip. He'd been patient, giving, and she'd been closed off and rude. It was a wonder he was still there, still with her.

"Kennedi, I didn't mean to upset you last night. I just thought if I told you about my experience with my mother you'd feel comfortable sharing your own experience with me."

Closing her eyes, Kennedi willed the tears that filled her eyes not to fall. She wanted to tell him, wanted to talk about it, but she feared if she did, it would set her back. She just couldn't do it. Not then. And she wasn't sure if she ever would.

Kennedi bolted up and turned to him, blinking back her tears. "I have to go."

He sat up, a concerned frown on his face. "Why? This is your house."

"Because!"

"Do you have somewhere to be?" He'd asked the question, but she knew he knew that she didn't have anywhere to go, or anything to do. "We're kind of in the middle of a conversation."

"I do have something to do. We still . . . I need to

see if Anny needs help at the nursery." Kennedi muttered a frustrated curse. She wasn't good at this, lying. She wasn't a crier either. And here she was, on the verge of tears and lying—badly.

Parker stood, inched closer to her. "Kennedi, you—"

"You don't understand, Parker. I don't do this. I don't cry. Yet, you keep making me want to cry." Parker reeled back as if she'd slapped him, and she pulled him back to her. "Not that way. It's just . . . you make me want to do things I shouldn't do, and I need you to stop."

"Kennedi, there's nothing wrong with crying."

"Don't you get it, I haven't cried since my parents died, Parker. I didn't even cry after my divorce. There was no wallowing with a pint of ice cream while watching sappy Hallmark movies to remind me of happier times." There were no pity parties after she filed the complaint. She didn't even tear up when Quincy accused her of being at fault for his infidelity. "You know what I did? I went to school the day after I found my parents slaughtered in their own house. After my divorce, I went to work. I won cases. I don't break down like some weak person."

The tear that finally broke free shocked her, and she stumbled backward.

He stepped closer. "It's okay, Kennedi."

Shaking her head, she held her hand up, preventing him from coming any closer. "It's not okay, Parker." When she squeezed her eyes shut, fresh tears spilled out over her lashes, down her cheeks. Then, the dam broke and she literally dropped to her knees and wept. In seconds, he was at her side, pulling her into his arms. She clung to him like a lifeline and sobbed so long and so hard it zapped her energy. And the entire time, he'd held her, cradled her in his arms, and let her.

They stayed like that for minutes, him holding her, rocking her, whispering words of comfort to her. Parker had given her the gift that few had given her over her lifetime. He accepted her for who she was, whether she was goofy, attitudinal, or weepy. He was okay with it, and, in fact, encouraged her to be herself.

Finally, she pulled back and he brushed his thumbs under her eyes. "I must look a mess," she said with a wobbly smile.

"You're beautiful. You always are."

Giggling, Kennedi dropped her head to his shoulder. "You have to stop."

He smoothed his hands over her back, stroking her, reassuring her. "What? Telling you you're beautiful?"

She wrapped her arms around him, squeezing him. "Yes."

"Never," he whispered, kissing the top of her head.

Parker's phone chirped and he pulled back to look at the caller ID. "It's Brooklyn," he said.

"Oh, answer it."

He hit the TALK button and said, "What's up, Brooklyn?"

Kennedi traced the crease that appeared on his forehead, then kissed him there. His hand dug in her hip, and he pulled her into his hardening erection.

"Okay, Brooklyn, slow down."

Hearing the concern in his voice, she hopped off his lap, choosing not to distract him when his sister needed him.

"I see," he said. "And Patricia?"

Kennedi noted the tension in his jaw and wondered who Patricia was. *Is she an ex-girlfriend?* Briefly, she considered the fact that they'd never talked about an *ex* of his. She made a mental note to ask him about his past relationships. It was only fair.

With a heavy sigh, Parker said, "Okay, Brooklyn. Anything else? Okay. You too."

Parker ended his call and looked at her. "Sorry about that." He stood, stretching.

"It's fine. Is everything all right?" Parker took a seat on the chaise lounge and bowed his head. Kennedi sat close to him, sweeping her hand up and down his back. "Are you good?"

"My father has an illegitimate daughter," he confessed.

"Is that Patricia?"

Frowning, he said, "No. Hell no. Patricia is my father's ex-wife. When you came to the office that day, I received a call that she was suing Brooklyn and me over the divorce terms."

Now, Kennedi officially felt like an asshole. She'd bulldozed into his office that day, intent on protecting her land and unwilling to even listen to him. She remembered him getting the call, recalled how he'd slammed the phone down. Yet, she'd taken it personally and dug her heels in, even after he drove all the way to the manor to apologize.

"I'm sorry."

He peered at her, a soft smile on his face. He seemed to sense that she was apologizing for more than the call he'd just received from Brooklyn. "Don't apologize. We're past that now. Right?"

She nodded, squeezing his knee with her other hand. "So, your father filed for divorce from his wife before he got sick?"

He shook his head. "No, we filed for divorce from his wife after he got sick. We went to the table, negotiated with Patricia, gave her more than my father would have if he'd filed, and she still won't go away."

"That sucks. Is there anything you can do?" Kennedi knew better than most how a divorce decree was often not the last hurdle one had to jump through to be done with a relationship. "My best friend is one of the best divorce attorneys I know."

"Really? I'll definitely keep that in mind. But I asked Brooklyn to handle it, and I think she pretty much has it under control. Except I'm just waiting to get that call from Carter telling me that Brooklyn has been arrested for kicking Patricia's ass."

Kennedi rested her head on his shoulder. "That might not be out of the realm of possibility."

He pulled back, tipping her head up to meet his gaze. "Are you speaking from personal experience?"

With a smirk, she said, "There were many nights when I considered clocking him."

"Want to share?"

"Not particularly. But I will say that divorce is not for the faint of heart. I'm just glad it's done, and my final spousal support check has been paid."

Parker frowned. "What? Spousal support? Please don't tell me that fool asked for spousal support."

"I wish I could tell you he didn't."

"Well, I stand by my previous assertion that he's a punk."

Kennedi threw her head back and laughed. "Stop. But enough about him. Tell me about this sister you have."

Parker told her about Patricia's confession the day she had to leave the family home. "Brooklyn was handling that, too."

"Go Brooklyn. I like her."

"She likes you, too."

Kennedi smirked. "She told you that?"

He shook his head. "No. But if she didn't like you, trust me, I would have heard about it."

"Well, I'm glad."

Parker finished his story, telling her that Brooklyn had hired a private investigator to find his sister, Veronica. The investigator recently found an address for Veronica in Indianapolis, but when he'd gone to her place of residence, she had disappeared. "So there's nothing else we can do at this point. He'll be in touch when he has an update."

"Wow, you have a lot going on."

"Sometimes I wonder if I bit off more than I can chew, taking the helm at Wellspring Corp."

"Parker, no. You were made for this, you worked for this. You said it yourself. You have a desire for the company that will take it in a direction that will honor your grandfather's legacy, one that will put you in a position to give back to the city everything your father took away. You can do this. It's just going to take a while."

"You just said I had a lot going on?"

She nodded. "Yes, you do."

"Not all bad." He looked her up and down, making her pulse race. "By the way, this morning, I had a chance to look over the offer for the Hunt land and nursery. I think your concerns were warranted. I want to have my personal attorney look it over, but there is no reason we can't make this happen."

Kennedi adored him. It was too hard to explain, to articulate just what he meant to her in that moment. Instead of being concerned about his family problems—and he had many—he still took the time to assure her about the sale of Anny's land.

"Yes!"

"Yes?" he asked, confusion marring his face. "I don't think I asked you a yes-or-no question."

Even still, *yes* was her answer. "I know. But, I just appreciate your work on this."

He flashed her a knowing grin. "Come here."

She leaned forward, and he placed a sweet kiss to her lips. Soon, the kiss grew in intensity, hard and wild. Without warning, he lifted her up and carried her inside the pool house, kicking the door closed behind him.

When he set her down on her feet, he cradled her face and pulled her into another searing kiss. He was taking her higher with every kiss, winding her up like a toy doll. She was so high, she felt like she was floating, like her feet would never touch the ground again. Every kiss, every brush of his fingertips against her skin lit a fire inside her that seemed to burn out of control.

She felt his knuckles on her skin as he unbuttoned her shirt, never breaking the contact. And although he hadn't touched her breasts, hadn't even kissed her below her neck, her nipples were tight with need. Hell, her entire body hummed in anticipation of more.

And that's exactly what she said. "More."

He chuckled, low and dangerous. The sound of fabric tearing pierced the room, and the next thing she knew buttons were flying and her shirt was a tattered mess at her feet.

Kennedi pushed back, peered up at him, unable to hide the smirk on her face. "Oh my God. That was Anny's shirt."

"Oh shit." He grimaced. "Sorry."

"I won't say anything if you don't."

"Sounds good. No more Anny talk. Turn around."

Kennedi did as she was told, letting her head fall back against his shoulder when he kissed her shoulder. He feathered fingertips over her back, over her ass, before he bent her over the table, tugging her leggings down. She was slick with arousal and pushed back against his erection. His low curse made her feel powerful, happy that she had that effect on him.

She heard the clink of his belt, and two seconds later, he was inside her, pounding her like his life depended on it, like she held the key to his survival. His thrusts were hard, but not painful. His hands were hot on her breasts, pinching and tugging at her pebbled nipples. *Oh God.* She was close. So close.

"Kennedi," he breathed against her back before placing a kiss to her spine. "Damn, I want this. I need this."

His words, his confession was enough to send her spiraling over the edge and she let go, letting her orgasm take her over.

Chapter 15

When the sun rose Monday morning, Parker was lying next to Kennedi's warm body. They'd spent the rest of the weekend holed up at his place, making love through the night and learning more about each other during the day.

Parker could hear her thoughts, believe in her dreams. He adored her, would even venture a guess that he was falling in love with her. But he'd known her only a short while. There was still a lot he didn't know about her. He also hadn't shared a lot about himself.

Never had he wanted to spend the entire night with someone. But with her , . . he didn't want her to leave. And she'd tried to leave. In her defense, though, she did have plans with Angelia and Fred at the manor on Sunday, which she'd ditched to stay with him.

"Parker?" He felt her lips on his chest.

Squeezing her tight, he said, "Kennedi."

"Don't you have to go to work?"

Work. Parker would rather stay in bed with Kennedi any day of the week, but she was right. Duty called. "Yes. I'm getting up in a few minutes."

She wrapped her arms around his waist and crooked her leg around his. "I can come to your office later today, to finish up the contract business."

"Sounds like a plan. You would be a welcome sight in the middle of my workday. Maybe we can have lunch?"

She perched herself up on her elbow, giving him a full view of her breasts. He brushed his thumb over her nipple. "I'm cool with lunch."

He rolled them over so that she was on her back, and took her nipple in his mouth, sucking gently. Kennedi arched her back off the bed, clutching the sheet in her fists. She was naked and wet and ready for him.

"Parker," she breathed. "Work."

He hushed her, slipping one finger, then two, inside her heat. "This is work, beautiful."

The sound of someone knocking at his door interrupted his "work," and he groaned, jumping up.

Kennedi sat up, her hair all over her head and her eyes glazed over. "Who the hell would be knocking at your door this early?"

There were only a few people who would do such a thing, and his sister was the first person who came to mind. "It's probably Brooklyn."

He slid a pair of sweats on and headed to the front of the house. Only, when he opened the door, it wasn't Brooklyn standing outside. It was Carter.

Frowning, he said, "Carter, what's up? It's early."

Carter pushed past him. "Did you see the papers?"

His brother-in-law pushed a newspaper at him. "I saw them when I stopped off at the store on the way to Wellspring Corp. Brooklyn is freaking out. She's on her way."

Parker scanned the front page, and his blood ran cold. The headline: WELLSPRING WATER EMBROILED IN ELABORATE LAND-GRABBING SCHEME. POLICE TO INTERVIEW NEW INTERIM CEO, PARKER WELLS JR.

Fuck. Parker smacked the paper down on his coffee table. He couldn't blame anyone but himself. He'd been distracted. He was supposed to step up his efforts to find evidence against Senior and Gary.

Kennedi walked into the living room, now fully dressed in a pair of sweats and a T-shirt. Carter did a double take when he spotted her, then turned to him. "I'm sorry, shit. I should have called first."

Parker waved a dismissive hand at his brother-in-law. "It's cool."

"What's wrong?" Kennedi asked, taking a seat next to him.

He handed her the paper and she scanned the headline, her eyes growing wide. "Oh no."

"Yeah. This is bad, not just for me but for the company and the town."

"Well, I hope that the person who leaked the information was doing it because they genuinely care about the people Senior hurt. I hate to say it, but if there is any truth to the rumors, then it's a good thing for the people affected that it came out."

Parker agreed. It would be good for the people

affected, if they got some relief, but bad for him and Wellspring Corp.

Twenty minutes later, Brooklyn was at his house, pacing the floor. "There has to be someone at Wellspring leaking this information. It can't be Gary because he's just as guilty as Senior."

Parker thought about what his sister said. It wouldn't make sense if Gary was the leak, but nothing about Gary Townsend made sense. Bottom line? He couldn't rule him out.

"I don't know, Brooklyn. He was outvoted when they named me interim director. He could have leaked the information to push the board to act and terminate me."

So far, Parker had discovered that Gary had known Senior for years, longer than either of them had let on. In fact, they'd served in the military together when they were in their twenties, had even enrolled in Michigan State after their discharge. But Senior had always acted like Gary was just a business partner.

And after they'd discovered that Senior had forged their mother's will to gain access to her money and controlling share of Wellspring Corp., Parker had always suspected Gary had more to do with that than anyone knew. Gary was an attorney after all, with connections in the court.

"I don't understand why you can't just fire him and remove him from the board," Kennedi said.

"Which is what I've been working on, but it's not

that simple. I want to get him out of the company and off the board all at once. It wouldn't make sense if I fire him and he's still able to make decisions as a board member."

"You could make a case for conflict of interest. He's the company's attorney, right?"

"Yes," Parker said.

Kennedi shrugged. "Prove that he's acted as Senior's personal attorney, at any time during the course of his tenure with the company, and that's grounds for termination. It's a conflict of interest."

"That's it." Parker had been so distracted with his new sister and Senior that he hadn't thought of the most obvious choice. Senior had done a good job of protecting Gary, but there was one action in which Gary had represented Senior—his sister. It was Gary who represented Senior in the paternity action filed all those years ago. "I've got it. Senior messed up when he had Gary represent him in the paternity action for Veronica. We've got him. But that only takes care of Gary. It doesn't solve the land-grabbing issue." Parker met Kennedi's gaze. "I don't know if I want you involved, Kennedi. If this shit hits the fan, I could be charged with collusion. I mean, they can't get Senior."

"I'm already involved. We were supposed to finalize the offer for the land."

Parker bowed his head. "Kennedi, in light of this, I'm not even sure we should go through with the land deal. I might need to leverage company resources to handle this."

"Even if the deal doesn't go through, you still

need help. This is what I do. I may not know the ins and outs of your company, but I know the law. Parker, I'm not worried about Hunt Nursery. If we have to find another buyer, we will. But this isn't going away for your company, and I'd like to help."

Parker tugged her forward and gave her a hard kiss on the mouth. Breaking the contact, he shot Brooklyn a sideways glance and found her and Carter watching him with their mouths wide open.

Clearing his throat, he said, "Let's get to work."

Parker's phone rang then. "Hey, Sandy," he answered.

"Parker?" Sandy was whispering. "You need to get here as soon as possible."

Standing, he asked, "What's going on?"

"Mr. Townsend just came to the office, with the newspaper in hand. The one . . ."

"I know, Sandy. What did he want?"

"The board wants to hold an emergency meeting. And I overheard him saying that they are considering asking you to step down because you're too high profile, being Senior's son."

Parker let out a long curse. "I'll be right in."

A while later, Parker arrived at Wellspring Water Corporation headquarters with Brooklyn, Carter, and Kennedi. They were met by a slew of reporters, snapping pictures and asking questions.

Sandy rushed to his side when he entered his suite. "Thank God you're here. Reporters have been calling all morning. This is a nightmare."

"It's okay, Sandy," Parker assured her.

"The board meeting is scheduled in an hour. I tried to delay it, but they're refusing. I think Mr. Townsend is leading the charge."

Parker shook his head. "I'll be ready."

Kennedi took a seat in the chair in front of his desk, while Brooklyn barked orders on the phone to someone. Parker handed Kennedi the Hunt land offer with his notes and watched as she skimmed the contract, a focused look on her face.

The fact that she was willing to step into the fray for him made him rethink his earlier assertion that he might be falling in love with her. He was already there. Parker had always had Brooklyn's support, and even to a certain extent Bryson's. But he'd yet to find a woman, one who was his equal, whom he wanted to share a part of himself with. And in less than two weeks, he'd given more of himself to Kennedi than any woman he'd dated.

He was addicted to her, lost in her. Now that he'd had a chance to wake up with her in the morning, now that he remembered how she looked when she first opened her eyes after a restful sleep, he wanted to do it every day. He wanted to hear the way she moaned when he touched her, when he kissed her, when he . . . *loved her.*

Watching her mark the contract with her red pen made him twitch with the need to pull her to his lap. *So sexy.* But he had to focus on the matter at hand. On the way to work, they'd strategized their next moves. Brooklyn would handle the PR with the company's public relations department. She suggested he do a press conference later in the day assuring the community that he was in no way connected with any scheme to steal land.

Parker had given Carter access to the cyber security software so that he could try to find out who in the company, besides Gary, would benefit from a shake up if the board terminated him. His brother-in-law was in another office working on that for him.

As far as Parker could tell, they had two separate problems: land grabbing and leaking secure company information to the public. And it could be one person, or multiple people involved.

There was a loud commotion outside the office and Parker jumped up just as Gary Townsend walked into the office.

Sandy was on his heels. "Parker, I'm sorry. He pushed past me."

"It's okay, Sandy."

After today, Gary Townsend would no longer be a factor. Gary glanced around the room before meeting Parker's gaze. "So you finally decided to show up for work? Convenient that it's the day all hell has broken loose."

Parker took his seat. "Gary, I'm glad you're here. We have business to discuss."

Gary scoffed. "What you need to be doing is figuring out how to save your job. In lieu of this latest news, I feel it's best that you step down as interim CEO until we can get this sorted out. I'll put forth a motion during today's emergency board meeting."

"After today, you won't have a seat on the board to put forth a motion on anything."

Laughing, Gary took a seat in one of Parker's chairs and crossed his legs. "Are you sure you want to have this conversation in front of your ungrateful sister and your . . . friend?" Gary's gaze raked over Kennedi and Parker wanted to jump over his desk and throttle him.

"I don't have a problem with them being here, but if it would make you feel better, they can leave."

"Parker, no," Brooklyn said, shooting Gary a hard glare. "I don't trust him."

"It's fine, Brooklyn. I've got this."

Brooklyn's shoulders fell. "Fine. But I'll be in the building. I'm going over to see Carter." Without another word, Brooklyn was out of the office.

Parker looked to Kennedi when she stood as well. "I'm going to head back to the manor," she told him. "Call me if you need anything?"

"I will." He smiled at her, then watched her as she left the room, shutting the door behind her.

Once they were alone, Parker leaned forward, arms crossed over his desk. "Gary, I don't appreciate you barging into my office, past my secretary. She's there for a reason."

"Senior wouldn't appreciate you bringing people into Wellspring Corp. who have nothing to do with the company. And that includes your little sister, Brooklyn."

"I'll tell you what. You continue to make snide comments about my sister, and you'll see a side of me that you don't want to see."

"Show some respect, Junior."

The sneer hit its intended notes. When he was a

kid, Senior would often call him Junior just to let him know who was in charge, that he would never be bigger or better than him. "Respect is earned, and you don't have mine."

"Listen, you—"

"No, you listen. I'm the interim CEO of this company, until the board votes me out. And you will hear me." Parker was done going back and forth with Gary. He pulled out the paternity action, filed in Indiana by him on behalf of Senior. He set it in front of Gary, smirking when the other man's eyes went wide. "I'm sure I don't have to tell you what this is, Gary."

Gary flicked the paper back toward him. "I don't know why you brought this out."

"It's simple, and you have my father's eaves-dropping ex-wife to thank for this, by the way. We found out that Senior has another child. I did some digging, hired an investigator, and came across this paternity action, filed on December 19, 1990, in Hammond, Indiana. Imagine my surprise when I saw that the attorney Senior had file the motion was you."

Gary shifted in his seat, but Parker remained still, his eyes never leaving the other man.

"As the interim CEO, I'm troubled by this infor-mation. As a member of the board and an attorney for Wellspring Water Corporation, you have sworn to disclose any conflicts of interest. Acting as Senior's personal attorney in any way, at any time, constitutes a conflict of interest."

"You don't know what you're doing, boy. I will bury you."

"Good luck with that. In the meantime, you're fired. Get your shit, and get the hell out of here. And don't get any ideas, because I'll have security waiting in your office for you. You are not to take anything that belongs to Wellspring Corp. out of this building."

"You're in love."

Kennedi clutched her cell phone in her hand. She'd called Paula to check in on her. The wedding was barreling down on them, and she wanted to make sure everything was going smoothly.

Of course, Kennedi also wanted to talk to Paula about the goings-on in Wellspring. She'd just finished telling her friend about Parker, and about how he'd shown her a good time. At no time in her conversation did she mention love. Adoration and appreciation, but love?

"I'm not in love."

"Well, what do you call it?"

"I told you—adoration. And I appreciate him for being there. He's also really concerned about Anny and her land. He even said that he doesn't want the deal to go through while he's going through the shit with the company."

"Mmm-hmm," her friend said.

"What? It's not love. I'm just going through something. Maybe a little departure from reality . . . for a bit."

Paula barked out a laugh. "What? You're so in denial."

"I'm not in denial. Okay, so he's fine. More than fine, he's . . . oh God, I want this man."

"I knew it," Paula shouted. "You don't even sound like the Kennedi who left Ann Arbor a few weeks ago."

"I still wouldn't say it's love. Infatuation. That's what I'm calling it. I'm attracted to him."

"Listen, Kennedi, I think it's great. It's about time you let yourself go. You're so . . . controlled. I want you to be happy."

"Paula, it's not that deep. Besides, he lives here. I live there. How would we make that work?"

"So you're thinking about it?"

Kennedi paused. She'd thought about seeing him after her vacation was over, yes. But she hadn't been able to figure out a solution that wouldn't leave her sad and frustrated. Not only did they live in two different worlds, they lived on opposite sides of the state.

It was the reason she'd tried to maintain some distance initially and not spend the night with him. But he'd blown that all to hell when he'd asked her to stay in that way he had.

"Should I be thinking about it, though?" Kennedi asked.

"I think you should. And I think you should bring him to the wedding. That way, you'd get to spend more time with him, see how he interacts with your colleagues and your friend. Me. Oh, and Lauren. She's the ultimate judge of character. If she gives him a hug, he's a keeper."

Kennedi smiled, thinking of her beautiful and spirited goddaughter. She was not forthcoming with affection. So when she'd immediately taken to Mark, Kennedi knew her friend had found the man for her. "I miss her," she told Paula.

This was the longest Kennedi had ever gone without seeing Lauren since she was born. That little girl was her heart. Kennedi had been in the delivery room holding Paula's hand as Lauren came out crying. She'd been a goner ever since, and her baby "Lo-Lo" knew it.

"She misses her Kenni Cakes, too. And so do I."

"Aw, you really do love me?"

"I do. And real talk, I'd be lost without you. But I meant what I said—you deserve to be happy and it looks like Wellspring has made my Kenni Cakes a happy camper."

"Shut up, girl. You're too much."

"Hey, you know I tell it like it is. I've been waiting for this day since I met you."

Frowning, Kennedi asked, "What day?"

"The day you finally, finally tell me you're in love. Because you know how I felt about Quincy."

Paula had never liked Quincy, and it was no secret. Her friend had told her countless times to leave him during their short marriage, but Kennedi hadn't listened. She'd only fought harder. But when she finally made the decision to divorce, Paula had handled the case with gusto, and a little mean streak toward Quincy that made Kennedi proud to have her as a friend.

"Yeah, yeah, I know. We don't have to rehash that."

"Oh, I gotta go. Due in a meeting in ten. I love you, Kenni Cakes."

"I love you, too, Paula."

Ending the call, Kennedi fell back on the bed. She couldn't discount anything her friend had said. After all, she was closer to Paula than her own sister. She glanced at the bedside clock and thought about Parker. *I wonder if he's fired Gary yet?*

She couldn't help it. He was on her mind. She wished he was with her, touching her and kissing her. Holding her. She wanted him to make love to her again. She missed him—and she'd just seen him an hour ago. That thought made her bolt upright and storm out of the room. Now in the bathroom, she peered at herself in the mirror. There was no use in denying it. *Damn, I'm in love.*

Chapter 16

Over the next week, Kennedi spent as much time with Parker as she could, when he wasn't in closed-door meetings with lawyers regarding the land grabbing. The board had voted Gary Townsend out and backed Parker publicly with regard to the allegations.

Today, Kennedi was spending the day with Anny at the manor. Fred was out of town visiting his cousin in Detroit, so it was just the two of them. They'd spent the day watching old movies and eating junk food. Kennedi was sure she'd gained ten pounds just being in Wellspring. Anny kept her fed at the house, and Parker seemed to want to fatten her up as well. He'd consistently brought her goodies and taken her to different restaurants. They'd recently attended the Wellspring Fall Festival downtown and she'd stuffed her face with food from several food trucks.

"What are you going to do when it's time for you to go home?" Anny asked.

Honestly, her aunt hadn't asked her anything she hadn't already asked herself. She had no idea what she was going to do when she left Wellspring and returned to her home. Because truthfully, she'd felt more at home in the last few weeks than she had since her parents were alive.

Kennedi hugged her knees, resting her cheek on them. "I don't know."

"And Parker?"

Anny and Fred, Kennedi and Parker had spent some time together before Fred left town. They'd driven to the Gun Lake Casino in Wayland, Michigan. The four had eaten, listened to live music at the casino's club, and played the slots until the wee hours of the morning.

"I don't know," Kennedi repeated. "We both knew from the beginning that I wasn't here for the long haul."

"Do you think he wants you to stay?"

"He asked if I'd thought about it," Kennedi admitted.

It was the night before last, after a pretty stimulating game of strip poker. She'd lost bad, but she still got the prize. They made love all night until she'd practically passed out from exhaustion. But before she'd closed her eyes, he'd asked her if she'd ever thought of moving to Wellspring. She hadn't answered him, but she'd thought about the possibility.

"What did you tell him?" Anny asked.

"Nothing. I didn't answer the question."

"I can't deny you living here would be great for

me." Anny grinned at her. "I miss you when you're not here."

"But you're going to be traveling the world with Fred, once you sell the land."

Parker had been so busy with the company's other troubles that she hadn't broached the subject of the land sale again. Which was just as well. It wasn't the right time for him, and Kennedi agreed. The good news was her aunt had options, and even though Anny wanted to sell to Parker and Wellspring Corp., if it didn't work out, she would be able to get a good price for the land.

"Speaking of the land," Anny said. "If this isn't settled before you leave, I want you to still be in charge of the sale. I would feel better if you were."

Kennedi nodded. "You know I will."

"But I'm still secretly hoping and praying that you'll stay."

The doorbell chimed, and Kennedi jumped up and answered it. It was a courier, who handed her a huge manila envelope. She thanked the man and closed the door.

The envelope was addressed to Hunt Nursery, LLC, in care of Angelia Hunt. The return address was Wellspring Water Corporation. Frowning, she held up the envelope so Anny could take a look. "Are you expecting something from Wellspring, Anny?"

Her aunt shrugged. "No. What is it?"

Kennedi studied the envelope one more time before opening it. She pulled the contents out, frowning when she realized it was a business sale agreement. "It's a contract for the sale of Hunt land. Did you talk to Parker about this?"

Anny sat up, shaking her head. "I haven't said anything to Parker since we talked about it that day in the pool house."

Kennedi browsed the contract. It appeared to be approved by the board of directors. And at the bottom of the document was Parker's signature. Kennedi picked up her phone and called Parker, but the call went to voice mail.

"What does it say?" Anny asked.

Kennedi continued to read, noting that several of the provisions she'd struck out of the original offer were there. As she flipped through the pages, she tried to tell herself that it was a mistake, that Parker would never do this, but that little part of her, the part that remembered being burned before, was loud and clear, telling her that it was possible.

Then, Kennedi's blood ran cold when she skimmed section eight of the contract, regarding the greenhouse on the property. Wellspring was planning to tear it down and build a pumping station on the stretch of land the greenhouse rested on.

Infuriated, Kennedi rushed upstairs to her room and dressed. She attempted to call Parker again, but there was no answer. Then she sent a text: Where are you?

His response came back within seconds: In a meeting. Everything okay?

No. Need to see you.

Give me five and I'll call you was his response.

No, I'm coming to you.

She then turned her phone off and rushed downstairs. "Anny, I'll be back."

Kennedi didn't wait for Anny's response before she grabbed the keys and rushed out to the car. She arrived at WWCH in twenty minutes and went straight upstairs.

"Hi, Sandy," she said, entering the suite that housed Parker's office. "Is he out of his meeting yet?"

Sandy smiled at her. "He was here for a minute, but got called out for an emergency. But he told me to let you know he'll be back shortly. You're welcome to wait in his office."

"Thanks. I'll just go in."

A few minutes later, Parker walked into the office, smiling when he saw her. "Hey." He bent down to give her a kiss, but she leaned out of reach. Frowning, he said, "What's up?"

Kennedi held up the contract. "This. We received it by courier today."

He rubbed his forehead before taking the contract from her outstretched hand. He reviewed it, a frown on his face the entire time. "Who sent this to you?"

"You did." She held up the manila envelope.

He shook his head. "I didn't send this."

"It has your signature on it."

Parker blinked, then turned to the last page of the contract. "I didn't sign anything, Kennedi."

"Well, someone did. Did you see the language in there about the greenhouse?"

He nodded. "This doesn't make any sense. We put this on hold pending the mess with the land grabbing."

"I know. So, either you're a really good actor or you have someone else on staff who's fucking with you."

He eyed her warily. "I hope you believe it's the latter option, Kennedi."

She swallowed, averting his gaze.

His eyes widened, even as his brows remained furrowed. "Really, Kennedi?" He shook his head slowly. "We're back to this? After everything?"

Kennedi closed her eyes, letting out a heavy sigh. When she opened them again, he was looking at her with hurt eyes. "No. I believe you. But you understand why I'm upset, right?"

"I do, but Anny didn't sign it, so we're good."

"That's not the point. I'm not going to be here after a week."

He grimaced. "And?"

"What if Anny got the contract, thinking that you and I had talked about it, and just signed it. She would have been sideswiped by this."

"But she didn't sign it."

"Parker, you need to figure out who it is in this company who's out to get you. Gary is gone, but obviously there is someone else."

"That's actually what I was in a meeting about. Sweeping changes in the company. Sandy is writing up the termination letters as we speak. We've identified several of Senior's old cohorts who were complicit in the land-grabbing scheme."

Parker told her of shady contractors hired to

give faulty inspections of businesses, bad office deals with other companies to drive business out of Wellspring for their own purposes. It was deep, and Parker was cleaning house.

Kennedi sighed. "That's crazy, Parker. I'm sorry all this is happening, but I'm glad you're taking care of it. Any word on who leaked the story?"

"Actually Brooklyn figured it out. It wasn't even an employee of Wellspring Corp."

Kennedi sat on the arm of a chair. "Who was it?"

"Patricia's ass."

"What? Why would she do that?"

"Revenge. Plain and simple. She's mad because the judge dropped the lawsuit, so she thought she'd hurt me—us—by leaking the story. Apparently, she'd heard about it by listening to Senior talk to his business partners."

Parker had been working with law enforcement, cooperating with their requests for information. And as the pressure mounted, people were folding, calling people out to avoid being prosecuted. The scandal was huge, and even reached up to the state Senate.

"I fully expect more charges in the coming months."

Kennedi still couldn't believe it. To think her Anny could have been caught up in that mess made her tremble with anger. "I guess it's a good thing I came when I did. Anny might have signed the contract."

"I agree. And you're right. I still need to find out

who let this thing go through, because they didn't think twice about forging my signature."

"Who has access to your signature stamp besides Sandy?"

"My weekend assistant. She comes in on Saturdays because I'm often here working. But that doesn't mean anything. It could be anyone who has access to the suite. She keeps it at her desk."

"Perhaps she should lock it up from now on?"

"We've already discussed this. I'll remind her and Dalia, the weekend assistant."

"Good."

He pulled her into a hug, kissing her forehead, then her nose, then her lips. "Want to grab dinner this evening?"

"I do. I'd better get back to Anny. She's probably worried. Just call me."

He picked up the contract. "I'm going to head up to legal and get to the bottom of this contract."

He walked her down to the entrance, gave her a quick searing kiss, and hurried to the elevator. Just before she walked out of the building, she spotted Gary Townsend standing against the far wall, looking right at her.

She rushed through the door, but he caught up with her. "Ms. Robinson." He grabbed her arm.

Yanking her arm from his grasp, she turned around to face him. "What can I do for you?"

"Now, now. That's no way to talk to me. I've never done anything to you."

"You drew up that land agreement for the sale of my family's nursery, didn't you?"

"I worked on it. It was a solid offer."

"It wasn't going to cut it. That's why we didn't sign it."

"I think you need to rethink that. You won't get another offer as good as ours."

"Don't you mean Wellspring Corporation's? As far as I know you're no longer employed by the company."

His eyes turned from faux concern to ice in a matter of seconds. He stepped closer, and she retreated backward. Leaning in, he sneered, "You think you're so smart, don't you. But you don't know anything. You're so trusting of Parker, but he's his daddy's son."

"You don't know Parker, Mr. Townsend. And I suggest you back up."

"I'm going to give you this warning and then leave you alone. You're nothing but a means to an end. He was only supposed to get you to sign the contract. Not sleep with you. But I guess you were just someone he couldn't pass up." He reached out to touch her, and Kennedi smacked his hand away. "I'd watch your back, Ms. Robinson."

Kennedi sucked in a deep breath. "Mr. Townsend, I suggest you leave me alone and get out of the building before I tell Parker to have you forcibly removed."

Gary backed away, held his hands up in surrender. "I'm going. But I meant what I said. You were a means to an end, sweetie. It would do you well to remember that."

Then, he was gone.

Chapter 17

Kennedi took her frustration out on the heavy bag in the gym, punching and kicking until her legs and arms felt like jelly, limp. She crashed to the ground and took in huge breaths.

It had been hours since she'd run into Gary Townsend in the lobby and she was shaken. She had no reason to believe him. Parker had been nothing but honest to her, but . . . *How do I really know he was being honest with me?*

There was a heaviness in her body, a tightness in her chest, that hadn't been there earlier. She just couldn't shake the feeling that there was something to what Gary had told her. *Did Parker come to me and apologize solely to get me to sign the contract?*

Anny walked into the pool house. "Kennedi?"

Peering up at the ceiling, Kennedi swallowed rapidly, willing herself not to panic, not to cry. Not over a man. She didn't cry over Quincy; she wouldn't cry over Parker.

She felt Anny get on the floor next to her,

smelled her soft perfume and felt comforted. For a minute. Then the doubts crept back in.

"Parker called," Anny said. "He said he'd been calling you. You were supposed to have dinner with him?"

Kennedi remained silent, because if she talked . . . she would break.

"He told me about the contract. He figured out what happened. One of the people on the legal team accidentally pushed it through. He reprimanded them, but he's not worried about it happening again."

Kennedi closed her eyes, relieved that she hadn't been wrong to trust him in that. But still . . .

"Babe, I'm worried about you. Tell me what's wrong. Is it Quincy?"

At that, Kennedi snorted. Because it *was* Quincy, to a certain extent. He'd played her, destroyed her trust, used her to get what he wanted. And the possibility that Parker had done that? It made her want to cry out, scream at the unfairness of it all.

"I ran into Gary Townsend at WWCH today," Kennedi said.

"That asshole," Anny said bluntly.

Any other day, she would have laughed at her aunt's cursing. But not today, not now. "He told me that Parker was only supposed to get me to sign the contract, not sleep with him."

"Oh." Anny's voice was low.

They lay there in silence for several minutes before Kennedi turned to Anny, a tear finally falling from her eyes. She cursed that damn tear to hell and back. "Anny," Kennedi breathed.

Anny glanced at her, her brown eyes boring into hers, and Kennedi didn't mistake the tears shining in her aunt's eyes.

Then, she turned her attention back up to the ceiling.

"Kennedi?" Anny said after a few moments. When Kennedi didn't answer, Anny continued. "Trust Parker."

"I do," Kennedi admitted softly. "I do trust him. That's the problem."

Kennedi couldn't describe her conflicting emotions about this. The mess with the contract was before *them*. It was before he'd made love to her, before he'd shared his life with her, before *he'd* trusted *her* with his family business. Logically, she knew she couldn't hold it against him. But with that logic came another hard truth. Was Kennedi really ready to be in a relationship? Could that trust hold if she went back to her home on the other side of the state?

"Why is that a problem, babe?"

"Because I trusted *Quincy*, too. And he was lying to me the entire time. He had a whole nother baby, Anny! He had multiple affairs. And I was home, trusting him. Praying for my marriage because I remembered Mom telling me that it was important for a wife to pray for her marriage a long time ago."

"I know how you feel, babe. Trust me, I do."

Kennedi nodded, knowing her aunt was telling her the truth. The two of them . . . bonded by blood and experience. "I need some time. I just have to think about everything. It's too much, too fast."

"Okay, babe. Parker will understand."

"What if he doesn't?"

"I don't know, babe," Anny said truthfully.

Kennedi heard the door open and knew it was Parker without even looking. She heard the click of his shoes against the tile as he neared her. His smell wrapped around her and held her tight, and she sucked in a deep breath, already wanting to revel in it, in him.

She opened her eyes and saw him standing there. He was staring at her, an off expression on his face.

Anny stood, brushed off her pants. "I'm going to leave you two alone," she said before making her exit.

"I've been calling you," Parker said. "You haven't answered any of my calls."

He was still dressed in his work suit—a black pin-striped suit with a burgundy shirt, no tie. "I had to think," she said simply.

"What happened, Kennedi?"

Deciding on the truth, she stood, faced him directly. "I ran into Gary Townsend at WWCH this afternoon."

With raised eyebrows, he asked, "He was there?"

"Yes. He cornered me." She noted the way his hand clenched into a fist and the tiny vein in his neck throbbed. "He didn't hurt me, though."

"Good," he said simply. "He's a problem that I'm going to fix soon enough. They're filing the first indictments soon. I've been told he's at the top of the list, along with Senior. And since Senior is . . . well, you know."

Even though Senior was in a coma, he could still be arrested and indicted. The court would then have to suspend the trial until Senior awoke from the coma. "How do you feel about that?" she asked, knowing it had to be hard to know that his father was in a coma and would more than likely die being arrested for the crime that almost destroyed him.

"It is what it is, at this point."

"Still, he is your father. You must be feeling some weird emotions."

"I can't even begin to describe what I'm feeling about Senior right now. I'm just happy Gary and those still conscious will be prosecuted."

Kennedi was happy to hear the good news, even happier to hear that Parker's name wasn't on the list. "Good news."

They stood there in awkward silence, and it made her sad. From the beginning, silence was never awkward with them. That's why she needed to get away—she needed perspective. Right now, it felt like they were so far apart. They were on different paths. She knew it was going to happen, yet she'd still gone in with both eyes open because she couldn't resist him. She couldn't resist the way he'd made her feel alive.

Kennedi felt full, like at any moment she would burst open from the pressure building inside her. She needed him to understand, needed to get through to him that he meant so much to her. But she needed to go; she needed time to get herself together.

"Kennedi."

"Parker."

They'd said each other's name at the same time, but neither of them made a move to continue. Until he asked, "What did Gary want?"

"He wanted to make sure that I knew I was nothing more than a convenience for you."

Parker stepped forward. "How would he know that?"

Kennedi shrugged. "He said that you were only supposed to get me to sign the contract, not sleep with me."

Parker's jaw clenched, and he let out an impatient sneer. "That fuckin' asshole."

Kennedi waited to see if he was going to deny it. But when he just stood there, his posture stiff . . . brooding, she asked, "Is it true?"

His shoulders fell. "You have got to stop doing this, Kennedi. Either you trust me, or you don't. You know who Gary is, you know what he's doing. He wants to cause discord between us because I hit him where it hurts. If you let him, he's winning."

"Parker, I don't believe him."

He closed his eyes and tilted his head toward the ceiling. "Good. Because I meant what I said. I never would have done anything that would hurt Angelia, or put her in a bad position."

"I know, and I appreciate that."

"But?"

A pang in her heart had her rubbing her chest.

"It's just . . . we lead very different lives. And it's time for me to go home." Because if she didn't, she would drown in him, and that scared her.

Parker couldn't believe his ears, so he leaned forward and asked, "What?"

"I'm going back to my house. In Ypsilanti."

"Your leave isn't over for another week," he argued.

"I know. But I want to go back and help Paula with wedding stuff, get back to work."

Parker knew that her best friend was getting married, but he also knew that Kennedi had already told her she wasn't attending the bridal shower next weekend. According to Kennedi, Paula had even encouraged her absence, wanting her get her full vacation in. But he didn't say that, he didn't argue with her.

Instead, he said, "I'll go with you. I can get away for the weekend."

They'd talked about him visiting her. She didn't live very far from Detroit, and he'd told her he wanted to go to a Detroit Tigers game, walk the Detroit RiverWalk. He'd heard about all the improvements to the city, and he wanted to check it out, see some sights.

"No," she said. "I'm leaving. You're staying here. I need time away from Wellspring. It's been an emotional visit."

"You need time." Parker tried not to sound bitter, but it had spilled out in his words. She needed time. "From me. In other words, we're done."

Kennedi averted her gaze, and Parker swore. "This is ridiculous. This is stupid. You're leaving.

After everything that's happened between us, you can just . . . bust up?"

"You knew my visit here was only temporary, Parker. I just feel like I need some space. Being here, being around you is messing with my head right now. It's too much."

"So, how about we go away together? Island vacation. Just me and you. To talk, to just be with each other."

Parker had never felt so desperate before, so unhinged, like she had pulled one tiny string and everything in him was falling apart. It didn't make sense. No, they hadn't known each other long, but he felt like his heart knew her. His heart saw her.

He was so in love with her, and every day was better than the day before. The thought of her leaving before they had a chance to really make a go of it made him want to shake her. Because he didn't want her to go. He wanted the feeling to last, he wanted to bottle it up and sell it, it was so good. But then he wouldn't want to share it, share her with anyone else.

Kennedi grabbed his arm, squeezed it. "Parker, please. I have to go."

Then, she turned on her heels and walked out of the pool house, leaving him there alone.

Parker pulled up at Lawson Garage a short while later. He picked up the six-pack of beer he'd purchased and slid out of his truck. He used his key to open the door. The place was quiet, dark. Turning, he locked up and headed toward the back of the building, where Trent kept a small apartment for his late nights.

His friend was sitting on the couch, watching television, when he walked in. "What's up?" Parker said, tossing Trent a beer from his batch.

"Shit," Trent answered. "I was surprised you called."

After Parker left Hunt Manor, he'd driven around for an hour, thinking. Going over every scenario over and over again had made him feel a little crazy, so he'd called Trent, asked if he wanted a beer.

Parker popped the top off of a beer and guzzled it down. Sitting on a recliner in the corner, he said, "Well, I needed a break from everything."

Trent eyed Parker. "It's Kennedi, huh?"

Parker groaned. "It's nobody. Can't I want to talk shit and drink a beer with my brother?"

Because Trent really was like a brother to him. They'd been through a lot together, and had still remained close. So close that Parker hadn't hesitated to help Trent with the start-up capital for the garage. It was one of the many moves he made to diversify his investment portfolio outside of Wellspring Corp. just in case Senior tried to kick him out of the company and disown him for some crazy reason. Parker had also bought several rental properties that were bringing in extra money.

"I call bullshit. But I'm going to let you have that one."

Parker sighed. Trent was his best friend, but they weren't the type of friends who talked about women troubles in a meaningful way. The most they shared with each other was an "I fucked up" or a "She talked too much" or an "It wasn't that deep."

But Parker wanted to talk to someone, and Brooklyn wasn't it. She'd go charging over to Hunt Manor and demand answers. He could've talked to Carter, but again . . . Brooklyn. And even though Carter would not intend to tell Brooklyn, she seemed to have a way of wrapping him around her finger.

"Kennedi is leaving," Parker blurted out.

"I know. She called. Her car has been ready for a while, but I told her I'd keep it here until she was ready to get it. She did have you carting her around everywhere. Her vacation is over?"

Parker nodded. It had actually been his idea for her to leave the car in the garage. It wasn't like she needed it, anyway. "She's cutting it short."

"Ah."

After a few minutes of silence, Parker slammed his bottle down on the table. "Ah? That's all you've got?"

Trent grinned. "Are you asking me for advice?"

"Well, I told you. I was assuming you'd say something other than 'Ah.'"

"Oh, is that what we're doing now? Giving advice? Because I distinctly remember coming to you about Maddie and you telling me to suck it up and go get my woman."

Trent got on his fuckin' nerves sometimes. He'd just thrown his own words back at him. "But there's a difference here. Kennedi is not *my* girl officially."

"That's not what I saw," Trent said with a shrug.

"She was your girl all right. You were willing to go to battle over her. I saw the way you looked at me when she came to the shop. Like you were going to beat the shit out of me. Or try at least."

"Oh, I wouldn't have to try," Parker retorted. "Anyway, we weren't really together."

Trent shot him a side eye. "Whatever, man. Keep telling yourself that. You fell in love with her."

Parker blinked. Now, this conversation was just getting weird. He scratched his head, wondering if he could admit that to his friend. Then, he waved a dismissive hand. "Shut the hell up. Let's play some cards."

"Nope," Trent said. "In all seriousness, my life without Maddie sucks. I would hope that you learn from me. Stop bullshitting around and make it work."

A few hours later, Parker pulled up at his house. After the serious moment at Trent's the two had reverted to normal and spent a little while playing cards and talking shit. He walked up to the door and frowned when he noticed the door was ajar. He pushed the door open and stepped in just in time to see a masked intruder barreling toward him. He felt the hard thump of something against the back of his head and then everything went black.

Chapter 18

Kennedi packed the last of her things and carried her suitcase down to the first floor. "All packed. Ready to leave first thing in the morning," she announced to Anny and Fred. "I called Trent and he said he'd have the car washed and everything for me when we go pick it up."

Anny nodded, gave her a wobbly smile. "I thought I'd have more time with you."

"I know. But I'll see you at Paula's wedding in a few weeks."

Fred rubbed her hair. "Kenni Bear, I wish you'd reconsider. Wellspring isn't such a bad place, and we'd love to have you closer."

Kennedi's heart ached at the sadness in Anny's and Fred's voices. "You know I'll be back to visit. We have to get this land sold after all."

"Yeah, about that," Anny said. "I think we're going to just sell to Wellspring Corp."

"Oh?"

"Parker. Um, I mean Wellspring Corp., is making

great strides to assure residents of the community that they want to keep our town the quaint haven it's always been. And I trust that they'll do right by the land."

Kennedi didn't doubt Parker would do everything in his power to make sure Anny was taken care of. "I think so, too."

"I wish I had known you were leaving earlier today. I would have made your favorite—short ribs."

Short ribs would have been nice, but Anny had hooked up dinner anyway. They'd had fried chicken, mashed potatoes, and sautéed spinach. Then, she'd surprised her with a homemade cream cheese pound cake that made Kennedi's mouth water.

"I know. But I have a Crock-Pot. You can hook me up when you come visit me."

Anny hooked her arm in Kennedi's. "I'm hoping you find what you're looking for."

Kennedi nodded. "I just need time, Anny. I'll be fine."

A loud knock sounded and Fred glanced at his watch. "It's late. Wonder who that is."

Fred pulled the door open and Brooklyn was standing outside, a worried expression on her face. Kennedi stepped forward. "Brooklyn? What's wrong?"

"It's Parker."

Kennedi gasped. "What happened?"

"He was robbed tonight."

Behind her, she heard Anny's sharp intake of breath. But it sounded muted, like it was far away. *Not again. Oh God, not again.* "Is he . . . ?" Kennedi couldn't bring herself to finish her sentence. The thought of Parker not being alive was too much to bear.

"Oh God, no. Girl, I would be done if anything happened to my brother."

Kennedi let out a shaky breath. Fred's strong hand was on her back and Anny was holding her arm. They must have known her knees were weak and at any moment she would have fallen to the ground.

"Thank God," Kennedi whispered. "Where is he?"

"At home. He wants to see you, and I promised I'd come get you."

Brooklyn and Carter drove her to Parker's house. As they pulled up, she saw the flashing lights of the ambulance and her heart fell. It was almost surreal, that Parker had been robbed and assaulted, around the same time her parents were six years earlier. If Kennedi didn't know better she would think the universe was fucking with her.

Carter stopped the car, and Kennedi jumped out, broke into a run toward the house. Sheriff Walker stopped her. "Whoa, Kennedi," he said. "Parker is not in there. He's in the ambulance."

"Thank you." She turned and ran to the ambulance, then stopped when she spotted Parker sitting up on a stretcher, just outside the back door of the ambulance. His back was to her, and he was talking to one paramedic while another was tending to him. He had no shirt on, and he was holding an ice pack to his side.

Kennedi recognized the moment he realized she

was near, because he tensed, then slowly turned. Her stomach twisted in knots when their eyes met.

His slow perusal over her face, down her neck, to her breasts, and then back up to her eyes stole her breath. She leaned into the ambulance. Even now, he seemed to see something in her that she didn't see herself.

The longing in his eyes mirrored her own. She wanted to wrap herself in him like a blanket and block out the rest of the world if only for a few hours. She wanted to go to him, feel his heart beating under her palm so she could be sure, so she could know for certain that he was really still there. But she remained rooted to her spot, as if her body, her mind, would not let her step forward.

He tried to stand, but the paramedic shook his head, telling him to remain seated. She heard Parker's grimace, and then she was moving, rushing to his side.

She reached out, cupped his cheek in her hand, brushed her thumb over the small bruise that was forming over his eye. Her throat closed up, and she couldn't seem to find the words.

"I'm fine, Kennedi," he said softly. He picked up her hand and pressed it to his heart, as if he'd read her mind earlier. She closed her eyes at the feel of the strong beat of his heart against her hand.

A sob tore through her, bubbling up until it came out. He pulled her to him, and she leaned into him, wrapping her arms around him, crying into his neck.

"Kennedi?" Anny said, from behind her.

Blinking, Kennedi turned, surprised to see Anny and Fred there. "You're here?"

Anny smiled sadly, brushing the tears from her face. "You know we wouldn't be anywhere else."

"Ma'am," the paramedic said, "we need to take him to the hospital to be looked at."

"I told you, I'm fine," Parker said.

"No, you're not fine," Brooklyn said, crossing her arms over her chest. "I'd feel better if you were checked out at the hospital."

"I need to get the house situated." Parker groaned in pain when the paramedic pushed down on his side.

"Parker, you should go to the hospital," Carter said. "I'll stay at the house."

"We'll stay with him," Fred said. "Just go."

"I'm going, too," Kennedi said. "Can I ride with you, Brooklyn?"

Brooklyn smiled and nodded. "Come on. We'll meet you at the hospital, Parker."

Kennedi hugged Parker again, and then brushed her lips over his before she turned and followed Brooklyn to her car.

Several hours later, Kennedi helped Parker into his home. Brooklyn was behind them. The doctors had examined him and let him go with instructions to take it easy. Kennedi was glad that he didn't have to stay overnight. She hated hospitals, hated the smell, hated the sounds of the machines. Nothing positive or good had ever happened in a hospital, and she avoided them whenever she could.

Carter, Fred, and Anny were still there, and Trent had joined them. Parker wanted an update on the case, and Carter told him that Sheriff Walker had collected some evidence, but there wasn't much to go on. The fact that the assailant hadn't stolen anything told them that the person might have been there looking for something specific.

"Well, Parker, you need to rest," Brooklyn said, giving him a kiss on his forehead. "We'll be over to check on you in the morning."

Carter said his good-byes as well before they walked out. And Trent also made a quick retreat, but not before doing the man-hug thing.

Fred stood then. "Let me know if I can do anything for you, Parker."

Parker nodded. "Thanks, Fred. Appreciate it, but I'll be fine."

Anny hugged Parker. "I'm glad you're okay."

Smiling, Parker said, "You know I'm not going to let anybody get the best of me."

Anny laughed. "I know." Turning to Kennedi, Anny mouthed, "Call me."

Kennedi walked her aunt and Fred to the door. Once they were safely in their car, Kennedi closed the door and locked it. Turning, Kennedi watched Parker stand. She stepped into him, wrapping her arms around his waist and leaning her forehead against his back. Even though he'd been the one who was hurt, he'd made sure she was good at the hospital, seeming to sense her apprehension. He was so strong, in mind and body. Kennedi needed that strength tonight.

He held her hands against his chest. "I'm glad you're here."

Kennedi circled him, stopping in front of him, lacing her fingers in his. She lifted herself up on the tips of her toes and kissed him. "Where else would I be?"

"Back in Ypsi," he said.

"Shh." Raising their joined hands to her lips, she kissed his knuckles. And then led him back to his bedroom.

Back in his room, she ran bathwater, pouring some Epsom salt into the water. When the water was ready, she undressed him, slowly, making sure she didn't hurt him.

Parker leaned down, placed a kiss on her forehead, then her cheek. She leaned back, peering up at him. Shaking her head, she said, "No, Parker."

He cradled her face in his hands. "I want to hold you."

"You can hold me later. But now, let me take care of you."

He dropped his hands to his sides, and she helped him into the tub. While he soaked, Kennedi changed his sheets and put some hot tea on in the kitchen. Once she was done, she walked back to his room, half expecting him to be up and trying to dress himself for bed. But she found him right where she left him, in the bathtub. Asleep.

Kennedi dropped to her knees. "Parker?" she whispered.

He opened one eye, smiling when he realized it

was her. He lifted a hand up, ran a damp finger down the bridge of his nose. "You're still here," he murmured.

"Did you think I'd leave you in the tub?"

Chuckling, he said, "I guess not. That would be cruel and unusual punishment."

Kennedi took a sponge and dipped it into the water. Then she washed him clean, taking her time to make sure she didn't rub against the angry red bruise on his side.

According to the doctor, Parker had a bruised rib, which must have happened when Parker was knocked out. Unfortunately, there's not a lot they could do to treat bruised ribs, so they'd given him instructions to use ice, take ibuprofen, and make sure he was moving around and doing breathing exercises.

Once he was clean, Kennedi helped him stand and fought back a groan. He was glorious, wet from the water, and hard. His eyes were on her, intense and seeing. He was all hard lines and muscles, and Kennedi felt desire pool low in her belly from just watching him.

When he stepped out of the tub, he tugged her to him and kissed her. The water from his body seeped into her clothes, soaking the front of her shirt and her pants. Kennedi reluctantly broke the kiss. "We can't. I don't want to hurt you."

"I'm fine." He coughed, and winced in pain.

"You're not fine. And it's okay."

She dried him off with a towel and then wrapped it low around his waist. Back in the bedroom, she held out a pair of pajamas she'd set on his bed. He shook his head. "I'm fine." He dropped his towel onto the floor and walked over to the bed. She stood by his side as he eased himself down on the bed, then tucked him in.

"You're not getting in the bed with me?" he asked.

"I'm wet." Her eyes widened when the words came out.

He laughed, grimacing while holding his side. "Oh, that hurt."

Worried, Kennedi approached the bed. "Can I do something?"

"You can take your clothes off and get in this bed with me," he said with a wink.

Kennedi smiled and stripped, pulling her clothes off right in front of him. The heat in his eyes as she undressed was palpable. He wanted her, and she wanted him. Unfortunately, they weren't in the position to do anything about it. Swallowing, she climbed into the bed. He was lying on his back and she scooted forward, nestling against his unbruised side.

"Better?" she asked.

"Much," he said wrapping his arm around her. "Kennedi?"

"Yes."

"I want you to stay."

Kennedi gasped and lifted herself up on her elbow. "What?"

He swallowed visibly. "You've been avoiding a conversation with me. I don't know what that's about, but I felt like I should tell you where I stand. Stay. Stay with me, and let's see if we can make this work."

Tears welled in Kennedi's eyes. "Parker," she whispered.

"I won't push you, but . . ." He trailed off, and she wondered what he was going to say.

"Sleep, Parker. You're tired."

"Just . . . think about it," he murmured, his eyes drooping closed. Soon, he was sleep.

Kennedi awoke clasping at her throat, trying to catch her breath. It felt like she was screaming, but no sound would come out. But that feeling, that fear deep in her gut was still with her. She turned to Parker, who was resting peacefully.

It was a stark contrast to the Parker in her dream. She placed her hand over his heart, closing her eyes when she felt the strong beat of his heart. *He's alive.*

She felt a tear fall to her hand, and it shocked her because she hadn't realized she was crying.

The dream had started out lovely. She'd decided to stay in Wellspring, build a life with Parker and start her business. But when she moved in with him, she'd discovered his lifeless body in his bed.

She'd howled in her dream, fallen to her knees, begged God to spare his life, but the blood was everywhere. Parker's blood had been smeared all over the bedroom and he was . . . Kennedi swallowed. Someone had shot him between the eyes.

The cold terror that she'd felt in her nightmare had felt so real, almost like it had really happened. *It could have happened.* Kennedy slid out of the bed and walked into the bathroom.

Visions of her parents, lifeless and bloody, mingled with visions of Parker. There was nothing she could do for them, not when they'd been dead for hours. There was nothing she could do for Parker.

Kennedi felt like she was unraveling, like at any minute she would split in two and then break into tiny pieces that would be impossible to put back together again. She loved Parker, she wanted him. *But what if . . . ?*

Parker had asked her to stay. And she wanted to be there with him. She wanted to say yes. But the cold fear in the pit of her stomach, that part of her that was scared of loving someone so much again and then having the person ripped from her, rang loud in her ear. And she had to shut that part up. She had to go, or she wouldn't have any peace.

She stood up and walked back into the bedroom. Parker hadn't moved. Glancing at the clock, she took a deep breath before grabbing her phone from the nightstand. Typing in the telephone number, she held her breath as she waited for her to pick up.

"Hello?" Brooklyn's voice was rough, like she'd been sleeping.

"Hi, it's me."

"Is it Parker?"

"Can you come here?" Kennedi didn't want to say anything over the phone. "I need you to come over to Parker's house."

Kennedi had been waiting outside when Brooklyn arrived.

"Kennedi?" Brooklyn said, as she approached the house. "What's going on?"

Swallowing, Kennedi met Brooklyn's worried gaze. "I can't do this." Kennedi bit down on her lip. "I have to go."

Brooklyn stepped forward, rubbed her back. "Are you sick? What's going on? Did you and Parker fight?"

Kennedi shook her head. "No. He's fine. Perfect. But I'm not. Please, don't hate me. But I can't stay."

Brooklyn's shoulders fell. "Kennedi, I wish . . ." The other woman studied her, then nodded. "Okay. Do you need me to take you somewhere?"

"No, Anny is coming to get me. I'll wait out here."

Brooklyn squeezed Kennedi's shoulder and walked in the house without another word.

Parker awoke the next morning, in pain. Groaning, he turned his head toward the other side of the bed. And it was empty.

Sighing, he let out a curse. He didn't bother calling out for Kennedi, because he knew she wasn't there. She'd left him. Again.

"Knock, knock," Brooklyn said, walking in with a tray of food. "I brought you breakfast, nothing heavy."

Parker struggled to sit up straight, making sure he held the cover over his naked body. Couldn't have his sister catching a glimpse of him in all his glory. She set the tray over his lap once he was situated.

"Kennedi?" he asked.

Brooklyn stared down at her hands. "She called

me this morning and asked me to come over and sit with you."

"She's gone."

Brooklyn slumped against the dresser. "Yes. Parker, I'm so sorry. I wanted to try and talk her out of it. But she was a wreck this morning when I came over. I don't think she wanted to leave, but something is pushing her to go."

Kennedi had seen so much tragedy in her life, it was hard to know what he could have done to change things.

"Did you tell her you love her?" Brooklyn asked.

Parker's eyes flashed to his sister. He remembered the conversation he'd had with Trent the night before. "Do you think that would have changed anything? She wanted to leave." And if he'd told her he loved her and she still left, it would have ripped him apart.

"But you'll never know, because you didn't say anything. You had the opportunity, but you choked."

Parker thought about their short conversation before he'd fallen asleep. It was on the tip of his tongue—all he needed to say were the words—but he'd choked. "I asked her to stay," he told his sister.

"Yes, but you didn't give her a reason to stay."

"You're supposed to be on my side, Brooklyn. She left me, without so much as a good-bye."

"I am on your side. Trust me, I wasn't happy with Kennedi when she called me this morning. But . . . I saw her. Then I wasn't mad anymore. Listen, I want you to be happy, I do. And I believe that Kennedi is the one who can do that for you.

Give it a little time. Let her deal with her issues. Then go get her."

Everything in Parker wanted Kennedi with him. He woke up every day thinking about her. He went to breakfast, to work, to dinner with her on his mind. He wanted to dive in face-first, immerse himself in her love. He wanted to chase away her fears and be the man she could trust with all her heart. But Kennedi wasn't the only one hurting. Waking up to find her gone—again—had hurt him. After everything they'd shared, she just walked away.

Parker considered Brooklyn's advice. He knew there was something bigger at play, something deeper that propelled Kennedi to leave. But . . . she'd still left him. And that made him question her feelings for him. Was she really his girl? Could he trust her not to hurt him again? Parker wanted to be secure in the fact that she would be there when he woke up in the morning. He needed to be able to fall asleep knowing that they'd make new memories together the next day. And right now, he wasn't sure he'd be able to do that.

Chapter 19

Kennedi had come full circle. She was sitting in her living room, a Hallmark movie playing on television and a bowl of peanut butter and chocolate ice cream in her lap. *At least, I'm not crying.*

She was lost, wandering through a haze of self-doubt and regret, after walking away from Parker. He'd asked her to stay, and she'd left anyway, propelled by the sight of that blood in her nightmare. Even now she could still see him lying in his blood. She knew it was just a dream, but it seemed so real. She couldn't explain it away, saying things like it would never happen. Because it did happen. It happened to her parents. She loved him so much, she couldn't bear it if something happened to him. And she couldn't live her life scared that the other shoe was going to drop. And so it seemed like the better solution if she just walked away. It hurt her, but a little time and distance, and she would be okay. She would be able to move on, and get back to work.

Sighing, she dipped her spoon in the carton and lifted it to her mouth.

"Girl, if you don't put that damn ice cream down, I'm going to strangle you." Paula walked into the condo and stood in front of her, hands on her hips. "This is not going to work, Kenni Cakes. You have to get it together, hun."

Kennedi gaped at her best friend when she snatched the carton of ice cream off of her lap. "Wait, I wanted that."

"Enough." Paula stalked over to the trash can in the kitchen, held the ice cream up, tapped the lid open with her foot, and dropped it in there. "Now, get up."

Kennedi stood. "Get out, Paula. You ruined a perfectly good night in."

"That's the problem. You're too young for so many nights in. I'm just going to say it. Go back to Wellspring. Go back to Parker."

Kennedi's first day back at home, Paula had brought Lo-Lo over to her house and they'd had a sleepover, catching up on the goings-on with the wedding and how things ended with her and Parker.

"I can't just go back to Parker," Kennedi said. "I messed up."

"Okay, I'm just going to say it. Yes, you fucked up. But you can still fix it. It's not too late, Kenni Cakes. Call him and invite him to the wedding."

Kennedi had picked up the phone to call him so many times but never pushed the button. "I'm a coward."

Paula sat on the couch next to Kennedi and pulled her into a tight hug. "You can't live your life

like this. You have to deal with your issues. You
have to deal with the death of your parents and
your divorce, Kennedi. Now, I love you. I'm here
for you. But you have to be here for you."

"You didn't break me, old man," Parker said, glancing down at his father's still body. The machines
were still keeping him alive, breathing for him.

After he'd visited his father weeks ago, during
the trouble he was having at Wellspring Corp., he'd
wondered if he'd spoken too soon when he'd taunted
his father about righting wrongs. But he knew that
even when he'd felt the weight of the world on
his shoulders, he wouldn't give up. He wouldn't let
Senior have the last word.

"And you tried," Parker continued. "All my life,
you tried it. You made my life hell."

Parker's eyes welled with the tears he'd held
back for years. Tears for the relationship that he'd
wished he had with his father, the relationship he
missed with his mother.

"And still, even after everything you've done, if
you had come to me and apologized for being the
father you were . . . I would've forgiven you. I
would have worked to move past it and try to have
a relationship with you. But you didn't. That's
your loss."

Parker touched his father's hand. "I still learned
from you, though. Some good things, some bad.
I learned to never let anyone see me sweat, to keep
my posture straight and maintain eye contact. I
also learned how to command a room, how to

handle opposition. Those are things that made me competent in business, but they had nothing to do with me becoming a man. I became a better *man* because I fought so hard to be nothing like you. And I'm not. I'm not a bully, I don't spend my time tearing others down, and I love my family. Not for what they will do for me, but because of who they are as people. So, I'm nothing like you and I thank you for showing me the type of man I didn't want to be."

There was a knock at the door, and Parker stepped back. In seconds, Brooklyn walked into the room, Carter on her heels. She walked up to him, wrapped her arms around him.

"They're here," she said.

Soon, the room was full of agents, from several law enforcement agencies. Parker and Brooklyn watched as his father was arrested, charged with corporate fraud and conspiracy. They'd just left the courthouse, where the indictment was handed down and the agent in charge of the case had allowed him and Brooklyn a moment with their father before they entered the room.

If Brooklyn was right, and Senior could hear everything said around him, Parker wondered what his father had been thinking. But in the end, he knew it didn't matter. In his heart, he knew that Senior wouldn't see a day of jail time. And he couldn't decide if he was happy about that, or just sad.

Several minutes later, Parker stood at the entrance of the Wellspring sheriff's station. Brooklyn had pouted and tried to deter him from coming. They did have a schedule to keep. But Parker had to see this through to the end.

It had been a week since the break-in, since Kennedi had gone back to her life, leaving him feeling empty and cranky.

But the bright spot in all of this was that Gary had been getting what he deserved. Mr. Townsend was finally arrested on charges of corporate fraud and conspiracy, as well as conspiracy to commit aggravated assault, and aggravated assault. Turns out Senior's best friend and cohort wasn't content to lie, cheat, and steal; he was okay with violent crimes as well. When Sheriff Walker and his deputies found one of the men who'd broken into Parker's home and assaulted him, it didn't take long for the guy to tell them who had hired him.

Parker watched Gary Townsend as he was led away in cuffs, with his attorneys behind him. Parker waited for the older man to look up, to see him. Because he'd purposefully positioned himself where he couldn't be missed. That man had caused him nothing but trouble, and he couldn't wait until the bars closed on him.

The street was full of reporters from all over Michigan, and even the national news media. Parker had done more than a few press conferences over the past few days, explaining Wellspring Corp.'s position on the pending charges.

Finally, Gary glanced up and met Parker's glare. Gary scowled at him, but Parker simply smirked and tipped his head in his direction. He wanted to add in a "fuck you" for good measure, but he refrained.

"You ready?" Brooklyn said from beside him.

He nodded. "I am. I just wanted to see it for myself."

"It's over, brother. Let's finish this."

Parker and Brooklyn had received a call from the private investigator who'd located their sister, Veronica. They were scheduled to catch a flight out that afternoon to go meet her.

On their way to the airport, Parker leaned his head back against the seat, closing his eyes.

"Have you called Kennedi yet?" Brooklyn asked.

"No."

"Are you going to call her?"

"No."

"Can you say something more than 'no'?"

Parker opened one eye, turned his head, and looked at his sister. "Hell no."

Brooklyn sighed. "You're still angry."

It wasn't a question. "Hell yeah."

"Parker, stop."

Parker had gone over it again and again in his head. As much as he loved Kennedi, what she did wasn't okay with him. And he hadn't called her because he knew his anger would come out over the phone and what he had to say to her needed to be said in person. He wanted her to look at him when he told her that she'd essentially wrecked him by walking out on him. He needed her to see the truth in his feelings. And she wouldn't be able to do it over the phone.

The only problem with that logic was he wasn't sure when or if he'd ever see her again to get the chance to tell her that. He doubted she'd come to Wellspring for a visit anytime soon, and he wasn't too keen on traveling to Ypsilanti to see her.

"Brooklyn, please. I don't want to talk about this right now. There are other things we can discuss— like what we're going to say to Veronica when we finally meet her."

Thankfully, Brooklyn got the hint and dropped the subject for the rest of the ride to the airport. When they touched down in Indianapolis, the driver they hired took them to Veronica's house.

They pulled in front of an upscale condo in the heart of Broad Ripple Village, a neighborhood about six miles north of Downtown Indianapolis. It was a quiet street, not a lot of activity. Brooklyn led the way up the stairs to the front door, then rapped softly on the white door.

Seconds later, a petite woman opened the door. "Come in," she said, letting them in.

Brooklyn had called earlier to set up the visit, so it wasn't a surprise to Veronica that she'd come. The house was nice, new. Hardwood floors spanned the downstairs area, and there were neutral-colored sofas in the living room. The kitchen was modern, with granite countertops and dark-colored cabinets.

"I'm Brooklyn," Brooklyn said, shaking Veronica's hand. "And this is Parker."

Parker held out a hand to Veronica and she clasped his hand and shook it. She looked familiar to him, but Parker thought maybe his mind was playing tricks on him. It wasn't like he'd ever met her before. She was similar in build to Brooklyn, with dark brown skin. She wore her hair long, in braids.

"Wow," Veronica said, breaking the ice. "I have siblings."

"And I have a sister," Brooklyn said. "It's so awesome to know I'm not the only girl anymore."

Then Brooklyn hugged Veronica. Parker could tell Veronica was caught off guard, but he had to hand it to his sister. She'd rolled with it, embracing Brooklyn.

The three talked for a bit. Well, Brooklyn did most of the talking. Veronica mostly listened, but every now and then she said something. Parker was surprised to find out that Veronica had visited Wellspring a few times with her mother, who had been another of Senior's mistresses.

When Veronica's mother, Sue, found out she was pregnant, she'd reached out to Senior, who had told her he wanted nothing more to do with her or her baby. But apparently his father had thought better of it when he thought Sue had had a boy. That's when Gary had filed the paternity action. They didn't find out Sue had been lying until the paternity test came back indicating Senior was the father.

Parker had to hand it to Sue. She was smart. She knew Senior was full of shit and played him. And since he'd paid for the paternity test, and had it established, he was required to support Veronica. Instead of sending monthly checks, Senior had paid Sue off with a lump sum and Veronica had been able to live a comfortable life.

"Are you married?" Brooklyn asked Veronica.

Veronica looked at Parker, then back at Brooklyn. "No. Never been married."

"I just got married this year."

"Really?" Veronica smiled. "Congratulations."

In that moment, Parker thought his sisters favored each other. "So, I heard you were a teacher?" he asked.

Veronica nodded. "I am."

Parker couldn't decide if Veronica was happy they'd reached out to her, or upset, or ambivalent. He knew it was appropriate for them to reach out to her, once they found out about her.

"Tell me about our father," she said finally.

He and Brooklyn exchanged glances, and he motioned for her to do the talking. Brooklyn gave Veronica the quick version of Senior, the G-rated version that told just basics like where he went to school and what he did for a living.

"Senior had a heart attack several months ago, and he's been in a coma since," Parker told her. They'd considered telling her over the phone or in a letter but thought it best that they told her about Senior's condition in person.

"I had read that he was sick," Veronica admitted. "I also read that he was indicted on conspiracy and corporate fraud charges?"

Parker confirmed with a nod. "I want to give

you the opportunity to come to Wellspring, to see Senior before he . . ."

Dies seemed too small a word, too final. Because long after Senior was dead and buried, his lies, his crimes would live on.

Soon, Brooklyn and Parker were saying their good-byes to Veronica and heading back to Wellspring. Carter picked them up from the airport and they decided to grab food at the Bees Knees, where he ran into Anny, having dinner.

"Parker." Angelia waved him over.

Excusing himself from Brooklyn and Carter, he walked over to Angelia. "Hi." He leaned down and gave her a kiss on the cheek. "How are you?"

"I'm well." She motioned to the empty seat across from her. "Have a seat. I've been meaning to call you."

"Where's Fred?"

"Out of town," she said. "I was supposed to go with him, but I plan on heading to Ypsilanti for Paula's wedding."

Parker picked up the sugar canister on the table and set it back down. "That should be a nice trip."

"I think so," Anny said.

"How is she?" he asked.

"Well, she's hanging in there. She's not back to work like she thought she would be. But she's busy with the wedding, and spending time with Paula and Lauren."

Parker imagined Kennedi smiling with her goddaughter. "Good."

He didn't have it in him to ask Anny anything else. His day had already been long enough, and he was sure he'd be haunted by dreams of her overnight.

"Parker?" Angelia asked. "I wanted to talk to you about the sale."

He rubbed his chin. Since Kennedi left, he hadn't reached out to Angelia about the sale of Hunt Nursery. He'd told himself he would wait until one of them reached out to him because he wasn't sure they still wanted to sell.

"Okay," he said. "Are you ready to move forward?"

"I'm ready to move forward, but just not in the way you think."

Leaning closer, palms flat on the table, he said, "Well, tell me what you're thinking and I'll see if I can swing it."

"There's just one favor I need from you," Anny said.

"Anything."

"Since my Fred is out of town, I sure could use a date to the wedding. I would be the talk of the town walking in there on your arm."

Chapter 20

Kennedi sat at the window in her suite at the hotel staring out at the street. In a few hours, Paula would be married to the love of her life. It had been a long time coming, but Kennedi was excited for her friend. She'd spent the night at the hotel—even though she lived less than twenty minutes away—in order to be on hand and help Paula with whatever she needed. Also, it gave her a chance to enjoy a hotel stay.

When Kennedi was a little girl, her parents had taken her and Tanya on a trip to Traverse City. They'd stayed in a small hotel on the beach of Lake Michigan. It was one of her favorite memories as a child, because that is where she'd realized her love of hotels. She enjoyed the idea of a getaway, one that relaxed and rejuvenated the spirit. In that particular hotel, her family had been treated to personal service. It seemed like every time they walked into the building the staff greeted them by name.

That trip had jump-started her dream of owning a
hotel, much like the one she was standing in.

Weber's Inn was one of the top hotels in Ann
Arbor. It wasn't a huge hotel, housing less than a
hundred rooms, but it was intimate. The inn had
a personality, a heady atmosphere that kept people
coming back. Attached to the hotel was a top restaurant and banquet center and Kennedi had been to
several events there. Paula's wedding ceremony
would be held in the Atrium Ballroom, which was a
stunning room with huge windows and dark wood.
The wedding colors were chocolate and champagne,
with a hint of gold. Everything had come together
beautifully. They had decided on an evening wedding, taking place by candlelight. She had no doubt
that the staff would do everything in their power to
make her wedding a memorable event.

In her dream hotel, she would make sure it
stood out as a destination where people could go
to be pampered, to be inspired. The décor would
be unique; classic, but contemporary. There
would be nothing generic about her hotel. Families would be able to enjoy themselves, but it would
also be a place where couples could go and relax.

It was a dream that she'd put in her back pocket,
only taking it out to look at for a few minutes
before she stuffed it back in. Once she'd become
an adult, she'd made decisions that seemed logical,
realistic—like law. Her father had been a talented
attorney, one who was lauded in his company as
sharp and an integral member of the legal team.
And he'd dreamed of her following in his footsteps,

becoming a lawyer so they could one day open up a private practice. Robinson Law. Wanting to please her father, she'd immersed herself into his world. After he died, she continued in it, studied hard, and became a pretty damn good lawyer. It seemed like the perfect way to honor his memory.

But now . . . her career choice seemed hollow. Or it made her feel hollow. Going to work, burying her nose in a case file, constructing multilayered contracts, or being in the thick of a tense arbitration didn't hold any appeal for her. And she found herself pulling that old dream of owning her hotel out of her pocket. The possibility had always seemed so far off, so impossible to reach. Until now.

Parker had asked her why she couldn't do what she wanted. He'd pushed her to ask herself why she couldn't do it. And the reasons she'd ticked off really didn't hold water. There was really no reason why she continued to pursue a career that didn't feel fulfilling to her. And Kennedi was at the point where she wanted to do something she felt passionate about.

Behind her, she heard a click at her door, signaling someone with a key was entering. It was probably Paula coming to check on her. Her friend was the epitome of a calm and collected bride. There were no Bridezilla tendencies, no crazy demands. Kennedi figured it had a lot to do with the fact that Paula got it. She understood that today was just a day, a memorable blip on the radar of a full life with the man she loved. In many ways it reminded her of Anny, and the quick wedding she'd had with Fred. Neither woman had been concerned with the details. They just wanted to get to the marriage.

"Hey, babe."

Kennedi leapt to her feet and rushed over to Anny, falling into her arms. "Anny."

"Whoa," Anny said, rubbing her back. "If I had known I'd get a hug like that, I would have come sooner."

Kennedi pulled back. "I'm so glad to see you."

Anny brushed a tear from her cheek. "You're crying?"

"Been doing that a lot lately," Kennedi admitted.

"Oh, babe. Come here," Anny said, pulling Kennedi over to the couch.

From the time she woke up at six o'clock that morning until now, at noon, she'd been running. Hair appointment, pedicure, and nail appointment. Paula had warned her not to wait until the morning of the wedding, but Kennedi hadn't listened. Luckily, she had a stylist who'd opened early for her. Now, all that had to be done was her makeup and getting the bride downstairs in one piece.

"I was just getting ready to go up and check on Paula," she told Anny. Knowing Anny was coming, Kennedi had asked the hotel staff to give her the key to the room since they were sharing.

"This is a nice room," Anny said, scanning the area. "Lovely flowers."

Kennedi was the keeper of the bouquets. They were arranged in disposable vases on the coffee table in her room. She was also the keeper of the rings, which were both on one of her fingers.

"How's Fred?" Kennedi asked.

Anny's smile widened. "He's Fred. But he's mine. He wishes he could have come with me, but his guys' trip with his brother had already been planned."

"How was the drive?"

Anny peered up at the ceiling and hummed. "Well . . . I thought it was good. Pretty quick. Had a good conversation."

Confused, Kennedi asked, "A conversation with who?"

"A friend," Anny said simply.

Kennedi shrugged, figuring Anny had been chatting on the speakerphone the entire ride with one of her girlfriends. "That's nice."

"I wanted to have a few minutes with you before the wedding."

"Why?" Kennedi asked. "Is something wrong?"

Anny waved a hand at her. "Girl, no. Well, not with me anyway."

Kennedi lowered her head. "I know what you're going to say."

Every conversation with Anny since she'd left Wellspring had consisted of questions about why she left the way she did, when she was going to come back, and how she could leave Parker when he obviously loved her.

Kennedi knew her aunt was worried about her, but she couldn't take anyone else asking her about why she left Parker. "And I hear you," she continued. "I heard you when you said it the first fifty times."

"So what are you going to do about it?" Anny challenged. "I've lived a life full of regret, full of safe choices. I don't want that for you. I don't want you to look back on your life and regret anything. And your mother and father wouldn't have wanted that for you."

Kennedi choked back a sob. "Anny, I'm sorry." It broke her heart to hear of Anny's regrets.

"But you know what?" Anny said. "For the first time in my life, I feel like I'm on the right track. Marrying Fred and deciding to sell the business was exactly what I needed. And today, I have no regrets." Anny cradled Kennedi's face in her hands. "I realized that I did you a disservice, babe. I told you not to cry, I showed you that it was okay to work hard, but not follow your dreams."

"No, Anny. You're amazing."

"Thanks, but I knew you looked up to me. I saw you. I knew you were doing something that you didn't love to honor your father's wish for you. And you did that because you saw me do the same thing for years. Not that you weren't good at it. You're an excellent lawyer, babe. But it's not what will make you happy."

"I know," Kennedi admitted. "That's why I quit my job."

Anny's mouth gaped open. "You what?"

"Taking a leave of absence to visit you was the best move I've ever made. And you're part of the reason I made the decision. Because I watched you stay firm in your decision to sell, no matter what I said to stop you. Because I saw my favorite person, my only aunt step out on faith."

A sob burst from Anny's lips. "Oh, Kennedi."

"I'm so serious. You did set a good example. You showed me that it's never too late to go after what you want."

"And Parker?"

"Anny, I regret leaving him. But leaving him forced me to take a long, hard look at myself. I asked myself how I can be good for Parker if I can't even deal with my problems. I've spent so long running from them, under the guise of pushing past them. I didn't think that I could face them head-on and remain productive. But you were right. You told me that I had to deal with the past, and I had to face Mom's and Dad's deaths."

"I'm glad you realize that, babe."

"Losing Mom and Dad the way we did . . ." Kennedi swallowed past the lump in her throat. She'd never really talked about it to Anny. She'd kind of talked about it with Parker, but she'd only scratched the surface of her emotional minefield. "I couldn't believe that God allowed them to suffer the way they did. And then to walk in and see it, to see the evidence of their struggle. It haunted me. I couldn't escape it, so I coped—or tried to cope, anyway—by marrying Quincy."

"Let's not talk about Quincy, babe." Anny patted her hand gently. "He's a nonfactor."

Kennedi laughed. God, she loved her aunt. "You're right. He is a nonfactor."

Because Kennedi had realized that he was never

for her. She'd plucked him out and tried to fit him into the space her parents had filled, and it ended up being a terrible mistake.

"Anyway, I want to move forward. I mean, really move forward. And that means asking the hard questions and dealing with the past."

"How did you come to this conclusion?"

"There were a bunch of reasons, but mostly because it's something I want to do for me."

"I'm proud of you. I was worried there for a minute, but I feel better about it now."

Kennedi squeezed Anny's knee. "I miss them so much."

It was the first time she'd said it out loud, allowed herself to feel the loss. But as her mother used to tell her, there was power in acceptance. And the fact was, her parents died in a horrific way. But they also lived. They enjoyed life, they enjoyed each other, and they loved them with everything they had.

"I know, babe. I miss them, too. But my sister would have been proud of her baby girl."

"I believe that," Kennedi said.

Anny held Kennedi's chin in her hand. "You look so much like her."

Kennedi felt the tear slide down her cheek and didn't rush to wipe it. "You do too."

Sometimes Anny would say something or look at her in the same way her mom would. It was weird, but strangely comforting.

"And your dad would, too."

Kennedi swallowed. "I know."

Anny pulled her into a tight hug and they cried together. After several minutes, Kennedi pulled back. "When you first told me you were retiring, I was devastated. I couldn't see past you leaving and someone else owning the company. It felt so final, like Mom and Dad, Grandma and Grandpa, you. . . . I wanted to hold on to happier times and I associated those times with a place when it's really an inside thing. It's my heart that holds the memories."

"Well, the place has something to do with it, too."

"It does, but I'll be okay if that place isn't ours anymore because I'll still have you. And I'll still be able to visit the manor and chill with my Anny."

"That's right," Anny agreed. "You can always come home, Kennedi. I'll be there."

"I'm seeing someone," Kennedi said.

Anny blinked. "What? Why? How? Oh God. What about Parker?"

Kennedi shook her head. "Anny, I mean a therapist. I've only had one session, but it has helped immensely."

After her chat with Paula, Kennedi had gone to see a therapist. She and Sacha had clicked immediately, and Kennedi found that having a session with her was more like talking to an old friend. The first and only session she'd had so far had been enlightening. By the time the session was done, Kennedi had a newfound respect for people who did that type of work. It was exhausting, gut wrenching, but oh so worth it.

Kennedi figured she'd get a few more sessions

in with Sacha and then go back to Wellspring, to Parker. She'd made her decision, and she knew what she had to do to get what she wanted.

There was an emptiness in her life when he wasn't near. And she hoped that he would hear her out when she went to him because a part of her would die if he didn't, if he'd given up on her. But she had no choice but to try to make it work.

"One more thing," Kennedi said. "I'm moving to—"

"Kenni Cakes!" Lo-Lo bounded into the room and jumped on Kennedi's lap.

"Lo-Lo." Kennedi hugged her goddaughter, rocking her back and forth until the young girl squealed in delight.

Paula walked in behind her. "She wanted to come see you."

"Kenni Cakes, look!" Lo-Lo held up the empty flower girl basket. "Flower girl."

"I love it," Kennedi said. "Do you remember my Anny, Lo-Lo?"

Her goddaughter gave her Anny the once-over and then lifted her arms to give her a hug. Kennedi grinned up at Paula. "I guess Anny still gets the seal of approval."

"I knew she would," Paula said, leaning down and giving Anny a peck on the cheek. "I'm glad you made it, Anny."

"I wouldn't miss this wedding for the world."

"I'm also sorry Fred couldn't make it. I was excited to meet him. I've always heard so much about him from Kennedi."

Kennedi rocked Lo-Lo slightly, enjoying the sound of her humming a made-up tune.

"You'll have to come to Wellspring and visit," Anny told Paula. "There is plenty of room for your little family."

"Well, I'm definitely going to consider it," Paula told Anny. Turning to Kennedi, Paula asked, "So, listen, do you mind keeping Lo-Lo with you while I finish getting my hair done? Your makeup appointment is coming up soon."

"I know. I'm on it," Kennedi said with a grin. "I won't be late."

Paula waved at them and snuck out of the room while Lo-Lo was reciting her ABCs.

"So, has this therapist helped you figure out why you left Parker the way you did?" Anny asked, steering the conversation back.

"You know why," Kennedi said.

"I have my ideas. But I'd really like to hear what you think."

"I told you I regret leaving. I wanted to stay," Kennedi admitted with a whisper. "But there was something in me, this blinding fear that I would lose him. I dreamed of him getting shot, of him dying and me finding him."

Anny gasped. "Oh no. That's awful."

"I know."

"So it had nothing to do with your lack of trust in him?"

Kennedi thought about that. Initially, her decision was made because she'd felt overwhelmed by everything. It was just one thing too much for her at the time. When Mr. Townsend had cornered her, it kind of felt like an easy way out. But she couldn't even bring herself to say that she believed that Parker was capable of hurting her like that. Because she knew he wasn't. She trusted him, and that scared her.

"No. I think it had something to do with the fact that I *did* trust him. I didn't know what to do with those feelings."

"That's . . . weird."

"I know. I'm a mess."

"A beautiful mess," Anny corrected. "We all are a mess from time to time. But we all have it going on from time to time as well."

That was what her mom would often say. It meant that we might be a little crazy at times, but we were awesome at times, too. One of many sayings that Kennedi had kept with her over the years. Her mother would say that people were independent little cities. Each organ was a building that had its own function: the brain was the hub, the local government, and the heart was the centerpiece, the thing that set the town apart. Kennedi once asked her mom why she'd left her family behind to chase her father's dreams. Her mother's reply was that the thing that set her town apart was her kids, her husband. Because her mother's dream was to have a family she could dote on, to take care of. Yolanda Hunt-Robinson had lived her dream, just like her father had.

"So now that we've had our 'come to Jesus

moment,'" Anny said, cutting through her memory, "I'm going to need you to do one thing."

"What?"

"Go to Parker, and don't look back."

"Kenni Cakes?" Lo-Lo's voice stopped her from telling her aunt what her plan was.

Kennedi tapped the little girl's nose. "Yes, love?"

Lo-Lo's finger brushed her cheek when a tear fell. "Why are you crying? You told me that boys were the crybabies, not girls."

Anny laughed, and Kennedi joined in. "Well, babe," Kennedi said, "sometimes it's okay for girls to cry."

The little girl pouted. "But it makes me sad to see you cry."

"Aw, don't be sad. It's just a part of life, just the heart's way of cleansing itself."

Lo-Lo frowned, confusion marring her flawless brown skin. She was all dressed for the wedding, in a white floor-length dress that was spattered with tiny jewels that glittered in the lighting of the room. Her hair was curled with tiny ringlets and she had on little diamond earrings, given to her by Mark last night at the rehearsal dinner. It had been his gift to her, and a promise to be the best dad she could ever have. The presentation had left no dry eye in the house, and Kennedi knew that her best friend and her godchild would be well taken care of.

"So if you don't cry, will your heart be dirty?"

Kennedi giggled, squeezing Lo-Lo until she burst out in a fit of laughter.

Anny reached out and brushed a finger down Lo-Lo's cheek. "You are a smart little girl. Just like your Kenni Cakes."

The alarm Kennedi had set on her phone went off, and she sighed. "It's almost time for me to head over to my makeup appointment."

Kennedi set Lo-Lo down and stood, then rushed to the bathroom to grab her foundation and concealer. Her one condition to being made up had been that she would wear her own light foundation and no fake lashes. She hated those things with a white-hot passion. It always felt like she had a spider on her eye.

Peering into the mirror, she patted her eyes. All the crying she'd done had left her eyes red and puffy. She dug through her bag, pulled out her eye drops, and dropped the solution in her eyes. Then, she washed her face quickly.

She turned in the mirror. Paula had chosen a one-shoulder, floor-length chiffon gown for Kennedi's dress. The champagne color went well with Kennedi's skin tone, and, as Anny would say, made her ass look great.

"Okay, Lo-Lo, we have to go," Kennedi announced as she walked back into the living area of the suite. "Your mom will kill me if . . ."

Kennedi gasped. Because standing in the middle of her hotel room was Parker.

Chapter 21

Parker couldn't take his eyes off of Kennedi, standing before him in a floor-length gown. Her hair was pinned to the side, and her curls cascading down her neck like a waterfall. She was a vision. He wanted to drink from her, to consume her.

Without her, he felt like he was going out of his head, which was crazy because he didn't even know her before last month. He couldn't think of anything but her. He couldn't explain his feelings because they weren't logical. At least, they weren't to a large segment of people who didn't believe that someone could be so connected to someone that it didn't take long to know it. He'd been that person. He'd been the type of person who scoffed at people who said they'd fallen in love over a weekend or at first sight because . . . it was impossible, right?

But standing there in that room, in that moment, he knew it was more possible than he'd ever dreamed. The woman in front of him made sense to him, and he needed her to be there.

Over the past few weeks, he'd realized that she was the missing piece of himself. For so long, he'd had a void in his heart that couldn't be filled with anyone or anything. Until she rear-ended him and blew into his life like a strong, but exhilarating wind. She'd snapped his infamous control, made him love her. *God, I love her.* He loved her more with every smile, every conversation, every kiss.

His sister had been right. He should have told her that night in his bedroom. He'd missed the moment, he'd been hesitant, almost fearful to speak the words. But no more.

"Parker," Kennedi whispered. "You're here."

"Someone needed a date to the wedding." He shot Anny a look. "And asked me to come."

Kennedi looked at her aunt. "Anny, you did this?"

"I did," Anny responded with a grin.

Kennedi met his gaze again, a whisper of a smile on her perfect lips. Then, she was in his arms, holding on to him as if her life depended on it. And he held her, lifting her up in his arms, enjoying the feel of her, the smell of her.

"I love you," she whispered in his ear.

Parker sucked in a breath, and then let it out slowly. He set her down on the ground but didn't let her go. He couldn't let her go ever again. He opened his mouth to tell her that he loved her, too, to plead with her to put him out of his misery and come home with him, to—

He felt a tug on his jacket and looked down to find a little girl staring up at him. *She must be Lauren.*

Parker looked up at Kennedi before bending low. Once he was eye level with the little girl, he waited as she studied him, her brown eyes assessing, knowing. Kennedi had told him that Lauren was a good judge of character, even at her young age. And he hoped he passed the "Lauren test."

"Hi there," he said finally.

Lauren blinked, tilted her head. "You hugged my Kenni Cakes."

Parker looked to Anny for help, and the woman shrugged. Then, he looked to Kennedi, and the woman he loved gave him a sheepish smile. When his gaze locked on Lauren's accusing eyes again, he said, "I did."

"And you picked her up. She's not a baby."

Parker chuckled. "I know." But Kennedi was definitely *his* baby. "I was happy to see her."

Lauren stepped back and hugged Kennedi's leg. "What's your name?"

"My name is Parker. I'm a friend of Kenni Cakes."

The little girl's face lit up, and then she smiled. "Kenni Cakes is my godmama. That means I have to come stay with her when she moves away."

Parker looked up at Kennedi, then back to Lauren. He didn't want to assume the little one was talking as if Kennedi moving away was something that was happening soon. After all, kids often talked about hypothetical situations. Right? "Is Kennedi moving away?"

Lauren frowned, stuck her finger in her mouth. "I'm a flower girl."

Parker nodded. "You're a pretty flower girl."

"And Kenni Cakes is a beautiful maid of honor."

He peered up at the beautiful Kennedi. "Yes, she is," he said.

Lauren tapped him on his shoulder. "You like her."

Anny laughed, and he couldn't help but laugh, too. "I love her," he told Lauren.

Kennedi gasped, her hand covering her parted lips. "Parker."

"I love you," he mouthed to Kennedi. "So much," he added in his full voice.

"Are you nice?" Lauren asked, drawing his attention back to her.

"I think I am. What do you think?"

Lauren looked up at Kennedi, then back at him. "Kenni Cakes is crying again. She cried earlier and said it's a part of life."

"Lo-Lo!" Kennedi exclaimed, covering her goddaughter's mouth. "Don't tell all of my secrets, now."

Then Kennedi bent lower and whispered something in Lauren's ear. When Lauren turned back to him, she said, "Kenni Cakes loves you, too. And she said I had to go with Anny to tell the makeup lady that she was going to be late."

Parker chuckled, sure that Lauren wasn't done feeling him out. He stood to his full height and watched as Lauren pulled Anny out of the room.

Kennedi stepped to him, wrapped her arms around his waist. He pulled her close, hugged her tight. "How are you here?" she asked.

"I told you. Anny needed a date."

She laughed. "I'm glad you came."

The car ride to Ann Arbor had been interesting, to say the least. Riding with Anny, learning from the older woman, had been priceless. She'd told him about growing up a "Hunt" and the expectations her parents had for her and Yolanda.

Anny said that her parents had only ever wanted them to be happy. The business meant a lot to them, but they didn't expect it to mean the same thing to their children. Sure, they'd hoped someone would carry on, but they had always told Anny and Yolanda to go where their dreams took them. Yolanda had done that, but Anny had chosen to stay behind and work their dream.

Parker realized that listening to Anny was like listening to Kennedi talk. Or even himself, to a certain extent. Kennedi and Parker were like two sides of the same coin, but Anny and Kennedi had led parallel lives.

The two women had so much in common. They'd both pursued careers out of a sense of honor, loyalty, even though those careers weren't what their hearts wanted. And Anny had shared with him that her fear was that Kennedi would wake up one day and wonder where her life had gone, just like Anny had done several months ago.

That "aha" moment for Anny had spurred her into action, and she'd told Fred that she loved him that same day. Then, she'd decided to sell the business. Parker was impressed with Anny, inspired by her story. The woman always made sense, and he was happy to know her.

"Kennedi, I want to talk to you."

She pulled back and peered up at him, biting

her bottom lip. He brushed his fingers over her mouth, releasing her lip from her teeth. He wanted to kiss her, taste her. But he knew he would get lost in her, and he needed them to have a conversation.

"I wanted to talk to you, too," she said.

"Okay. Normally, I would let you go first, but I need to say this."

He led her to the couch and waited for her to sit down before he joined her. She scooted closer to him. It was one of the many things he appreciated about Kennedi. She always sat close to him, touching him, letting him feel that she was present and listening. It was downright arousing.

"You hurt me," he admitted.

"I know. I will always regret that."

"It took a lot for me to let go of that to come here." He figured honesty was the best policy. He'd never lied to her, and he wanted her to know that.

"Why did you?"

"I love you. And I never told you that. I probably should've, but those words aren't exactly the easiest to say."

It had been easier for him in other relationships with women to keep them at arm's length. Yes, he'd dated often, spent time with women. But he'd seen his father hurt his mother so badly throughout the course of their relationship that he never wanted to see that hurt in another woman's eyes because of something he did.

"Tell me about it," she agreed.

"Something changed when you rammed my truck."

"I didn't ram your truck," she argued. "I—"

He placed a finger over her mouth. "It's okay to admit it. It's over and done."

"Fine," she grumbled. "I rammed your truck."

"See, how hard was that?"

"Very," she admitted, running her hand over his leg.

He laughed. "Anyway, back to this sappy moment. When I met you, there was something that drew me to you from the very beginning. I couldn't stop myself from wanting it, wanting you. It caught me by surprise. Then, you left. I felt like I'd misjudged the situation, like I'd tricked myself into believing there was something there that wasn't. Then, of course, I felt like a fool. And then I got angry."

Because how could he love someone who would hurt him like that?

Prior to Kennedi, he'd never imagined being filled to the brim with emotions for a woman. But Kennedi . . . he'd never seen someone so beautiful. She fed a part of him that he didn't know was starving.

When she left, he'd never felt so alone. When he was alone in his house, out on his boat, or even playing poker with the fellas, he'd felt helpless, lost. He'd missed waking up with her, laughing with her, cooking with her.

"I wanted to lash out. I wanted to call you and yell at you for walking out on us before we could really get started."

"What changed your mind?"

"Anny," he said simply.

When Parker had talked to Anny, everything had

clicked. That conversation had penetrated the fog of anger and resentment he'd been walking in. She'd asked him to be patient with Kennedi.

"I realized that just because I was ready that didn't mean you were. So I made the decision to come here and tell you in person that if time is what you need, then I'll give it to you. But I only ask one thing."

"What?"

"That when your time is up, you come to me. Even if you decide that I'm not the man you want, that you had time to think about it and realized that it's better that we cut our losses and move on."

Being in love, wanting to be with someone so completely was a game changer for them both. If they decided to make this work, they were risking a lot for it. So, he would try to understand if she wasn't willing to take the risk.

"I'm not going to lie—it will wreck me if you did that," he continued. "But when I said I love you, I meant it. And that means I'll love you even if I'm not the man you choose to be with."

Kennedi was in full-on sob mode. Parker had basically given her all of the control. He'd laid it all at her feet, pushing himself aside to make sure she had everything she needed.

"Kennedi? Beautiful?" He tilted her head up, peered into her wet eyes. "Did you hear what I said?"

She nodded.

"Can you do that for me?"

Kennedi guessed he was talking about coming to

him after she'd had her time. But the thing was . . . Kennedi didn't need time. She knew what she wanted.

"Talk to me," he implored.

There were no words that described how she felt. So, she kissed him, pouring everything into that kiss—her hurt, her joy, her sorrow, her pain, but mostly her heart. She wanted him to take it, to feel how much he meant to her.

His fingers dug into her hair, holding her to him. She wrapped her arms around his neck, tilting her head and deepening the kiss. Kennedi didn't know how it happened, but she wanted to risk everything to be with Parker. She didn't expect it, hadn't even necessarily wanted it or looked for it. But it was there. Without him, she was destroyed, a shell of everything she could be. He made her laugh, made it comfortable for her to let go. He saw something in her that made her feel invincible and she never wanted to let him go.

Reluctantly, Kennedi pushed back, holding her hand to his chest. But he leaned in and planted another searing kiss to her lips. "Wait."

But Parker didn't wait. His hands were like heat-seeking missiles, roaming her body, driving her crazy with need. As much as she wanted to let him have his way with her, she needed to finish the conversation. Then she needed to go to her makeup appointment. There was a wedding going on in a few hours, and she was the maid of honor.

"I need to tell you," she said, still attempting to hold him at bay. "You asked me a question."

"I think you just gave me your answer," he said, sucking her bottom lip before biting her gently.

Parker inched her dress up, slipping his hand under the fabric and straight to her core, where she was wet. Oh so wet, and throbbing. "Parker," she groaned when he slipped one finger into her heat. "Oh God, you have to stop."

"I can't," he murmured against her neck, as he slipped another finger inside her. "I want you."

Her head fell back against the back of the couch. "Shit."

It was all she could get out. She didn't have it in her to make him stop, not when her body was screaming for him, for release.

"Open up for me, beautiful," he coaxed.

"But my dress," she whined, even as he rolled her hips with his motions.

"Let's take it off, then."

Then, he was up, pulling her to her feet, turning her around and unzipping her dress inch by inch. When her freshly steamed dress hit the floor, she couldn't bring herself to care. It was Parker who picked it up and laid it out on the couch.

When he looked at her with so much longing, so much love, Kennedi had to force herself to breathe. He stood there for a minute, his eyes touching every part of her body. She was only clad in her strapless bra, her thong, and her strappy sandals.

"You're so beautiful, Kennedi."

His words sent a spark of electricity through her body, and she let out a shaky breath. When he finally touched her, her heart kicked off at a fast pace, beating wildly in her ears.

"Just so you know," she said, her breath hitching in her chest when he smacked her ass lightly, "I don't need time. I know what I want."

"Really?" he asked, trailing a finger up her arm to her shoulder, then up her neck to her ear. He tugged at her earlobe. "Care to tell me?"

"I was going to tell you, but your hands . . ."

His chuckle was low. "They missed you." He licked her jaw before sucking it softly, then nipped it with his teeth. "There are other parts of me that missed you, too."

She ran her hand over his strained erection, giggling when he muttered a curse. "I can tell," she said, squeezing him in her fist.

Parker looked at her then, his eyes sincere. He brought her hand up to his chest, above his rapidly beating heart. The gesture, so tender, so beautiful, brought tears to her eyes. He didn't have to say anything for her to know that his heart missed her.

He leaned his head against her forehead. "I love you, beautiful."

She wrapped her arms around his neck, hopped up in his arms, and wrapped her legs around his waist. "I love you more, Parker. Now, make love to me."

He walked her into the suite's bedroom. "You're so bossy," he said as he dropped her on the bed.

"You love it," she said pulling him on top of her.

* * *

An hour later, Kennedi hurried into the bridal suite, where there was chaos around her. The bridesmaids were running around in a tizzy, and Paula's mother was eyeing her suspiciously. She rushed over to Paula, who was sitting in the makeup chair, her back to her.

Kennedi eyed her best friend's reflection in the mirror. Paula was stunning. "Oh my God, you look beautiful."

"Thanks, Kenni Cakes." Paula turned, looked her up and down. "Kennedi, what happened? You don't have makeup on. And your hair is a mess."

Kennedi scratched the back of her neck. She'd tried to fix her hair, but Parker had done a job on it during their hot make-up session. "I'm running late."

"An hour late?"

Kennedi heard whispers from behind her but plowed ahead. "Yes. I'm here, now."

Paula looked behind Kennedi, a frown on her flawless face. "Where's Lo-Lo?"

That was a good question. Anny had left with Lo-Lo, giving Kennedi and Parker some alone time. And Kennedi hadn't seen them since. "She's with Anny."

"Okay, but we have to go down soon. The ceremony is starting in two hours. I don't think you'll be happy with the pictures if you don't do something with that hair at least."

Paula waved over her stylist, who was still in the room. "Can you fix her hair, Donna?"

Her best friend stood up and gestured for Kennedi to sit in the seat she'd just vacated. Once seated, Paula leaned down and whispered in her ear, "Don't think I believed your flimsy excuse of running late. You have freshly fucked hair, and I want the deets."

Kennedi swallowed, meeting Paula's gaze in the mirror. "You'll be happily married in less than three hours. You won't even remember this conversation later."

"Don't bet on it."

With her hair fixed and makeup on fleek, Kennedi rushed to the door. She had to find Anny and Lo-Lo. They still hadn't turned up, and she hoped Anny had gone back to the room to get dressed, or there would be trouble.

As she swung the door open, her eyes widened at the sight of Anny, Lo-Lo, and Parker on the other side. Anny was dressed, Lo-Lo was happily eating grapes, and Parker . . . well, he was looking at her like he wanted to eat her for dinner.

"You're back," Kennedi said.

"You're pretty, Kenni Cakes," Lo-Lo said. "Want a grape?"

Kennedi snatched a grape from her goddaughter's outstretched hand and popped it into her mouth.

"Oh my, you're gorgeous," Anny agreed. "Not that you aren't always beautiful, but for some reason, you're glowing."

Kennedi shot Anny a wary look. Her aunt knew good and well why she was glowing. "Don't start, Anny."

"What?" Anny asked with a wink. "Doesn't she look beautiful, Parker?"

Parker's gaze traveled from Kennedi's head all the way to her feet, and she shifted. Placing a hand over her quivering stomach, Kennedi said, "Lo-Lo, your mom is waiting for you."

"Is that my Lo-Lo?"

Oh hell. Kennedi turned just as Paula approached the doorway. "Paula, I—"

Lo-Lo ran into her mother's arms. "Mommie!"

Paula scooped Lauren up and gave her a kiss before setting her back on her feet. Then, her friend turned smoky eyes toward Anny, then Parker. "Who are you?" Paula asked.

Lo-Lo answered for her. "His name is Parker and he loves Kenni Cakes. He picked her up."

Kennedi clapped a hand on Lo-Lo's mouth again. "Lauren, remember what Kenni Cakes said about telling her business?"

Parker stepped forward. "I'm Parker, and you must be Paula."

Paula shook Parker's offered hand. "I am."

"You look lovely," Parker said.

Kennedi had to agree with Parker. Now, fully dressed, Paula was the picture-perfect bride, in her ivory-colored, mermaid-shaped dress.

"Thank you," Paula said, her smile wide. "It's nice to finally meet you, Parker. I've heard a lot about you."

"It's good to be met," Parker said with an answering grin.

Paula took a minute to give Parker the once-over before leaning back and whispering, "He's so hot," in Kennedi's ear.

Kennedi shushed Paula, because her friend was many things, but "good whisperer" was not on the list. "You're so stupid."

Someone from inside the room called Paula's name and she excused herself. Lo-Lo ran after her mom, announcing to the entire room that Kennedi's friend Parker was outside and he was hot.

Kennedi dropped her head, shaking it in amusement. "Oh God."

"It's okay, babe," Anny said, wrapping her arm around Parker. "I don't mind if people think my date is hot." She looked up at Parker. "Kennedi is hot, too, isn't she? Did you see her ass in that dress? You know she got that from me? Her mother didn't have a single piece of butt fat."

"Anny!" Kennedi shouted.

Parker laughed. "It is pretty nice. And you're right, she's definitely hot."

"Don't encourage her, Parker."

"It's cool," Parker said, leaning forward to place a kiss on Kennedi's neck. "My girlfriend is hot."

Kennedi brushed her lips over his. "Your girlfriend also loves you."

Parker stroked the spot behind her ear with his thumb. "I love you, too."

Chapter 22

Parker awoke the next morning with Kennedi's naked body pressed against his. After the wedding, he'd stolen her away from the reception and brought her up to his room, where he'd worshipped her body all night.

After being with her again, making love to her, he didn't know how he'd managed to go even one day without touching her. They still hadn't really talked much since he'd arrived. The only thing she knew was that he loved her, but he had so many other things he wanted to say.

Next to him, Kennedi stirred and her eyes popped open. When she smiled sleepily up at him and kissed his jaw, Parker knew she was where she wanted to be.

"What do you want to do today?" Parker asked.

Kennedi's smile widened. "Oh, I can think of a lot of things."

He rolled over on top of her and kissed her,

reveling in the feel of her underneath him. "I can get used to this."

"I hope so. I'm not going anywhere."

Parker traced the lines of her forehead, then down the side of her face, and over her lips. "Are you real?"

"Real as in 'keepin' it real' or real as in am I really here?"

Parker buried his face in her neck, taking in her sweet scent. He could stay in that spot forever, between her legs, his body on hers. She was so warm, so soft. "Are you really here?"

"Parker?" Kennedi asked.

He smiled. "Yes, beautiful."

"We should talk."

Parker sat up, pulling her onto his lap once he was situated with his back against the headboard. "I agree."

Kennedi's stomach growled, and she held a hand over it. "Well, maybe we should eat first?"

"That's probably a good idea. Don't want you to starve."

After Kennedi checked on Anny, who was staying in Kennedi's suite, he ordered room service. Kennedi tugged on his dress shirt and climbed into bed with him.

"You don't need that," he said, dipping his hand into the opening of his shirt and brushing one of her nipples with his knuckles.

Her eyes closed in response. "That's exactly why I need this on. We'll never be able to talk if I don't put a barrier between your skin and mine."

Parker tugged on the shirt. "This is not a barrier. You're still open and ready for me."

"Stop," she said, scooting to the foot of the bed. "How's this for distance?"

"I'd prefer if you were closer to me for this conversation, beautiful." Even with the distance between them, he was able to pick up her foot and kiss the top of it, then each of her toes before he sucked one into his mouth.

Kennedi fell back on the bed with a moan. "Oh God. Parker, you're killing me."

He kissed his way up her body until he was right back on top of her, wrapping her legs around his waist. "I can't resist you, beautiful."

Parker could read her body language like he wrote the book of Kennedi. He knew when she was happy, when she was sad, and when she wanted him. Now, she wanted him. And he would never not give her what she wanted.

He pushed forward and soon he was buried in her heat. "Parker," she moaned, tugging him down to her mouth in an intense kiss.

Slowly, he pulled out before thrusting into her again, enjoying the hitch in her voice and the way she breathed his name.

"I can't get enough of you," he said, kissing her neck, her chin, her jaw, then her mouth.

Kennedi felt so good, like she was made just for him. Parker wanted to stay there forever, buried to the hilt inside her. But the pull, the need to climax spurred him into action. Soon, their pace quickened as they raced to completion. When her eyes fluttered closed, he knew she was close.

"Parker, don't stop. Harder."

He happily obliged, pushing into her with abandon. Her head was hanging over the edge of the bed, giving him access to her nipples. Taking advantage of their position, he sucked one nipple into his mouth, circling the hard nub with his tongue.

His name sounded like a tortured cry on her lips as she came, closing her legs tight around him. Then, he snapped, pumping hard and fast until he exploded inside her and they slid off the bed and onto the floor with a thud.

"Oh shit." He looked down at her, worried that he'd hurt her with the landing.

Her face was red, flushed, and she was laughing. "Parker," she said, a gleam in her brown eyes, "we fucked our way off the bed."

Parker dropped his head to her forehead and chuckled. "I know."

"That was amazing."

He lifted his weight off of her. "It was."

They stayed there for a few minutes, staring at each other, communicating in a silent language all their own.

Parker couldn't love her more if he tried. He'd be forever grateful that she crashed into his truck that September day. Because that was the day his life changed forever. Now she was his life and he hoped she would soon be his wife.

* * *

Wrapped in a plush hotel robe, Kennedi walked out of the bathroom. After breakfast, and another round of lovemaking, Kennedi had insisted she hop in the shower—alone.

Parker was seated on the edge of the bed, a pair of sweats on. There were few things more beautiful than Parker in a pair of low-riding sweats. She grinned. "My boyfriend is a hottie," she teased.

He laughed. "You're funny. Come here please."

Kennedi grabbed Parker's hand and let him pull her to him. Once beside him, she nestled into his side, smiling when he wrapped an arm around her shoulder.

"Kennedi, we really do have to talk," he said.

She knew that. They hadn't said anything about her plans to move to Wellspring or about her opening a hotel. He still didn't know she'd quit her job.

"Can I go first?" she asked.

"Sure." He kissed her brow. "I'll wait."

Kennedi pulled back so that she could see his face. "I quit my job."

Parker's brow lifted. "You what?"

Nodding, she repeated, "I quit. I gave my notice this week, when I decided I wanted to move to Wellspring."

He closed his eyes and leaned his forehead against hers. "I don't think you realize what you just did to me," he said.

Kennedi tilted her head back to look at him. She saw his love for her shining back at her, in full color. "I think I know," she said. "Parker, when I told you I didn't need any time, I meant it. I made my decision days ago. I just needed to get through the wedding."

After Kennedi had given her resignation to Jared, she'd contacted a property management company. She wasn't ready to sell her condo yet, so she would rent it out for a while. It was actually Parker who'd unwittingly given her the idea when he'd mentioned owning rental properties.

"I'm going to rent my condo out, and I should be there by Christmas. I told my boss that I would assist with the transition of my caseload, so that will take a while to get situated."

Jared had done so much for her, mentoring her and getting her the job at the firm. She wanted to be sure they had time to find her replacement or at least make sure that her cases were in capable hands.

"I already told Anny. She's excited."

"I can't believe it," he said. "Now, I don't have to ask you to move to Wellspring."

"Is that what you were going to do?" she teased.

"You know it. I want you near me, Kennedi."

"Parker, when I came to Wellspring, I never intended it to be more than a visit. But I didn't just fall in love with you. I fell in love with the town. And I realized that my dreams involve being close to family and living in the town that gives me peace, that feels like home. Wellspring does that for me." She cupped his chin. "You do that for me."

Parker kissed her—hard. "I'm glad."

Kennedi opened her eyes. "Wow. I'm glad you're glad." She rested her chin on his shoulder, and kissed his cheek. Out of the corner of her eye, she saw an envelope on the bed. She picked it up. "What's this?"

"Open it."

Curious, she tore the envelope open and pulled the paper out. It was an offer for Hunt Nursery. "Why do you have this?"

"Angelia and I talked. If you're okay with it, I'd like to buy her out of the company."

Kennedi's mouth fell open. "You? Or Wellspring Corp.?"

"Me. Parker Wells Jr. She still wants to sell, and I want to keep the nursery open."

"But why? Isn't the land worth something to your company?"

"Because the nursery, the greenhouse, is a part of Wellspring. Business is good, and it's a top employer of the town. I want it to stay that way. I propose that you sell the plot of land closest to Wellspring territory to the company, which is about an acre. But the other Hunt land and the nursery should remain in your—our—hands."

"I'm speechless."

"I've also talked to your Anny about turning the greenhouse into a botanical garden."

It was a great idea, and one that Kennedi had considered before. "Is Anny wanting to run it?"

He nodded. "Yes. She's willing to help."

"I think my grandmother would be happy." Kennedi's grandmother had often talked about creating a botanical garden on the property.

"Your Anny told me that."

Kennedi wrapped her arms around him. "Oh, Parker. You're amazing."

"I have something else for you."

She stared at him. "You've already given me so much."

He smiled. "As far as I'm concerned, I have given you half of what you've given. I was going through my father's assets."

Kennedi had been keeping up with the news. She knew that Senior had been indicted and arrested on conspiracy and corporate fraud charges. She also knew that he hadn't regained consciousness.

"Brooklyn and I are trying to determine what needs to be handled in the event he dies."

"I get that," she said. "He's been in a coma pretty long. I know there are some people who wake up after long comas, but it's pretty rare."

"Exactly. But while we were going through his paperwork, we found the deed to the hotel. Turns out, the hotel was really owned by my mother, which in turn is now mine and Brooklyn's."

Kennedi smiled. The Wells Inn was an amazing hotel. She could see herself getting in there and turning it into a luxury boutique hotel. "That's pretty awesome."

Parker handed her another piece of paper. "Here."

"What is this?"

"I bought Brooklyn out of the hotel."

Kennedi frowned, peering at the deed. But instead of Parker's name, her name was on the document. She gasped. "What is this?"

"A gift. To you."

"No." Kennedi shook her head. "Parker? You're giving me the hotel? I can't accept this."

"Why?"

"Because it's too much. If you want me to purchase it from you, I'll do that. But giving it to me?"

"Kennedi, I want you to have this. You have a vision, and I want you to be able to live out your dream in Wellspring. With me."

It was the biggest and best gift anyone had ever given her. But it still was too much. "Parker, we have to . . . I can't."

"I want you to consider it a wedding gift."

Kennedi was glad she was sitting. Because if she had been standing, she'd have toppled over onto the floor. "A wedding gift?"

"I don't just want you to move to Wellspring, Kennedi. I want you to move in with me in Wellspring."

"Okay, but that's not the same as marriage. And you just said that the hotel was a wedding gift. So can you elaborate, counselor?"

"Only if you call me into your chambers for a recess."

Kennedi laughed then. "You're crazy."

"Seriously. I know you've been through a lot in your life, Kennedi. But I want to make you forget every disappointment, every doubt. I want to be the family you need. I want to be everything for you."

"Parker," she breathed.

"I'm not saying we have to get married tomorrow. But I do intend on making you Mrs. Wells sometime in the near future."

"Are you asking me to marry you?"

"I'm asking you to marry me," he repeated. "I can't live another day without you, in my bed, in my home, in my life. And I figured since we moved at hyper speed with this entire relationship, we might as well keep up the momentum."

Tears welled up in her eyes. Kennedi had turned into a crybaby over the past month, and it was exhausting. She couldn't believe that Parker had basically just proposed—after he bought Anny out of the business and after he'd given her a freakin' hotel.

Part of her wanted to put the brakes on it, because they still had so much they had to learn about each other. But the other part, the part that was winning, was telling her to go for it.

"I have no idea how I got so lucky when I rammed into your truck," Kennedi said.

"I think I was the lucky one. When I met you, I thought you were beautiful and I wanted to take you out. But I had no idea what you would come to mean to me. Or that I'd love you. But I do. I love you so much, Kennedi A. Robinson."

"I love you, too, Parker Wells Jr. You have meant more to me in this short time than anyone else in my life. And if you want to do this, I'm all in."

Epilogue

Three months later

Kennedi walked into the Wells Hotel and scanned the lobby area. It was empty, save for a few staff members, closed for the Robinson-Wells wedding reception.

A strong hand slipped around her, hugging her close from behind. "Mrs. Wells, do you love your wedding gift?"

After Parker had proposed, she'd told him that she wouldn't officially take ownership of the hotel until they were actually married. She hadn't expected him to spring into action as soon as he made it back to Wellspring.

Within a day, Brooklyn had contacted her and welcomed her to the family, then proceeded to tell her not to worry about anything, that she was helping Parker with the wedding and the reception. When Kennedi had questioned Parker about it later, he'd told her that he knew what she liked and not to worry.

Anny and Brooklyn had visited her in Ypsi so they could go dress shopping with her and Paula. The ladies had had a great day, pampering themselves at the MGM Grand Detroit Spa, and spent the following day trying on gowns. Kennedi found a dress that had taken her breath away. She immediately knew it was the dress for her, even before she'd tried it on. It was love at first sight, almost like her and Parker. And it felt right.

While she'd finished up business in Ypsilanti, he was working at Wellspring Corp., planning a wedding, and driving to see her every weekend. It was a testament to his devotion to her, because she wasn't sure how he had time to do everything. She knew he had help, but Brooklyn and Anny had told her that he'd come up with all of the ideas for the wedding.

When it was time for her to move, Parker and Trent had rented a moving truck and picked her up. She'd officially moved to Wellspring and into Parker's home right before Christmas.

It was now mid-January, cold, and there was a foot of snow on the ground, but Kennedi and Parker had exchanged vows at Hunt Manor, in the backyard, inside a heated tent. They had been surrounded by her family and friends. Tanya and Bryson hadn't been able to attend, but both of them had sent their best wishes.

Anny had stood up for her as her matron of honor and Brooklyn had stood up for Parker as his best "sister." Lo-Lo had been the flower girl, and Paula the hostess. Fred had walked her down the aisle, with every intention of giving her away. But Parker had kissed her senseless before the pastor could even say, "Who gives this woman to be married to this man?"

They'd said their vows in record time, and then Pastor Locke had pronounced them man and wife. It was the best day of her life.

After the wedding, Parker had taken her home. Confused, Kennedi had asked about the reception and he'd told her he'd purposefully scheduled the reception for a later time so that he could have uninterrupted time with her.

When they'd entered their home, he'd peeled off her dress and made slow love to her until it was time for them to leave.

Kennedi turned in Parker's arms and glanced up at him. He was perfect. Strong and graceful. Serious and funny. Sexy and sweet. And he was hers.

She imagined her parents up in Heaven hand picking him for her because it felt like something Heavenly had led her to him. When he looked at her, with love brimming in his brown eyes, she swore he was an angel, Heaven on earth.

He'd slowly breathed new life into her body, with each kiss, each touch, each time he'd told her he loved her. He'd wrapped her up in his enduring, endless, timeless love. And she couldn't wait to spend the rest of her life with him and their children.

"Ready?" he said against her ear, as they stood at the entrance to the reception ballroom later.

"Before we go in, I have something to tell you," she said.

"What is it?" he asked, concern in his eyes.

"I figured it was only fitting that I give you your wedding gift now, while we're standing in your gift to me."

He smirked. "You gave me my wedding gift at the house, beautiful."

Kennedi laughed, dropping her head on his chest. "Parker, you are insatiable."

"And you love it."

Kennedi wrapped her arms around his waist, hugging him to her. "I do love it. You love me so completely that I never want to let you go. I'm sure you'll do the same for our baby."

"You know—" Parker pulled back, gazed into her eyes. "Our baby?"

Kennedi nodded as happy tears filled her eyes. "Yes, our baby."

"You're pregnant?"

"I am."

Kennedi figured it was the Thanksgiving sex on top of the poker table that had sealed the deal. When she'd arrived for a visit to Wellspring for the holiday, he'd surprised her with a huge poker table in the middle of the living room. And after a pretty hot game of strip poker, he'd slid all the chips off the table and taken her right there.

He pulled her into a tender kiss, and she let herself relax into his body.

"Are you happy?" she asked.

"I didn't think I could be happier than I was when I saw you walking down the aisle in that dress, but you've managed to do it. I can't wait to be a father to our child." When she saw the tears shining in his eyes, she felt her heart open up even more for him.

Kennedi knew how much it meant to Parker to be a good father. He'd made a vow to himself that if he ever had the chance to be a father, he would show his son or daughter the love they deserved. He would be someone they could depend on to have their backs in everything.

Senior still hadn't regained consciousness, but the doctors had recently told Brooklyn and Parker that his organs were deteriorating at a rapid pace. Kennedi hoped that when the day finally came that Senior left this earth, Parker would have some peace about it.

She cupped his head in her hands and kissed him. "You will be an amazing father, Parker. I have no doubt."

He kissed each of her palms. "Thank you for my gift. It's perfect."

"So are you. I love you, Parker."

"I love you, beautiful."

DON'T MISS THE FIRST BOOK
IN THE WELLSPRING SERIES

TOUCHED BY YOU

Enjoy the following excerpt
from *Touched by You* . . .

Chapter 1

The ground was wet. Cold.

But Carter Marshall couldn't bring himself to move, to walk away. He clutched the weathered copper ornament in his hands. It was the only thing he had left of his old life, the only tangible reminder that they both existed. Everything else was gone, charred beyond repair.

"I'm not sure how to do this," he mumbled to himself. He knew he had to let the anger go now. It had consumed him, filled him to capacity and pushed him to keep going. He wondered what would take its place, or if he'd even be able to let go of the hate he had in his heart for the man who had taken away everything.

The rain pounded on his head, drizzled down his face. It had been an hour since he'd arrived, but he couldn't bring himself to complete his task. Instead, he'd sat there, his expensive Tom Ford suit soaked and his Cole Haan shoes muddy. Nothing mattered anymore. Not his wealth, not his name, not his work. Everything that he'd once held dear seemed like a curse now.

"I'm sorry," he muttered. "I'm sorry I wasn't there. I was too obsessed with work, too driven, too focused on my damn money. I thought if I just worked hard enough, I could give you the life you deserved. I only wanted to make you happy."

His eyes welled with fresh tears. As if he hadn't cried enough already. The loss of his beautiful wife and daughter had devastated him to his core, weakened him. Even now, almost two years later, he could still smell the gasoline, taste the smoke in the air, hear the screams of the neighbors as the fire burned. He recalled the determination on the firemen's faces as they worked to put the blaze out, and he remembered the exact moment they all realized that it was too late.

You're the best part of my day, my hero.

Her words still haunted him. *Her hero.* His wife of three years, his college sweetheart, had told him he was her hero. Only he didn't feel heroic. What was the opposite of hero? Coward. Loser. Nobody.

Instead of being home with his wife and new-born daughter, he'd been working. Late. It seemed his work had eclipsed everything in his life, despite his denials. Krys had told him time and time again to live a little, to enjoy life. But the lure of the prestige, the money, the connections that his business guaranteed was important to him. He'd worked too hard, too long to let it go. He'd been distracted, meetings all day and projects to finish.

When the phone rang, he'd moved it to voicemail with a little text that said, **Give me a minute.**

To think that was the last thing Krys heard from him . . . He'd been so busy he couldn't even pick up the phone and answer. Was she scared? According to the arson investigators, the fire had started around seven o'clock. The call from her came through a little after seven. What if that one phone call could have changed something? Countless hours in therapy, numerous assurances that he couldn't have known, did nothing to quell the guilt he felt every time he looked at her response to his text. The worst part was that he hadn't even seen her response until hours later, after he'd been ushered from the scene of the crime. It read, **I love you. Always remember.**

Even in her last minutes, she'd been thinking of him. And he'd been thinking of his next project, his next dollar. *What good is all the money in the world without her, without them?*

Closing his eyes, he willed himself to move, to do what he came to do.

He scanned the area around him. It was *their* spot. Krys had insisted they visit as often as possible since it was the place where he'd proposed.

Today would have been their wedding anniversary. Remembering her beautiful face on the day he made her his wife made his heart ache. Krys was beautiful, in a classic "Clair Huxtable" kind of way. She was a good woman, believed that taking care of the home, being a wife and mother was the best job in the world. They'd been so young, so full of hope.

People had questioned him about the choice to marry so soon after college graduation, for even being with the same woman for so long. Even his best friend and business partner, Martin Sullivan, had been wary. And he'd known Krys for as long as he'd known Martin. Carter couldn't explain it, though. He wasn't an impulsive person. Everything Carter had done in life had been carefully planned. It was the reason he and Martin had been so successful. Neither of them played around when it came to business.

Marrying Krys, though, was his destiny. At least, he'd thought so at the time. She'd supported him through some of the worst times of his life—the death of his youngest sister and his grandmother and his parents' subsequent divorce. Krys never wavered, never wanted him to be anybody but himself. She'd never complained when he traveled for work or forgot to take the trash out. She was perfect, and he didn't deserve her. He'd broken the promise to love and to cherish, to have her and to honor her. If he had, he would have answered her call. He should have been there. Especially since she'd always been there for him. Krys had given him the best gift he could ever have—her heart, her body, her soul. He'd promised to protect her, to be there for her. *Except I wasn't, not when she needed me the most.*

Time hadn't made this wound better, hadn't healed him like they told him it would. He'd started to resent them—his parents, his friends, his employees . . . everyone. The questions were becoming unbearable. The sad looks infuriated him. Most of all, when people told him *It will be okay*, he wanted to slap them. Because he was not okay, and wasn't sure he would ever be okay again. He knew he had to try, though. For them. For Krys and for his baby girl, Chloe.

Carter closed his eyes and inhaled the wet, night air. It was too late to be the father Chloe needed. She wasn't even a year old. He'd never heard her say "Da Da" or had the pleasure of watching her toddle into his waiting arms for the first time. *It's not fair.*

The tears fell freely down his cheeks and his stomach lurched into his chest. *I failed.* Carter looked down at the Christmas ornament in his hand. It was shaped like a heart, personalized with their names and their wedding date. Krys had purchased it for their first Christmas as a married couple. Sighing heavily, Carter dropped the ornament into the small hole he'd dug, next to the tree where he'd dropped on one knee and proposed to his first love, his only love.

"I made them pay, Krys."

Within days after the fire, the Detroit Police Department had arrested the young men that were responsible. But pressure from city officials had them backtracking on the investigation. Of course they did, because one of the men, the main culprit, was the college-aged son of one of the most influential business owners in the city.

The McKnight family was well-known in the Detroit area. Carter had effectively launched a smear campaign, blasted them on every social media site. Through his own computer skills and those of his partner, they'd crippled the McKnight business. Revenge was best served with a depleted bank account. A guilty verdict wasn't enough for him. He'd just been awarded a settlement in the civil lawsuit he'd brought against the city and the family for hampering the investigation.

Money wasn't his motive, though. He wanted them to lose everything, just like he had. Those young men had destroyed his life on a whim, because of a bet. They'd targeted his house because it was on the corner lot in a mostly African American neighborhood—because they could.

"I donated most of the money to the burn unit at Children's Hospital and set up a foundation to help burn victims and families who've lost everything to a fire."

It would never bring them back. He knew that, and he'd certainly paid the price of the personal vendetta he'd waged against the culprits, with his family and his work. The criminal and civil trials had taken a lot out of him. Now, it was time for him to let the anger go, let them go. That was the hard part.

He covered the glass ornament with mud and stood to his full height. By all rights, he should be celebrating. He'd won. His mother had set up a family dinner, and his brothers had mentioned a hookup he had no intention of taking advantage of. What would be the purpose? Sex? Because that's all it would be. He was empty, a void that would never be filled.

"Everyone wants me to move on, but how? Is it even okay to love someone else?"

And now he was officially crazy, talking to the night air, to Krys like she could actually answer. At the same time, if he had a sign, maybe he could let go fully. His wife and child died, but his love never would. That much was certain. *I don't have room for anyone else.*

"I love you. Take care of each other."

Sighing, he made his way back to his car and, after one last glance at the tree, sped off.

A houseful of people awaited him when he arrived at his mother's place about an hour later. There were old friends, cousins, and more cousins. The smell of fried chicken wafted to his nose, and his stomach growled.

"Carter, get your butt in here."

Iris Johnston was a loud, formidable woman. She pulled him into her strong arms and squeezed tightly. Carter wasn't an overemotional person, rarely gave out hugs, but he couldn't help but wrap his arms around her plump waist and relax into her embrace.

"Ma, I thought it was only going to be family." He pulled back and kissed his mother on her cheek. "You promised not to make a big deal about this."

Iris shrugged and gestured to the table of food in the corner. "Eat. You deserve this. You've had a tough few years."

His stepfather, Chris, joined them and patted him on the shoulder. "She's right, Carter. Have a seat and relax yourself. This is the least we could do for you."

Carter walked through the house, greeting the people who'd turned out for him. One by one, they hugged him, gave him sad glances before they offered more congrats and condolences. *Shit.* It was like Krys and Chloe had just died. His thoughts flashed back to all the food his mother insisted be dropped off to the house, all the stares.

When he finally made it to the kitchen, he grinned at the sight of his brothers.

"Carter, I'm glad you're finally here," Kendall said, giving him a quick man-hug. "Mom has been worrying the shit out of us." Kendall was the baby brother, and officially a college graduate as of two months ago. It had been a happy day when he'd walked across the stage, because they all thought he wouldn't make it.

"Yeah, man. She was a nightmare." His brother, Marvin, leaned against the sink. Carter reached out and clasped his hand in their signature hand-shake. Marvin was the middle son, the lawyer of the family.

"Well, I'm here. Not sure how much longer, though. I told her I didn't want a party."

"Baby brother, if you leave, we're all going to have to pay for it." Carter turned to see his older sister, Aisha, standing behind him. "And let me tell you, I'm sick of y'all fools leaving me behind to clean up your messes."

Carter pulled his sister into a tight hug. "I'm sorry, sis. But you know crowds are not my thing. I'm getting antsy just listening to the chatter."

Aisha's expression softened, her brown eyes wide with unshed tears. "I know. But you have to start living again. You know Krys would want that." She rubbed his cheek. "You can't die with her. You're still here for a reason."

Carter blinked and prayed for an intervention, anything to stop the pain in his sister's eyes. She was worried about him. Being the oldest of five siblings, Aisha had been a sponge her whole life, taking on their emotions like they were her own.

"I don't want to talk about this," Carter said, leaning down and kissing his sister on the forehead. "Where's the food?"

Aisha's shoulders fell, and she nodded. "I'll fix you a plate."

Moments later, he was sitting at the small table in the kitchen, eating while the party roared on in the other room. Aisha sat across from him, watching him eat.

"I've been calling you. When are you going to come back to the office?" she asked. Aisha worked as the chief financial officer of Marshall and Sullivan Software Consulting Inc. She basically kept the company up and running while he and Martin traveled the world. His sister had been calling him for weeks, every single day. "Martin needs you back in the office."

Carter knew he'd been a lousy business partner. Martin had basically picked up all the slack in the last two years. It wasn't right for him to continue this way. And with his best friend recently tying the knot, Carter wanted to be able to step up again to let him be a happy newlywed. "I know, Aisha. I plan to go back soon."

"Soon? The office has been inundated with calls, requests for proposals. You're on the verge of something bigger than you ever dreamed, especially with the Wellspring offer. Don't give it all up."

"Aisha, please shut up!" he snapped. His sister's mouth closed in a tight line, and he immediately regretted his outburst. "I'm sorry. It's just . . ." *Forget it.* She wouldn't understand. Work was the last thing he wanted to do, because work was what he'd allowed to get between him and his wife for too long.

"I get it," his sister said, picking at the table with her thumbnail. "You're hurting, and I don't want to take that away from you."

He was such an asshole. Aisha had only been trying to help, to take care of him like she'd always done. It wasn't her fault he was incapable of being social. He had never really been the type of person that enjoyed being around a lot of people. Carter had always been more solitary, preferring to be by himself than go to the club.

"I didn't mean to yell." He dropped his fork on his plate. "But Krys is gone, Aisha. She's dead, and so is my baby girl. It takes a huge effort for me to get out of the damn bed in the morning. I just . . . I need some time."

"I know Krys is gone, Booch. I get it."

Carter rolled his eyes at the use of his childhood nickname. Only a few people still used it, but it always reminded him of being a kid. He wasn't a child anymore. He wasn't going to conform to everyone's ideas on how he should handle his grief. Shit, he was the one that had to go home every night to an empty house, an empty life.

"No, you don't get it, Aisha." Carter pushed away from the table and stood, pacing the floor. "Please stop pretending you do." He pointed at his chest and whirled around to face her. "I'm the one that has to deal with the fact that some ignorant prick decided to set fire to my freakin' house. With *my* family inside. I'm the one that has to look at myself in the mirror every day, knowing that my wife was scared and needed someone to talk to her and I didn't answer the phone."

"You can't be everywhere at once, Booch. You were working. Krys understood that about you."

"How do you know what Krys understood?" The anger that rose up in him was irrational and directed solely at the one person who didn't deserve it. "She needed me." Bile rushed up his throat and he fought to control it from coming out, spewing over his mother's hardwood floor.

Aisha stood and approached him, fire in her brown eyes. She gripped his chin and twisted it downward to meet her gaze. "You want to know how I know? Krys called me."

Carter's eyes widened. "What?"

"I didn't want to tell you because I knew it wouldn't help you at the time. You had the trial and then the lawsuit. It was keeping you going. Now that it's over, I need you to hear me, Carter."

He swallowed roughly, clenched his hands into fists.

She sighed. "Krys called me that night. She knew she wasn't going to make it." His sister's eyes filled with tears. "She needed to talk about some things. One thing she made sure she said was that she loved you. Carter, she loved you. Everything about you. But she knew you. She knew that you'd let her death consume you, she knew you'd let this ruin you. Your wife, my sister-in-law, wanted to be sure that you didn't. She wanted you to live, to have a life even though she wasn't here. She made me promise to tell you when the time was right. I'm telling you now."

Exhausted and emotional, Carter gave in, letting the tears that had filled his eyes spill. He fell back into the chair. His head bowed, he whispered, "I don't know how to do this, Aisha. How can I live without her?"

Aisha pulled a chair in front of him and sat down, tilting her head to meet his gaze. "It won't be easy. But you have to. You deserve to live. That's what she wanted for you. God didn't keep you here so that you can die a slow death, in your grief."

"What else did she say?" His voice cracked. "Was she scared?"

Shaking her head, his sister squeezed his knee. "Krys cried, but not because she was scared for herself. She didn't want Chloe, your baby girl, to suffer. She was scared for you, for the family she'd leave behind. I, on the other hand, was hysterical with tears."

Knowing that Krys wasn't scared for herself didn't surprise Carter. His wife was never scared. It was something he'd always loved about her. During labor, she'd refused to take pain meds. But she'd squeezed the shit out of his hand. So bad, he'd needed it iced afterward. "I can imagine you bawling. You're such a big baby."

"Hey, I'm still the oldest."

The room descended into silence as they sat there. Finally, he said, "I miss her." The admission was probably obvious to his sister, but it was the first time he'd said it out loud to anyone. It was like he'd been walking in a haze, refusing to show anyone that he was affected. Only the people closest to him could tell, and that was because they knew his routine, his personality. Everything about him had changed that October night.

Aisha pulled him into a strong hug. "I know."

They stayed like that for what felt like an eternity, him being held by his big sister. They'd grown up, but remained close. As children, they were joined at the hip. Only two years apart, Aisha had dragged him everywhere with her, to all the parties. She'd been taking care of him since they were toddlers, when she would sneak him cookies under the kitchen table.

When he pulled away, he brushed her tears away. "Thank you," he mouthed.

She gave him a wobbly smile. "Always."

"What's going on at work?"

"So much. Martin is handling everything, but I don't want him to get burned out. He's finally settled with Ryleigh and they're happy. They deserve some time to just be newlyweds. Traveling to Wellspring, Michigan, is not ideal for him right now."

Carter thought about Aisha's plea. She was definitely right. Martin did deserve to enjoy his new marriage. And he had to step up and let him.

"Who was scheduled to go with Martin to Wellspring?" Carter was so out of touch he couldn't even remember the Wellspring project particulars.

"Walt." Walter Hunt was the new software engineer they'd hired a few months ago. "He's not strong enough to handle point on this project. Handling a project of this magnitude is too much for him."

Carter rolled his eyes. Parker Wells Sr., president of Wellspring Water Corporation, had hired Marshall and Sullivan because they were the best in the state, and they'd designed an excellent Enterprise Resource Planning system. And his sister was a big part of that. *Aisha is right. This is too big a job to trust to anyone other than me or Martin.*

"So what are you going to do?" Aisha asked, a mixture of worry and challenge lining her face. "Someone is supposed to be in Wellspring on Monday to meet with the players. We've pushed the date back already. If we don't do this—"

"Calm down, Aisha." Carter had the perfect solution—one that would give him time and space from the emotions that surrounded him in Detroit. "I'll go. I'll head the project myself. And I'll leave in the morning."

Carter and Aisha talked for several more minutes,

working out the details of his trip. Aisha also gave him updates on a few other issues with the company. He would leave first thing in the morning and drive to Wellspring, which was approximately a three-hour drive from Detroit. A hotel had already been booked for Martin, so Aisha was charged with switching the reservations to Carter's name.

"Aisha?"

His sister turned toward the door. "Hey, girl!" Aisha stood and hugged the woman who'd interrupted their conversation. "Long time, no see. Carter, remember Ayanna? We went to high school together."

Carter smiled at the woman. He definitely remembered Ayanna. The woman standing before him, with her light skin and light eyes, was still as beautiful as he remembered. Instead of the trademark braids she'd rocked in high school, her hair was wavy and flowing down her back. But the attraction he once had to her was long gone.

Ayanna was also his "first." And judging by the way Aisha was singing her friend's praises, his sister didn't know. There were rules, after all. Back then, Aisha had banned him from ogling her friends. Little did she know or even realize, her friends weren't exactly shy when it came to him. Carter might have been a one-woman man when he met Krys, but he hadn't always been that way.

Aisha was yapping away, catching up with her friend. And Ayanna was checking him out. The heat in her eyes told him exactly what she was thinking.

"How have you been, Carter?" Ayanna asked, batting her long lashes. "You've been in my prayers."

"I'm good. And you?"

"I've been enjoying life." Ayanna inched closer to him and wrapped her arms around him in a tight hug.

Carter inhaled Ayanna's scent. She still smelled the same. It would be so easy to take it to the next level. The look in the woman's eyes when she pulled back and shot him a sexy grin was an invitation. Any other man would have run with it. All Carter felt was cold. But this could be what he needed to move on. He just wasn't sure he believed that.

"I didn't know you were coming," he said, wondering if Ayanna was the "hookup" his brothers had told him about. Only Marvin knew of their dalliance all those years ago.

Ayanna folded her arms over her breasts. "I actually was in the neighborhood, saw the cars and decided to stop. Your mother sent me in here to give you best wishes."

Aisha piped up. "You should totally stay. There is plenty of food, and we'll be playing cards later. It'll be good to catch up."

"I'd love to," Ayanna said. "It's a shame that we grew up together and barely see each other."

Detroit was a large city, with a population of almost seven hundred thousand people. Plenty of people he'd grown up with still lived in the city, but seemed so far away. Many of the kids he went to school with had left, though. Some had moved to the suburbs, and others had left Michigan altogether.

Growing up in Detroit was a good experience for Carter. His parents both worked good jobs, and their neighborhood was a safe haven for him. Everyone knew each other and looked out for each other. He remembered block parties and going to the skating rink with friends. No matter what the outside world thought of his city, it was his home. Although he'd had plenty of offers from different companies, he'd never considered moving. It helped that Krys was also from Detroit. They'd actually grown up fifteen miles away from each other, but had never met.

Thinking of Krys brought him back from the walk down memory lane. Even if Ayanna was giving him "the eye," he had no business even considering it. Especially today.

Taking a deep breath, Carter grabbed his still-full plate and tossed it in the waste bin. "I'm going to go out and talk to Mom before I leave," he announced to the two women. "I'll call you in the morning, Aisha—before I leave."

Even if he hadn't believed it was a good idea before, he was sure that taking on this project was the perfect solution—a new town, a new opportunity where no one knew him. Wellspring might be the welcome change of pace he needed.

Chapter 2

Brooklyn Wells hated charity functions. *But I love chocolate*, she thought.

She snatched a chocolate éclair from the tray as the waiter passed her, and stuffed it into her mouth. Moaning in delight, she chewed the piece of heaven as if it was the last one she'd ever eat. Damn, that was good.

"If you don't slow down, you're going to turn into an éclair, Brooklyn."

Rolling her eyes, Brooklyn assessed her step-mother as she walked by with a wealthy benefactor. The sound of her fake, monotone laugh echoed in the massive ballroom. The woman was as stiff as a board. Or was it boring as a stiff? She snickered to herself. It wasn't funny, but she'd been forced to amuse herself all night. Between countless handshakes, fake smiles, and polite nods, she'd had enough. But her father, the almighty, had mandated that she attend—for the family. Never mind that the charity was in the top twenty-five of America's worst charities. Despite her countless emails and pleas to donate to a more deserving charity—one that didn't line its executives' pockets with cash and one *not* connected to her father—her domineering father dismissed her requests and told her she'd better "shut up and show up."

"Can I talk to you?"

Sighing heavily, Brooklyn looked at her ex. Sterling King used to send a shiver up her spine with one look from his startling gray eyes. But the puppy-dog look he was sporting at that very moment only made her want to shove him into the tray of caviar right behind him.

"I have nothing to say to you," she hissed. "We've been through this so many times, Sterling. If you—"

Her words were cut off by his hands pressing urgently against her back as he guided her toward the back of the room, away from the stares of Wellspring society.

When they were tucked away from the crowd, behind a pillar, she jerked out of his hold. "What are you doing?" She folded her arms across her chest. "I told you I didn't want to t—"

Before she could finish her thought, he was on his knees. In his hand was a box holding a solitaire marquise-cut diamond. Absolutely stunning. But not her style.

"Brooklyn, I love you. Will you marry me?"

She glanced behind her, hoping her father wasn't lurking in the shadows. It would be just like Parker Sr. to have planned this entire thing. For all she knew, he'd purchased the ring himself. Her father had been trying to get her to marry Sterling since she'd graduated from college. Something about building an alliance between the King and Wells families. Brooklyn could care less about the business and her father's interests, so she hadn't intended to follow her father's directive when it came to Sterling and marriage.

"Um . . ." It wasn't like her to be rendered speechless. But she couldn't seem to find the words—well, the one word she needed to say. "I-I have to . . . pee." She turned on her heels and dashed through the ballroom without a backward glance.

Brooklyn breezed past a group of investors, lifted a glass of champagne from a moving tray, and headed straight to the private bathroom in the hallway. Once inside, she locked the door and gulped down the sparkling drink.

Gazing at herself in the mirror, she turned on the water and pulled out her cell phone. When her brother picked up, she whispered, "Parker?"

"Sis, where are you? Didn't I just see you?"

"I need you," she pleaded.

"What is that in the background? Water? Where are you?"

"I'm in the private bathroom."

"Um, you're crazy. Why are you calling me from the bathroom?"

Brooklyn knew he was on his way to her. After their mother died, her older brother took care of her when her father never bothered. He took her everywhere with him, introduced her to all of his friends. He'd threatened all his fellow football teammates with bodily harm if they even dared to approach her. So, she ended up with twenty brothers and no boyfriends.

Even now, as adults, she recognized that they didn't have the same philosophy in life. Parker was all about the family business and name, being the guaranteed Wells heir, and she couldn't care less about her trust fund or the perks her last name provided. But she never doubted her brother would be there for her, no questions asked. She heard him greet someone, excuse himself from another person, then . . . There was a knock on the door.

She rushed to the door, unlocked it, and swung it open, pulling him inside with her.

"What the . . . ?" he said, brushing off his charcoal-gray designer suit and straightening his tie. Parker crossed his arms over his chest. "You've really flipped out this time, sis. Why are you holed up in the bathroom?"

"Sterling proposed," she blurted out.

Instead of the fury she'd half expected in her brother's eyes, she was shocked to see the light of amusement in his brown orbs.

"Are you . . . Parker, did you hear what I said?"

Then, a smirk? Her dear brother thought her predicament was funny.

Clearing his throat, he said, "Sis, calm down." He gripped her shoulders and squeezed. "You had to know this was coming sooner or later."

"Sterling and I haven't been together in years!"

she yelled. "I can't even stand him, let alone want
to marry him. What was he thinking?"

Although she and Sterling had grown up in the
same circles, and were great childhood friends,
their attempt at a relationship went up in flames
after three months. Unfortunately, his handsome—
almost perfect—face and physique weren't enough
to keep her interest. Not only was he as boring as
glue, he was horrible in the sack. As if that wasn't
bad enough, his incessant need to call her "Brooksie-
lynsie" made her want to throw up. God, she hated
stupid pet names with a white-hot passion.

"You know this is all Senior, right?" Parker told
her. Her father had insisted that they call him
"Senior" instead of Dad, although Brooklyn was
the only one that could get away with calling him
Daddy at times. She guessed it had a lot to do with
her father's need to be superior to everyone else in
the world. "Just tell that idiot hell no, and keep it
moving. This isn't the end of the world." Her older
brother barked out a laugh. "I can't believe you
locked yourself in a bathroom. Get it together." He
shook her gently for emphasis. He wiped the
corner of her eye with his thumb. "Fix your face,
baby sis. You are looking rough."

"You get on my nerves." She pouted, turning to
the mirror and pulling out her compact. She eyed
her brother through the mirror. "I panicked, okay?
I'm allowed to panic. We can't all maintain control
like you, big brother."

Parker stared at her and gave her a small smile.
"You remind me of Mom."

Averting her gaze, she busied herself with her makeup. "I can't add tears to this night, Parker." She missed her mother, Maria, with everything in her. Her mother had been dead for fourteen years, but the grief was still just under the surface. Especially since her death was so tragic. "Let's just concentrate on getting me through the night without killing Sterling."

He placed a kiss on the top of her head. Her brother had more than a few inches on her in height, but he never made her feel small, like some of the other people in town. "Point taken. Stay clear of Sterling for the night. We can't have a scene. But tomorrow, make it clear that you'll never be Mrs. King. No matter how our father has conspired with his father to make it happen."

Her father had been cultivating a business relationship with Sterling's family for years. When Sterling's father was elected to the state senate, Brooklyn's father practically salivated with glee. Although Brooklyn wasn't involved in the daily business of the family company, she knew her father thought that having political allies would further strengthen his hold on the town and the state. For years now, Senior had been attempting to buy land in several counties to tap into the springs, and expand the company. It was obvious Senior had something up his sleeve, but Brooklyn would not be a pawn in any game her father wanted to play.

Parker picked up her empty champagne flute and opened the door. He held the glass up to her.

"You need another of these. And go find that man with the chocolate puff things you love so much. It's going to be okay."

She waved at her brother as he strutted out of the small bathroom and followed him a few minutes later. Spotting a cute server with a tray full of those yummy chocolate eclairs, she grabbed one and smiled at him as he strolled by. When he returned her smile with one of his own and a wink, she averted her gaze and pretended to look for someone in the crowd. She was not in the mood to be propositioned or hit on.

"And please try not to get drunk tonight, Brooklyn." Senior's fifth wife stopped right in front of her and scowled. "This is a charity event, not a Super Bowl party."

"Leave me the hell alone," Brooklyn muttered under her breath.

"I heard you," Patricia hissed with a hard roll of her eyes. The woman, barely ten years older than Brooklyn, smoothed a hand over her messed-up blond wig.

"I'm sure you did. Did I stutter?" Brooklyn said between clenched teeth.

"Look, I'm not playing with you," Patricia snapped. "Be good."

"You are not my mother, so stop acting like it."

"Well, I married your father."

"So did his last few wives, before he dumped them."

Patricia grumbled incoherently before she stomped off, probably in search of Brooklyn's father. At any minute, Senior would come over and berate her for daring to talk to his child bride that way.

Shrugging, Brooklyn scanned the room, looking for her brother. Parker was standing with one of her father's board members. They were talking in hushed tones, probably about some business deal. Parker was always talking about business, always trying to please their father. For the life of her, she couldn't understand why. It's not like he didn't loathe him as much as she did. Unlike her, though, Parker thrived on business and he was good at what he did. One day, he'd run the company— Wellspring Water Corporation.

The music faded and the chatter dimmed. Parker Sr. approached the podium, Patricia close to his side and . . . Sterling right behind him. Dread coated her insides as she watched the trio on the stage. *What the hell is going on?* When she met Parker's concerned gaze across the room, she guessed he felt the same way.

"Hello, ladies and gentlemen," her father's baritone voice greeted over the microphone. "I'm so glad that you've joined us tonight. We're on target to meet our fundraising goal for such a worthwhile organization. But I hope you don't mind me taking a few minutes to make an announcement and a toast. The servers will be around to make sure your glasses are filled."

With a smile, Brooklyn took the offered glass of champagne from a short server and waited for her father to speak again. Something told her that what was coming next was a game changer.

With his glass held high, her father smiled and wrapped his arm around Sterling. "I've watched this young man grow into quite a remarkable young man, capable of greatness."

Brooklyn gulped down her champagne.

"I want to congratulate him and my beautiful daughter on their engagement."

Brooklyn choked on the champagne and it sprayed out on the woman in front of her.

"Congratulations, baby girl," her father announced before turning to Sterling. "You will be a fine addition to the Wells family, son."

She glared at her father, standing in front of the crowded room with a satisfied Sterling. That son of a—

"Brooklyn, come here," her father commanded from the stage.

Before she could stop herself, she shouted, "Hell, no!"

Gasps from the crowd filled her ears as her gaze met her brother's across the room. Parker started toward her, but she backed away. Out of the corner of her eye, she saw appalled older women frowning at her. But she couldn't care. She didn't care.

I have to get out of here. But her legs didn't seem to want to work right. As she stumbled toward the door, as if she was stepping in quicksand, she tried to block out the loud whispers from the guests. Focused straight ahead, she finally took off at a sprint, intent on getting as far away as possible. Vaguely, she heard Parker calling her name, but if she stopped to look at him or speak to him, she'd never make it out of there.

The cold, bitter temperatures smacked her in the face when she made it outside. She hugged herself, rubbing her arms. Glancing back to see if anyone followed her, she shuffled down the street. Her dress was long, her toes were bare, and the snow was coming down, but she had to keep going. To where, she didn't know.

Grabbing her phone, she tried to dial her friend Nicole. No answer. She typed a quick 911 text to her friend. Distracted, she started across the street. She heard the blaring horn before she saw the truck heading straight for her. She tried to run, but slipped and fell on her side. Opening her mouth to scream, she frantically searched for someone. The street was empty. Bracing herself for the impact, she prayed for mercy and forgiveness for being such a bitch sometimes.

Only there was no pain. Instead she felt like she was wrapped in a warm, heavenly cocoon surrounded by trees and ginger and . . . Gain detergent? Was she in heaven?

"Are you okay?"

Her eyes popped open and she was met with beautiful, brown, unfamiliar ones staring back at her. Her mouth fell open when she realized that she wasn't sitting at the Lord's feet. She was still, in fact, outside in the brittle Michigan cold, lying underneath a stranger. She bucked up and the man stood to his full height.

She peered up at him and back at his waiting

hand. Sliding her hand into his, she let him pull her to her feet.

"Are you okay?" he repeated, surveying her face with a worried expression. "You were . . . I thought that truck was going to . . . I picked you up and pulled you out of the way, but slipped on ice and we both went down."

"It's . . . okay." Suddenly, she felt warm again and it wasn't because the man had taken his own coat off and wrapped it around her shoulders. She had a strong feeling it had something to do with the man himself standing before her. Brooklyn had never seen him before, but she was immediately intrigued by him. Maybe it was because he'd saved her life? Or maybe it was because he was fine as hell. Either way, she wanted to find out more about him.

He swayed back and forth on his feet and scanned the immediate area. "Do you need me to call anyone?" he asked, shoving his hands into his pockets.

She shook her head and waved a hand in dismissal. "No, I'm just going to head over to my friend's place. It's right around the corner. I'm . . . I can't thank you enough for saving my life. I thought for sure that truck was going to take me out."

"No worries." His full lips held her attention as he asked her . . . Lord, she didn't even hear what he'd said. Was it weird that she was focused on some strange man's mouth after she'd barely escaped death?

Shaking herself from her haze, she asked, "What did you say?"

He chuckled. "Just that I'm glad you're okay."

"I'm sure I have a few scrapes and bruises from the fall. But I feel okay."

"Good to hear," he said, glancing at his watch.

"Thanks again. I wasn't paying attention. I was distracted," she babbled on as she brushed the snow off her dress. "I don't know what got into me. It's just . . . I was trying to get as far away as I could, but I didn't bring my coat, and Nicole didn't answer her . . ." The rest of her sentence died on her lips when she looked up and realized she was talking to herself. The mystery man was gone.

Connect with  Us

Visit us online at
KensingtonBooks.com
to read more from your favorite authors, see books
by series, view reading group guides, and more.

Join us on social media

for sneak peeks, chances to win books and prize packs,
and to share your thoughts with other readers.

facebook.com/kensingtonpublishing
twitter.com/kensingtonbooks

Tell us what you think!

To share your thoughts, submit a review,
or sign up for our eNewsletters, please visit:
KensingtonBooks.com/TellUs.

31901063558748